Fantastical Visions
Volume II

Edited by
W. H. HORNER
and
Courtenay N. Dudek

Wilmington, Delaware
2003

Book design and layout by W. H. Horner. Yes, folks, he's available for parties.

Fantastical Visions Volume II
Copyright © 2003 by Fantasist Enterprises.

ISBN 0-9713608-1-2

Fantasist Enterprises
PO Box 9381
Wilmington, DE 19809

www.fantasistent.com

This book was printed using Print On Demand technology. It is available for wholesale through the publisher and through Ingram Book Group. It can be ordered for retail at most booksellers, both online and off, and is available from the publisher's website.

For orders other than individual consumers, Fantasist Enterprises grants a discount on the purchase of 10 or more copies of single titles for special markets or premium use, such as reading groups or educational endeavors. For further details, please write to the publisher, care of "Special Markets."

Why are you still reading this? Get to the good stuff!

To Amelia
for her patience, understanding,
encouragement, and hard work
through two anthologies.
-WHH

Contents

Perchance to Dream
by Jean Graham

Once upon a time, humankind dreamt of flight, and Icarus took wing. When later we conjured fantasies of dragons and elves and eventually, space travel and time machines, something called a genre was born. We gave it a name then: fantasy.

Many believe that fantasy literature began with the works of Jules Verne and H.G. Wells, and that it further came into its own a century later with the arrival of Tolkien's masterpieces, *The Hobbit* and *The Lord of the Rings*. The genre, they say, languished for a time, but has enjoyed renewed popularity in recent years due to the major media influences of *Star Wars*, *Star Trek*, and the book and movie exploits of a certain pint-sized wizard named Potter. While all of the above may well be the prevalent fantasies of our modern era, they are very far indeed from the genre's beginning. Not even Wells and Verne can claim that honor, because in truth, in one form or another, fantasy has been with us since *our* beginning.

From the earliest cave art to the very first civilizations of Egypt and Cathay, and in every age since, myth makers everywhere and in every culture have filled our world with gods, demons, heroes, villains, leprechauns, sprites and fairies. Whether they perched on cloud-high Mount Olympus or lived secretly somewhere in our midst, creatures of the fantastic have always been with us. To those who first listened to the oft-repeated tales, these were not mere stories, but great truths. And while we may think ourselves too "sophisticated" or too "educated" these days to call the exploits of Gilgamish or Odysseus true, we nonetheless carry, somewhere deep in our being, the inherent *need* to believe it. Call it the fantasy gene. We're all born with the need to imagine, to dream, to be something more than what we are—even if some of those dreams may exist only in the pages of a book or the flicker of a movie screen.

Not that our fantasies haven't often become reality. Could those who first imagined winged Isis or fleet Mercury ever have dreamed that one day, mankind would not only fly, but set foot on the moon? Conversely, it's doubtful that those who first wrote of the Apocalypse could ever have foreseen the harnessing of the atom and our subsequent ability to literally annihilate ourselves at the push of a button. Nightmares, it seems, can come true as easily as their more benign dreamland counterparts.

Light and fluffy or dark and brooding, our fantasies remain with us for good or ill. They may sometimes serve as dire warnings or political commentary (*1984, Brave New World, Lord of the Flies*), but more often of late, they simply become our temporary means of escape from the stressful, the tedious, the boring and the mundane. In our high tech, high stress world, we may need our fantasy gene more than ever before.

Alas, not everyone appreciates the vision. Fantasy, mystery, romance and all other genre literature is quite deliberately cold-shouldered by reviewers writing for the so-called "literary" magazines. It is, however, worthy of note that in spite of these rather glaring omissions, science fiction, fantasy and horror novels frequently dominate the best-seller lists. Then there's the Motion Picture Academy of Arts and Sciences, which consistently snubs every nominated fantasy film for all but the most minor technical awards. They're both representative of a very old bias, one that relegates all genre fiction or film to the dismissive category of "popular." In the lofty land of ivory towers, anything popular is automatically deemed anathema, and the tower keepers strictly and stubbornly forbid that anything read, watched and adored by millions should ever seek to set foot in their hallowed halls. All the same, while the literary snobs continue their snubbing and the Academy fogeys go on turning up their collective artsy noses, fantasy in all its forms has grown more popular than ever.

The conceit that fantasy should not be classified as literature is naive at best. At worst, it's just insufferably elitist, with the rather ludicrous result that for centuries, institutions of higher learning have assigned such classics as Milton's *Paradise Lost*, Dante's *Divine Comedy*, Shakespeare's *A Midsummer Night's Dream* and Spenser's *The Faerie Queene* without ever acknowledging the fact that all of these works belong to a genre—fantasy.

It's an even sadder comment that literary elitism is not the only prejudice fantasy is forced to endure. A misguided but adamant subset of Protestant Evangelical Christianity labels virtually everything imaginative (including Mother Goose and Grimm's Fairy Tales) "Satanic," "psychologically damaging," or both. These spiritually timid souls contend that all fantasy is evil, that children should be sheltered from even the most innocuous of fairy stories, and that all those who indulge in fantasy of any sort expose themselves to the very real threat of demonic possession. They're serious. They live in genuine fear that this is indeed possible. They even publish books instructing the faithful to "cleanse" their homes of any and all "demonic vectors," including crystals, cat statues, pyramids and of course, fantasy novels, by burning or throwing all of these items away and then holding elaborate prayer/cleansing ceremonies in the house. (An exorcism by any other name?) They see no irony in such a dictum. To imagine, they firmly believe, constitutes a sin.

Their children are staunchly denied the wonders of *Pinocchio*, *Alice Through the Looking Glass* and *The Wonderful Wizard of Oz*, and grow up saddled with the paranoid notion that something as innocent as reading "The Cow Jumped Over the Moon" or "The

Owl and the Pussycat" might well cause fire and brimstone to rain down upon their nurseries (a fairly horrific fantasy in and of itself). Theirs is an age-old dogma, a brand of Puritanical thought that is, tragically, so insecure in its own foundation (fearing the loss of what surely ought to be an "un-loseable" salvation) that it demands the essentially impossible, namely that all "true believers," in order to be "good Christians," must amputate the intellect, the sense of humor, and above all, that oh-so-bothersome imagination.

Incredibly, the fantasy-is-Satanic crowd has, with fervid fanaticism, resurrected both book banning and book burning, spectacles which, for most of us, connote not righteousness, but repression and outright mind-control. Devils in Narnia? Demons lurking in Shangri-La? One is tempted to point out that someone in this pitiful equation fails utterly to differentiate between fantasy and reality—and it isn't the children.

No matter how loudly the naysayers may deny it, we still need to dream. We can't help it. It's in our genes. There is empirically nothing wrong, sinful, psyche-damaging or demonic about fantasy in its proper place. Yes, there is the occasional fan who goes overboard, but that's hardly the entire genre's fault. And whether the literary magazines want to admit it or not, fantasy does indeed qualify as literature. It always has. The genre encompasses many of the greatest stories, written and oral, in human history, and we wouldn't, in fact, *be* human without it. We will always be dreamers because it's plain and simply a part of what we are.

Honed by the fertile imaginations of all those myth makers who came before us, our theater of the mind, our fantasy, can take us literally anywhere—or any *when*—we wish to go. The book you now hold is evidence of that legacy. Because no matter how "sophisticated" we may become, we are still very much like the children of Peter Pan's Never Never Land. We still want very much to believe in fairies.

One of the world's most notable fantasists probably said it best when he wrote, "We are such stuff as dreams are made on."

And so we are. So we are.

We hope you enjoy *Fantastical Visions II*!

The Grass Witch
by Lisa Swanstrom

The grass witch has scabs for eyes and a lizard for a tongue. Her hair is thick with chiggers; she has arms of sticks; her thumbs are red from grinding bone bread. She eats babies, Julep says, and I mean to find out, for the grass witch has stolen my son.

I was sleeping when she took him—when her fingers, long as moss, pulled him from the river's edge and swam him down to her mud-thatched hut in the fens. When I woke, my babe was only an echo of ripples from where the grass witch had been.

Some people saw her, but did they stop her? No. Did they even try? Not a chance. Nor would I, if it were someone else's child. But Ashlar was formed in the folds of my belly, and my womb trembles when I think of my sweet child held in the pointed thorns of the grass witch's palm. My Ashlar.

People looked at me like I'd gone all daft when I said I was going to get him back. Even Julep, my sister, pulled my arm as if to stop me. "Fens will kill you, Jilly," she said, her eyes wide. "Sure

1

enough before the old crone will."

Well, that's easy for her to say, with her belly so big she might give birth to twin cows any day. But Ashlar is my only child, and I've no man to give me another. Don't want one either.

So I've got my longbow, newly strung, and a quiver of silver-tipped arrows slung at my side. That's how I shoot—straight from the hip. No reaching behind my back with my elbow over my head, chest open and exposed, not for me. I hunch when I draw, bend at the knee and pull. Strange, you might say, but we've never gone hungry, Ashlar and me. And I've been hunting this way for thirteen years. From my tenth spin on.

Walking the fens is a dance on quick-sand. One wrong step and I'll feed the frogs, I know; and their low, hope-filled croaking isn't helping. I keep to dead trees, walk on logs, jump on twisted branches, and pray that Ashlar hasn't been crushed yet to make her bread.

I slip once, shoat-skinned boots sinking thigh deep; but I've got long legs, and one arrow tied to a rope. It's not easy shooting from the hip in the middle of a bog, but one bite from a lance-toothed frog gives me the incentive I need. The arrow sticks to the wide trunk of a banyan, and I pull myself to a log that's covered in the black slime of north star moss. Slippery, but better than drowning in wet acid.

My heart's pounding hard, like it's moved to my throat. I look at my boots and watch them smoke. The fen waters are oily with poison, burning everything they touch; which is why the trees are charred here, only the strongest roots surviving. And the Banyan trees, and only these because their roots grow backwards, skyward down, falling like ropes from the topmost branches.

Our Auntie used to say the Grass Witch's blood runs thick with swamp water. That her mud-thatched hut's just for show; she really lives in stygian depths of foul water, sleeps with the frogs and adders, rises with the stinking sun. But I've got my own ideas about the grass witch.

I wait till my boots stop hissing, glad again I chose pig skin instead of the thinner, prettier doe to cover my shins, and begin my trudge towards the grass witch's home, pretending like I'm not afraid.

Was a time she only took girls. Pretty ones with curly hair. Soft the way only a baby's hair is. She was more careful then, hunting at night with her long fingers. I only saw her once, when I was six, and she tried to come for Julep.

She came through our window, fingers first. Moving like creeping moss towards Julep's crib. Quiet as a sigh. I only stirred because Julep cried out in her sleep. Our Da put me in charge of Julep when our Ma'am died. She was a good baby, even then, and never cried. So I knew something was wrong when her soft voice pierced the night.

I jolted from my cot when I saw her. Scabs for eyes, lizard for a tongue, its tail flickering as if to smell the air. Moss for fingers, brambles for bones, she tangled about Julep's crib with her loose limbs, making a basket with her arms.

She had no skin, I remember. Just a body of branches and leaves, sticks and mud. And grass, of course, long threads of marsh grass threading across her body like veins. Her face peered over Julep's crib with an expression that looked almost tender—the twigs rising over her scab eyes; her brown lips parting wide.

I was only six, but I kept a dirk under my cot even then. My Da gave me that knife, and the bright steel of it shone like only a first blade can.

I palmed it, quiet, as the grass witch enfolded my sister. She was blind but swift, and she held my Julep in the bundle of her arms. I waited until her grasp was firm and I flicked my wrist, let fly my dirk.

It hit the grass witch's left eye, or the scab where the eye should have been; and she let out a high-pitched wail of pain that sounded like the wind ripping the branches of a tall tree; the lizard in her mouth quivering violently.

She dropped Julep back to her crib, surprised, and turned towards me, sightless and pained, and tried to grab me with her mossy fingers.

My dirk was still in her eye, and I had no other. So I did what a child of six has no shame in doing. "Da!" I screamed. "Da, come

3

quick! It's the witch, Da! The witch the witch the witch!"

I heard him stumbling down the hall. He opened the door as the grass witch made a grab for me. He held the longbow in his arm, the same one that I hold now, and he drew it back. Not a good weapon for close range, but in the short walk down the hall he'd managed to light his arrow with poison flame, and he let it fly, his face twisted with rage.

It hit the grass witch square. And she fled our small house the same way she came, out the window, fingers first, running for the dark waters of the swamp.

We never slept with the windows open again, but others weren't so cautious. Since that year, the grass witch has taken a child each season. And this was only my Ashlar's second spring. Today the day I gave him birth.

The picnic at the river was Julep's idea to celebrate her nephew's birthday. Oh, she'd made enough sweets to feed us sick, and I was tired from chasing my bairn from tree to tree, prying rocks from his fingers so he wouldn't swallow them. And him tired too, from being chased. So we fell asleep together on the river's edge, his little body making a nest of my skirts.

Ashlar would often laugh in his sleep, and it was the absence of his laughter that woke me. That, and the sudden, too still silence. Julep at my side when I jolted from sleep. Her green eyes bright from weeping. Her fine blue skirts knotted in her fists. "She came and went, Jilly!" she cried. "Too late!"

She never said who, but I knew all the same. The men went searching the other side of the river with half-hearted pokes of their swords. Julep's husband, our Da, our little brother Lupa with angry kicks of his dirty brown feet. But no one would go after her. Into the fen.

Last time someone went to chase her down, his bones washed up on our riverbank. We only knew it was him by the missing front tooth in his skull. His little girl got took last season, robbed from her cradle while he slept on the rocker at her side.

The witch came at night that time, in the purple-shadowed winter. He said he heard a noise, but it only sounded like bending

4

branches, and he paid it no mind. I don't remember what else he said, because he wept so hard as he spoke. I was touched by his tears. Never seen a man so big cry so hard.

But now I know why he wept. I can feel it in my own bones. The fear, the loss, the sickening emptiness. My cornerstone, my girding, my sly brown bobbin. Gone! He was the reason I lived when my own man died.

Gored by the horns of an eight-point stag. They'd been drinking, he and my Da, and my foolish Laird thought he'd kill the beast "hand-to-hand." "It was a good death," my Da insists, even now, but he doesn't believe it any more than I do, for he quit drinking that day, and I do all the hunting now.

I wonder who'll do the hunting if the witch takes me.

~~~~~

Once I cross the river delta, I've gone further than anyone from our village. The men walk heavily upon our land; the women too light. Few have the balance necessary to walk the fen. Except the dead man, big though he was. Something tells me that he went all the way.

The soil's rich here, wet and black, and now's where the walking gets tricky. There're some stones to help me, but the earth's too soft to trust even the biggest rocks. I find myself shooting that rope more times than I'd like, switching arrows so the shafts won't bend too much from my weight, hugging the giant trees so I won't sink.

I walk on for an hour or so, only covering a mile, at the most, as I shoot the rope, pull for balance, mince steps, leap to the trees, and listen.

I don't know where she lives. Not exactly, but already I'm hearing the sounds of bending branches, whispering leaves. And there aren't any proper trees in the fen. Just banyans, quiet as round stone walls.

And then I hear a familiar cry raise above the fen. My Ashlar! I tense, ready to run. That sweet voice is only one hundred yards away, due west. I check my arrows quickly, dip their sharp tips for second helpings in my poison sack. And then I run toward my child, tipping rocks as I scurry.

5

I miss a quicksand pit by inches and try to ignore the rock that disappears into the churn. There's no time for arrows or ropes now. I push aside all fear, ignore my sweating limbs, my pounding heart, and trust in my balance, and my trust is not in vain. I've reached the grass witch's hut, and I hide behind a banyan to look for a way in.

Her walls are thick with mud and marsh grass, her roof smothered in rushes. There's a small window on the side, and a hole in the front, dark as death. I listen and hear the cries of my son. Not in the cottage, but close by. And something else that speaks in low moans, creaking as it moves.

I hunker down, crawling on my belly, and move to the closest wall.

The window is crude—just a hole, no glass, but did I expect polished sheets of stained glass to adorn the Grass Witch's hut? No.

Our Ma'am used to spin yarns about the Grass Witch's beauty. Said she was no crone at all, but a shining lady with flowing hair like waves on a river. That's just how she'd say it, too, brushing her own long hair with a small tin comb as if she wished she were the grass witch herself, her gray eyes distant and too old for her smooth skin.

"And what about the babies, Mother?" our Da would ask. "If she's so fancy and fine, why'd she take young Emmie last spring?"

And our Ma'am would smile from her silver face—that serene, quiet smile that charmed and enraged our Da in equal portions—and shrug. "It's lonely in the fen, my Laird. Companionship is all for she takes the bairns." Never stopped brushing that hair, our Ma'am.

But she never saw the grass witch true, as I did, that night when I was six, so when I look through the rough window of her hut, I don't shudder in surprise at the squalor. I know the grass witch is no beauty. And I am beginning to sense that the grass witch is no witch at all, only sticks and mud that somehow rose from the swamp to walk one day.

The grass witch keeps a poor house. Dirt floors, uneven and wet, a rough stone table, and a cot. Heaps of white rocks lie in cairns about her floor, and she has no door. Her sagging roof is filthy, I see creepers in the rushes; and peeking my head into the window

6

deeper, I notice a large net hanging above the doorway, gathered up with a cord and hung by rusted nails. For rats, I wager. Or babes that try to crawl away.

Her hut's empty now, but I know she's near with my Ashlar, so I creep to the front and duck in the hole, quiet as a beastie, and hide myself under her stone table, holding my bow and arrows close.

I don't know what my plan is, not exactly. I aim to kill her, if I might, and save my son. But if arrows won't kill her, what will? My breathing's heavy now, any minute the crone could find me squatting under where she grinds her bread. My eyes dart around the room, looking for a better spot, but there's none. And I notice, peering closer, that the little heaps of white aren't rocks at all, but bones, picked clean and blanched white. Tiny bones, no bigger than mice. Our babies' bones. Neatly stacked and quiet. Little fingers, little toes.

I can't control my stomach. All the sweets that Julep made for Ashlar's birthday pour right out on the Grass Witch's floor. I want to weep, but that won't help the wee bairns now. Wiping the sweat from my brow, I pull my limbs tight to my body, try not to shudder, and wait in the dark for the grass witch to bring my boy.

It's not long before she comes skulking through the hole, a bundle in her arms. Ashlar, I think, and hold myself close. I'll rush her when she sets him down, and she'll never know what struck her. But I can't control myself when I see her face, and I let out a cry that is low and filled with pain.

The grass witch has eyes now. Mismatched and blue. One wide and round, one the shape of a young almond flower. And skin! Patches of fresh skin have been sewn over more than half her body. Varying shades of peach, yellow, tan, and brown cover her arms, small branches poking out where the stitching's uneven. Her head swings towards my cry.

But eyes though she has, they do not work for her, for the witch pulls her bundle close and tilts her head, listening and sniffing the air for my body. Blind.

Sweat's pouring from my skin in sheets, I can smell it; that and the sour mess I've made on her floor. And if I can smell it, it won't

7

be long before she will too. Slowly, I reach for the pile of bones closest to me and throw one across the room, near the door.

Her head spins where it clatters, and she holds her bundle closer. I've got to be careful for that bundle's sake. I am still as stone under that table.

She stands still, too, her mouth moving slow, chewing air. She sucks it in, and when she exhales, she moans. "Come out!" Her vowels blowing like wind. The word "ouuuuuuut" echoing in her dark hut. A wail of frustration.

I didn't know she could speak; but I keep silent just the same. Her voice is a bellows of pain. I'll do nothing to hurt that bundle she holds so close to her body. Quiet though it may be, too quiet for my boy. I hold my fears in check. Waiting.

She holds a moment longer, and then, understanding something I don't want her to understand, she turns away from me, pulls up the bundle over her head, and dashes it to the ground.

"My Ashlar!" I scream, my hiding place revealed, and I rush towards the door to save my son.

Something like a smile spreads across the witch's face as I run, and with a swift move she loosens the cord that holds her net. It falls from the rusted hooks that hang above her door, trapping me in tangles. To my side, the bundle I thought was my son is only kindling, smashed and wrapped in strips of swaddling.

I twist my body, trying to free from the net; but it's thick and twisted marsh grass, impossible to escape. The filtering sunlight just beyond my fingertips.

She stoops to the ground and picks up a smooth round stone, edges towards me.

"Where is he?" I shout, pulling away from the darkness, struggling against the net. It's hard to see her clearly, but I know the strike's coming. "My child!"

Her arm raises back, slow and rickety, and she strikes me once, twice, three times, and I meet blackness.

~~~~~

I wake to darkness, and I'm tied. My wrists behind my back, my ankles forced together by a clumsy knot of marsh grass. She's placed my bow and arrow in the corner of her hut, as if she's trying to decide what to do about them.

Not much light in the cottage, only a low fire under a copper pot she must've filched from town, her arms making large shadows as she moves. On her square stone table my Ashlar rests, still but alive, breathing and lovely as anything I've ever seen.

I'd cry out to him, but my mouth's filled with mud and watercress, stuffed full and smeared shut with wet grass. I'm on her cot, laying on the soiled fabric of her bed; and a large rat eyes me with its beady eyes. I make a feeble kick at it, and it scurries away, its whip-cord tail disappearing into the wall.

I'm chewing on mud, swallowing in gulps. It's poisoned, I'm sure, but my life is nothing without Ashlar. If I can swallow all this mud, she'll not know, whereas my spitting's sure to warn her. And if I can just get enough room in my mouth to speak, I can tell Ashlar what to do, where to kick so he can at least have a chance to run.

She bends over him, that strange look of tenderness on her borrowed face. Eyebrows raising, brown lips parting. She chews the air again, gulping it in and breathing out moans. "My pretty one," each word a grinding of her jaw.

She reaches with one twig finger to caress my child. She hasn't enough skin to cover all of her, but if she takes Ashlar, she might be close.

He stares up at her, his brown eyes large as ladles, drinking the sight of the grass witch in. He's a trusting boy, my Ashlar, and he reaches hesitantly to touch her, wraps his hand around her kindling fingers.

Tears well up in his eyes when his skin does not meet with skin. "Ma'am!" he wails. "I want my Ma'am!"

And he doesn't even know I'm here. I chew and swallow as fast as I can, still not enough. I'm almost choking.

The witch reaches for the knife that rests on her table next to Ashlar. The rusty blade blends in with the shadows, almost becoming a part of her hand.

Ashlar cries harder, but thank God he's not tied. He squirms on the table, and she holds him down with her bramble arms, the

9

patchwork skin draping off a bit so some branches poke out.

I swallow down mud to a manageable lump. The wet ball in my mouth is slowly melting to a handful of pebbles. I taste a wet string slide across my tongue. Worm. It slithers down my throat, alive. Tears form in my eyes as I hold down the gag. I've only a marble left of the mud now. I can feel the poison working through me, but I have enough strength to yell. Almost there. The rat's back now, and I kick harder this time, so it makes an eeking sound and burrows into the wall.

The grass witch tilts her head to the cot. I make myself still, stop my chewing and swallowing. But I think I've got enough room in my mouth to yell.

She turns her attention to Ashlar, draws her rusty blade over her head.

"Her face, Ashlar! Pull the skin and kick!" I scream.

And my son only hesitates a moment, twisting to his side so her blade hits stone, jarring her wooden bones. He reaches with his small fists, grabs the loose skin, and kicks the scabs beneath her borrowed eyes.

She reels back, screaming, her knife still in hand. There's something familiar about that blade, but I'm too busy to think about what. "Untie me, boy! Quickly!"

He runs to the corner of the room, tries to bury himself in my lap.

"No time!" I bend and show him my tied wrists.

The grass witch is lunging towards us now, swinging the dirk in the air in random sweeps. Her wooden jaw chewing air, grinding out wails of pain.

Ashlar works with his tiny fingers, clumsily tearing away the knot of marsh grass. His curls are plastered against his head in sweat, his body trembling. Only a few threads left. I look to the corner of the hut. "Grab my bow and quiver. Go!"

She's close now, and Ashlar just misses a sweep of her knife as he runs to my gear.

I fall on the floor and roll. Cut the last of the knot with the rough rocks in the mud. I grab my bow from Ashlar's shaking arms and pull him to my hip. I bend and cut the cords that hold my feet with the tip of one of my arrows. Free at last, we run out the hole.

She follows us, blind and howling. "My child!"

It's a heavy darkness that fills the fens, and I can't shoot without light. I can barely make out the hut we've just escaped from, let alone the grass witch who follows. I pick her cottage for my target and set Ashlar down.

~~~~~~

When he taught me to hunt, my father said one thing: "Don't think about killing. Shoot. To linger is to starve." And those words ring in my head as I draw my arrow from the hip, strike it to flame, bend my knees, hunch slightly, pull back, and let the arrow fly.

The roof is the first to burn. Like a pile of slag in a dry wood, it explodes. The flames crawl swiftly across the rushes, burning and cracking, scorching. Black smoke pours from the roof of her hut as the fire flowers across the walls, burning the marsh grass and mud.

The grass witch wails as her hut burns behind her. She's draped her face back on, but it hangs lopsided from her branches.

I shake my head and aim to shoot her, my arrows digging urgently against my hip. But even as I want to let the shaft fly, I pause. Her face so wretched, her eyes dismayed and weeping real tears. Human. I open my mouth to speak, to distract her, but she moves swiftly, flicking her wrist, throwing my own dirk at me so it hits my thigh. Just above my right boot.

I grimace and pull my blade from my own leg just as she must have pulled it from her eye that night, so many years ago when she crept upon Julep. I stare at the thin steel of it. All these years. I draw an arrow.

She howls. She wanted to kill me; and instead I'm only wounded. Her wrists are thorny with branches, tearing the patchwork skin from all the rapid movement, and she has nothing left to throw.

She makes a lunge for my Ashlar, but he grabs my left leg (smart boy!), picks up a rock, and pelts it at the grass witch.

I strike my arrow so it flames.

She screams, tearing at her hair with her fingers, broken twigs and hanging skin. Real hair, too. Soft and curly, as only a child's hair

11

can be. I ignore the sickness in my gut and release the arrow.

She's slow to burn, and I hold Ashlar's head down so he cannot see her melting flesh. The skin she's reaped flows like wax, her hair scorches and straightens, cornsilk yellow. No end to her screams. Finally the grass witch burns, her branches and brambles, her marsh grass veins and kindling legs catching fire. They spark, popping as they burn. But her lopsided eyes are watery till the end, human and blue, until nothing is left except brief scabs which also turn to ash.

~~~~~

I scatter her ashes along the fen as Ashlar and I walk, careful and slow, back to our village. The poison coursing my blood, I vomit every half mile.

"What was she?" Ashlar asks, his small hand tight around my wrist, his brown eyes black from fear.

I lean against a banyan, hold my bairn close, and remember how it was when he was yet unborn, sleeping in my belly—two hearts under one skin. The grass witch longed for that connection. Our Ma'am was right after all. I make a note to tell my Da.

"She wanted to be human."

"But what was she?" His hand squeezes tighter. He has to know.

"She was nothing but tinder and sticks, my boy. And mud and grass that somehow rose from the swamp to walk one day. There're no more like her, I wager. And she was all alone."

He stares at me, not understanding. And he never will, not anymore than I will. I pick him up and swing him against my hip, hold him close.

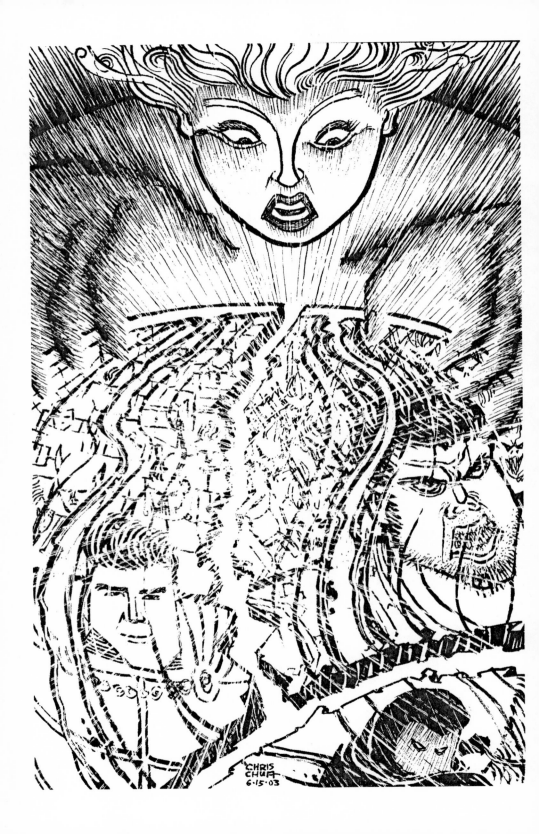

The Enchantress of Isgor
by Angeline Hawkes-Craig

Lightening cracked sharply, sending a shock wave through the huddled women who were concentrating on the struggling woman lying in the bed. A few jumped, jarred by the crashing of the thunder outside the tower window. Rain beat against the walls with such a fury that the midwife wondered if the old stone tower would remain standing long enough for this difficult babe to be born. How many hours had it been? The poor woman couldn't go on much longer. Her fight had been a valiant one, but her strength was waning fast. The midwife shook her head, sadly acknowledging to herself that she was going to lose one of her patients on this foul night. She hoped to save the babe before the mother expired.

"Push now, My Lady," the Elvin midwife said gently, but firmly.

The beautiful woman in the bed, her long blond hair plastered to her face with sweat, her eyes wide in a mixture of fear and determination, grabbed onto the ropes tied around the end posts of

15

her gilded bed and heaved her swollen body forward. She called upon every ounce of strength in her body to aid her in her task.

She screamed as she heaved with all her might. One of the nurses wiped the perspiration from the woman's furrowed brow with a wet cloth. Her gown was soaked from sweat and blood. The bed and the floor were blood-splattered as well.

"Here's the head now, one last push!" the midwife called over the thunder and the crackle of lightening which shot like skeletal fingers across the night sky.

The exhausted woman gave one last push and collapsed as she felt the baby expelled from her battered body.

"Ah! A girl!" the midwife said with a laugh, her pointed ears bobbing. "A girl with golden eyes!"

"Gold eyes, did you say?" the new mother asked, her voice weak—barely a whisper.

"Aye, gold."

"She is the one," the young mother breathed jaggedly. "Send for my mother in Isgor, she needs to be told. She foresaw the babe's coming."

The midwife handed the baby to the nurse and tried to stem the flow of blood from the mother. If she had been full Elf, she would not have bled like this—there were potions and charms that the midwife knew, but the mother was also half-Human, and Humans were very bad about dying in childbirth.

"Let in Rafmiel," the midwife said as she cast a watchful glance at the limp woman lying motionless on the crimson-soaked linens. She would not last much longer now.

A servant girl scurried to the heavy wooden door, unbolted it, and waved the tall, thin Elf into the chamber—a chamber that smelled of blood, sweat, and fast-approaching death. His head turned in every blood-soaked direction, near panic, his eyes large and questioning. This is why they kept the door bolted and him standing in the hall like a waiting servant boy. This was not a birthing room! This was the room of a butcher!

"I cannot stop the bleeding," the midwife said softly. "I have tried everything I know. The charms do not work on her—perhaps it is the Human blood in her. She has asked for her mother. Perhaps if Lamrea of Isgor gets here quickly—maybe she can save her, otherwise . . ." the midwife's voice faded off into the stale air. Everyone knew that Lamrea would not get here in time. Her duties as one of Isgor's most powerful sorceresses had prevented her from making the long and arduous journey to her daughter, and those same duties would more than likely postpone her departure further.

Rafmiel's eyes were wide with disbelief. His pale face grew even paler at the horror of losing his wife. He knelt by her side, burying his face against her breast. He could not remember her ever having looked so frail.

"Rafmiel?" she said.

"Save your strength, my love," he said tenderly.

"She is the one. The one the elders speak of. 'A girl with golden eyes born in the midst of a storm.' Mother was right," Limil said, breathing raggedly.

"The Enchantress of Isgor?" Rafmiel asked.

"The one," Limil said, flinching in pain.

Rafmiel looked across the bed towards the cradle carved in the shape of a swan, towards the swaddled bundle of pink flesh asleep in comfort. He smiled.

Then he looked down at Limil, his beloved wife. She stared towards the vaulted ceiling.

"Sleep my dove," he whispered. He felt as if a hole had been carved out of his heart and all that was left was a great crater of emptiness. Life without Limil. How could there be such a thing? He tried to stand up, but could not. His knees were bolted to the cold ground on which he knelt—beside the bed of his lover—his friend, his wife—the mother of his baby who lay asleep, unaware in the sheltering warmth of the cradle before him. Lightening flashed. The thunder rattled the walls, but still he could not move.

The midwife frowned and pointed to the cradle and then to the chamber across the hall. The nurses removed the baby, cradle and all to the alternate chamber, and Rafmiel was suddenly very alone with his very dead wife who was now resting in the Realm of the Spirits, waiting for the day they would be together once again.

17

He remained on the floor beside the bed and sighed. He was soon choked by sobs that matched the intensity of the crashing of thunder outside the tower window. Rain poured in through the open window, the shutters pounding loudly against the walls. Wiping his eyes on the back of his sleeve, he got up and closed them. The room went completely black save the few sputtering candles that had burned low through Limil's ordeal. He sat near her bed on a red velvet-covered stool and stared at her still form and pondered his motherless child. Lamrea would be here soon. She would know what to do. If only Lamrea had been here sooner. She might have been able to save Limil. Rafmiel covered his face with his hands.

~~~~~

Many years passed since that night, and though Rafmiel had been certain that his heart had been ripped out and he would never know happiness again, he discovered that Limil lived on in spirit through the tiny babe she left behind. The baby's name was Elsinore, named for Rafmiel's mother, and though motherless she did not go without a mother figure. Lamrea loved the child as if Elsinore were her own daughter. In a way, Elsinore was the thing that mended Lamrea's broken heart after her precious Limil died. And for Rafmiel, his daughter became his constant companion until she grew of an age that Isgor had need of her, and she and her grandmother left to live in that veiled place. His Elsinore returned to him often though, and he sought comfort in the life they had created together. His beautiful girl with the golden eyes.

~~~~~

Elsinore blinked and cupped her eyes from the glare of the blazing sun. She had been reading the account of her birth again. She had known of her tragic birth all of her life, known of the ultimate sacrifice her mother had paid. If only the midwife had known that one touch from baby Elsinore could have ceased her mother's hemorrhaging. But, the prophecies were vague with details.

Along with her inborn powers, every high wizard and sorceress in Isgor and the surrounding lands had trained the girl. She learned Elvin magic, Dwarven magic, Human magic, and the magic arts of other exotic peoples. She learned to counter the dark arts and

18

the evil magic of the Goblins, Orcs, and Trolls. Her life was one of constantly expanding knowledge.

She closed the large, old leather book with a dusty pouf! She locked the little golden lock on its side with a key she wore on a velvet cord around her neck. The book had been her grandmother's—a powerful sorceress in her own right—a book of all her charms and spells and her account of Elsinore's birth and everything else that Elsinore should know. It was part spell book, part history, and part familial recollection.

In the window seat, she looked out over the horizon to see a dot growing closer. It drew nearer and its massive pure white form became clear. Her dragon. He circled before her window to greet her and soared to the castle roof. Elsinore set her heavy book down, pulled her ermine-lined cloak on and softly pattered up the spiraling stone staircase to the roof where her dragon would be waiting in all of his snow-white splendor, ever faithful, ever true. One of the last of the Great White Dragons. They had once been as plentiful as horses, soaring majestically over the sapphire skies. Soon they would be gone—the ending of an era.

Elsinore greeted him with open arms and nuzzled her head against his white neck. He snorted his affection and threw back his silver-horned head. His eyes came back to meet her own, and then he held up his hand. In his talons he clutched a scroll sealed with the wax seal of Rowlfghorm, the leader of the Human and Elvin Allied Nations.

"What is this, my old friend?" she cooed while removing the scroll. He had already been very old when she had been entrusted to his care as a child. He had been Lamrea's dragon even in her youth. Now, Elsinore and he communicated in a silent language, he sensing her thoughts and she knowing his. The dragon snorted and lifted its huge head as if to say he did not know the contents of the message.

"Did Rowlfghorm call you to him? Or is he within Isgor's boundaries?" Her eyes lit up. Her heart pounded madly in her breast. She sucked in a great deal of air and tried to calm herself. She held the parchment scroll and, closing her eyes, looked across the rolling green hills of Isgor, through the dense forests, over the bountiful

19

fields—her seeing powers sought out this Human man . . . this man that stirred her heart. Was he here? She jolted. He was.

There he stood next to a giant silver steed. A few Elvin council members in long, flowing green robes stood along his side. Rowlfghorm turned and looked right towards the castle as if he saw her seeing him. She smiled. He could sense her. He had odd powers for a normal mortal. She breathed in sharply and her mind suddenly left Rowlfghorm and focused on the letter she held in her hand. She broke the blue wax seal and unrolled the crisp page of the scroll. Rowlfghorm's scrawled writing danced across the parchment in bold blue ink: "As you know already, I am here." She laughed happily. She patted her dragon on the side as he snorted once again, acknowledging her bemusement. She stroked her dragon's neck, lost in thought.

"Go now! Go and be fed!" she said suddenly to her dragon and watching him go, her thoughts returning to Rowlfghorm and his arrival.

Elsinore practically flew down the stone stairs in an excited frenzy. She bounced into her room and flung back the green velvet curtain that separated her room from her wardrobe of lavish gowns. The Enchantress of Isgor never dressed in tatters. Gowns and baubles arrived almost daily from provinces and territories and individuals attempting to curry favor with her for this or that cause. Exasperated, she went from gown to gown; unable to find one that she felt would be suitable, one that would make her stunning. Finally, she held her slender arms arched over her head, palms touching, and breathed out deeply.

"Este es Bonitias!" she chanted and a sparkling cloud of mist surrounded her as she whirled around, arms outstretched above her head. The mist settled to her feet and floated away into the air leaving her clad in a silvery dress studded with white pearls from sleeves to hem. Her hair was wound with ropes of pearls and diamonds and she laughed at her appearance in her looking glass. Yes, she was beautiful! The charm had worked.

Elsinore knew that she shouldn't use her powers on such frivolous matters—the world was full of real problems with real people who needed real solutions. If she exhausted herself on trivial whims, she would have no strength left to solve the problems that really mattered. But she was young and in love and all that mattered to her heart was Rowlfghorm. Rowlfghorm was a true leader, but he was a man foremost. All men love a beautiful woman, even if that woman was still mostly a girl. She lived in the confines of Isgor voluntarily, but nowhere was it written that she had to remain here alone. Elsinore sometimes wondered if he loved her for her, or if he was in love with her power and position—but when she really thought about it she knew that Rowlfghorm loved her for her own sake and not for the destiny she had to fulfill.

The horses were approaching. Billowing clouds of dust rose up above the winding road they traveled. The clank of the chains lowering the heavy iron gate of the castle could be heard above the noises of the courtyard. And suddenly the blaring of the trumpets signaled the arrival of important visitors. Elsinore looked down into the cobbled courtyard. Rowlfghorm sat upon his horse, staring up at her window—waiting. It had been many moons since she last saw him, was last in his arms.

In velvet slippers she ran as fast as decorum permitted down the dimly lit stairs, down the twisting stone steps, down to the cobbled courtyard outside. She walked out, the sun reflecting off the silver of her gown and the diamonds glistening in her hair. Rowlfghorm sat there dignified.

He dismounted. He lifted his arms in a welcoming gesture. She, forgetting her position of power, forgetting that she was the ruler of all Isgor, ran into his waiting arms and embraced him in bubbling laughter more fitting a silly girl, than a powerful sorceress. He didn't seem to mind. His face was loving, but grew serious.

She frowned, knowing why he was here. She sent dispatches to him earlier in the week concerning a rising disturbance. She had been uncertain of where it had originated at the time. She had sensed a shifting in power and had consulted the Orb. Little by little it began to reveal a gathering army and Elsinore knew that attack was eminent. Some dark force was clouding the Orb, however, and she was having a difficult time seeing through the fog that was protecting whoever was mounting the army for an attack.

"Is it the Orcs?" she asked disdainfully.

"Aye. That it is. Up to no good—again," Rowlfghorm growled.

"Thought as much. The Orb of Orion has glowed red for a fortnight. It took me a while to break through their cover of fog, but their magic is no match for Isgor's. There is an army of Orcs moving from the North," Elsinore said. "It seems they are ripe for battle again. I had planned to send word to you this day, until I learned of your arrival and could deliver the information in person."

Rowlfghorm had not known about the Northern army. His Elvin Captain, Tristan, who had been standing near enough to hear all that had been said, met his eyes with an intensely worried look.

"We had no reports of this?" Rowlfghorm turned to Tristan and asked.

"No. You would have been informed immediately. Something must have happened. If the Orcs found our spies and scouts, they would have cut them down before they had a chance to report."

Rowlfghorm frowned. With the amount of magic the Orcs were using it was likely that they had in fact identified their spies and eliminated them before any leaks or reports could reach his ears. Whatever the Orcs had been planning they had managed to pull it off in secrecy and with much apparent loyalty. A feat in itself for the self-serving Orcs. They must have an incredible leader to have been able to gain both unity and loyalty. Rowlfghorm scratched his head in thought. He studied Tristan's face, which was furrowed, his thin lips pinched even thinner.

"There's no time to speculate now. Take this news to Aldaetan immediately. Take my mount, he is fastest," Rowlfghorm said to Tristan and then looked at Elsinore who seemed troubled. "Is there more?"

It was Elsinore's duty to determine how much she should reveal and how much she should conceal. It was a hard task made even harder still when faced with the man she loved. It was difficult to hold anything back from Rowlfghorm, but her duty was to Isgor first and she had always followed the laws of Isgor. For her responsibility was not just to the Human race, but to the entire world.

"Aye. There is a Human who leads these Orcs."

"A Human?" Rowlfghorm and Tristan both said in startled unison.

Elsinore nodded her head slowly, her eyes fluttering as she sought out the images through the Realm of Enchantment. It was more difficult to use her seeing powers without the aid of the Orb. She could see much with her own skills, but she depended on the Orb for exact details. It was reassuring to rely on the Orb's powers rather than on her own. She doubted her abilities at times, afraid that her own wishes might cloud what she saw, but watching the events as they unfolded within the Orb assured her that what she saw was reality. She breathed slowly and searched the realms for her information. She stood motionless. "His name is Garren of Rimeal," Elsinore said.

Rowlfghorm turned to a worried-looking Tristan. "Rimeal is Orc territory."

Tristan frowned. "He is only half-Human then. No full-blooded Human would be given an Orc name without Orcish blood."

"His mother was probably some poor wench dragged off by one of those damned beasts," Rowlfghorm said, his face growing red with anger. Too many young girls had been abducted and killed throughout the years by the Orc savages.

"Probably," Tristan agreed.

"What does he seek?" Rowlfghorm turned his attention back to Elsinore, wanting to know more. The Orcs far outnumbered their ranks, but they were full of rage and lacking sense. The Allied advantage lay in knowledge, strategy, and above all, intelligence.

"Blood. Gold and slaughter to appease his armies. But, for himself, and another—I know not who—he seeks vengeance."

"He's definitely half-Human if he wants more than simple slaughter. Damned Orcs are satisfied with a few heads. You say you do not know for whom he is seeking revenge? Is that person with him?" Tristan pressed.

"I cannot see. The other one is cloaked by powerful magic. They do not want to be known. Garren acts for this person as well as for himself, but the power lies in this other person."

"Does this Garren have power of his own? Magic? Or just armies?" Tristan asked, trying to get Elsinore to dig deeper.

"He has some power, yes. Skills and learned magicks. But it is this dark person that protects him and is his source of power. This dark one has pure magic, inborn power. If I could just see the other being!" Elsinore struggled, her mind in the mists, but she could not see beyond the black blanket thrown in front of her.

"Well, I can't fight magic, but I can fight Orcs. Bless me, Enchantress. I must take my leave," Tristan dropped to one knee before Elsinore and she lightly touched his brow in silence. He kissed her hand and leapt up, mounting Rowlfghorm's horse and though eager to deliver his bad tidings, waited hopefully for further information. Elsinore stood quietly.

Rowlfghorm cleared his throat, breaking the silence. "Get news to Azrear somehow. Spies, leaks, whatever works. Maybe if those bloody Goblins know the Orcs are passing through their lands, they'll attack and divert the Orcs from Aldaetan, giving our armies a chance to prepare for an attack," Rowlfghorm said, holding the horse's reins as he spoke to his trusted friend.

"May the gods help Aldaetan if they don't!" Tristan said.

"Fleet of foot, my friend!" Rowlfghorm said to his trusted mount. Slapping the horse on the flank, he sent Tristan bolting off in a spray of pebbles and dust.

Rowlfghorm turned to Elsinore. The news that Elsinore had told him seemed to have aged him right before her eyes.

"You know more, don't you?" he asked her quietly as she was shaking off the daze of the enchantment.

Her golden eyes began filling up with tears. She had hoped that the distraction of her crying would stop Rowlfghorm from pressing her for more information. She found herself praying to her mothers and to the Spirits of the Realm to give her strength to do her duty and keep her mouth shut when she needed to. She loved Rowlfghorm, but she loved Isgor as well. She had been a daughter of Isgor, long before she had been the love of Rowlfghorm.

"Tell me," Rowlfghorm said firmly.

"Aldaetan will fall. None will be spared," Elsinore breathed out

24

jaggedly. More images began to flood her mind, images that sought her through the veils of time and place. "The Orcs will put every last soul to the sword. There is no hope."

"Tristan will intervene. He has this knowledge; he will get word to the troops and to the Goblin spies. The Goblins are sure to attack. They have been waiting for an excuse to start up another war with the Orcs. If we're fortunate, perhaps the Orcs will never reach the walls of Aldaetan."

Elsinore shook her head. "Aldaetan will fall."

Rowlfghorm's arms dropped to his side like dead weight. So spoke fate.

"And then where?" he asked, envisioning the marching armies of rampaging Orcs crossing the countryside, bringing death and destruction like a wave of all-consuming fire. Compared to the armies of the Orcs, the Human and Elvin Alliance looked like a bunch of weak boys dressed in their father's discarded war attire, waving wooden swords. There was little time to recruit new soldiers. Their best bet would be the Goblins attacking first and weakening the Orcs, perhaps stopping them altogether.

"The Goblins will stop the Orcs . . . but at a price. Aldaetan and the surrounding territories will be annexed into the state of Azrear," Elsinore said as if she had been reading Rowlfghorm's very thoughts and had anticipated his need for answers. She could tell that he knew she knew more. She could also tell that although he wanted to make her tell him more, he tried to hold back on his questioning. He knew she answered to Isgor and he could only pry so much. He didn't want her to give up information she would later regret giving him.

"Goblin territory," Rowlfghorm growled deeply.

"Aye," Elsinore said sadly. "My heart. It breaks." She sat down on a nearby stone step and clutched her bosom as if trying to stave off an actual physical pain that pierced her breaking heart.

"Your Father?"

"He is in Aldaetan," Elsinore said, her words nearly carried off in the wind.

Rowlfghorm punched his hand with his fist. "Our armies will be there shortly, they will leave as soon as Tristan delivers this news.

Perchance your father will escape! Any number of scenarios can play out in a battle!"

Elsinore's head dropped to her knees, her arms encircling her head in sorrow. "There is no escape for an Elf in Orc hands."

Rowlfghorm knew this to be true. It was common knowledge that above all, Elves were the most despised by Orcs. The Orcs did not even keep Elves as sex slaves as they did most races. Their hatred ran deep and was ancient. And they would take the city before the Goblins finished them.

"Maybe the Goblins will get there first. Elves make prized slaves, surely they will spare his life!"

Elsinore looked at him woefully. She had already seen what was to come. Rowlfghorm sat down beside her, his armor clanking against the stone.

"You must go," Elsinore said. "Your duty is to your men. They need your strength now."

Rowlfghorm put his gloved hand on her gowned knee. His face was marred with worry and concern.

"Go my love, and take this." Elsinore took an amulet on a gold cord from her pocket and pressed it into Rowlfghorm's hand. "It will protect you in battle."

Rowlfghorm stared at the chunk of amber, and then looked back into Elsinore's face. "I will return to you."

Elsinore smiled crookedly. "I know," she said softly.

Rowlfghorm laughed a little and stood. Elsinore followed him to the waiting horse and stood, hands clenched before her, as he mounted.

Elsinore suddenly said loudly, "Make no treaties with the Goblins. The Orcs will come to you—later—when they are needed."

Rowlfghorm thought there was a riddle in this warning, but he heeded it and nodded.

"I will do as the Enchantress of Isgor commands," he said boldly and lifted his hand to her, then spurred the horse to top speed. He didn't look back. It was hard enough to come and go like this without having to watch Elsinore crying as he left.

Elsinore watched him go. She knew before he had arrived what would take place. And the longer she had spoken with him, the more details had come to her. Vivid and vibrant, showing her the things that were to come as if she were standing in the very midst of the unfolding events. She had just hoped that somehow, for once, Fate would be wrong and she would get to spend a few precious hours in Rowlfghorm's company before he had to speed away again. Their visits were far too few. She turned and went back up the stone steps and entered the castle.

"I am to have all news delivered immediately to my chambers, no matter the hour, no matter how trivial. And meals too. No one is to disturb me for anything else," she barked to the servants as she trudged up the stairs, to her chambers. She entered her rooms and closed the heavy door behind her, leaning against its roughness for a minute, trying to regain her confidence and strength.

She threw back the heavy blue curtains that shrouded the Orb of Orion from the room. There it was, glowing red, bright like fire, so bright it lit the room with its glow. She hovered her hands above it in swirling motions, beckoning the powers within to reveal its secrets. Tristan had reached Aldaetan. In reality, he wouldn't reach the city walls for four more hours, but she was peering through the thick veil of time. Tristan would die fighting. She watched as four Orcs attacked him simultaneously, hacking him apart as he struggled to stand. She had known this when she was talking to Rowlfghorm, but she also knew that the prospective loss of Rowlfghorm's most loyal captain would cause him to act rashly and dangerously. She had chosen to withhold this information from Rowlfghorm out of pity and to safeguard the people Rowlfghorm would be protecting.

She fought the urge to see her father. She struggled with the Orb's forces that tried to part the veil to show her his fate. She used her strength and power to cloud the images. She did not want to see her father's end, to hear him call her name. The most powerful Enchantress foretold by prophecy and she could do nothing to save her father from an Orcish frenzy of destruction. She prayed to the goddesses and to the Spirits of the Realm to take him quickly so that he would not suffer.

The Orb gave up. Instead, it showed her the Goblin army moving out of the Northern Goblin Nations of Azrear. They marched to Aldaetan. Goblins marching. Orcs marching. Equally evil. Equally chaotic . . . Goblins met Orcs with devastating intensity. Blood ran in torrents through the city, through the streets—Elves and Humans fought side by side, in doorways, and alleys, on rooftops and in streets but still they were no match for the hoards of swarming Orcs. The citizens of Aldaetan were outnumbered plain and simple. No sword was powerful enough when every man fought two or more Orcs apiece. The Orcs kept coming, more and more of them in chaotic, violent numbers. And right on the tail of the Orcs the Goblins poured over the walls slaughtering the Orcs. It seemed to Aldaetan that their numbers would never cease—but what of Garren of Rimeal?

Elsinore suddenly became aware of his glaring absence. Had he slinked off like a coward? Did he turn tail and run before the battle had ever begun? Theoretically, the leader should be visible somewhere in the battle. Even if he was unmarked, she should be able to sense his whereabouts in the midst of the carnage that unfolded before her. So, she waited, as the hours passed and the veiled time became the now. She waited for the Orb to see more.

Elsinore stirred the mists of the Orb, but it would not yield Garren's fate. She had encountered powers that had tried to veil her eyes before, but the Orb always fought and revealed what she sought. This force she felt was new. The Orb was holding back information. There was nothingness where images should be. She felt an apprehension from the Orb as if it was avoiding her requests. Was the Orb sheltering her, or someone else? She waved her hands over the Orb, commanding it to let her see. A feeling of fear seized her, clutched her heart, and sent shivers over her flesh. This was not the Orb. This was evil. There was a stirring in the Orb. For a moment she sensed the interference of an unknown power equal to her own. The Orb fought to reveal the outsider tampering with Isgor's implement and Elsinore's mind. Black swirling mists revealed nothing. Elsinore was furious. Who was it that possessed such powers and how had they escaped the eyes and ears of Isgor?

Who had such audacity to attempt to gain control of the Orb? Who believed themselves powerful enough to wrest control of the Orb from the Enchantress herself? She continued to struggle in the dark mists, to crack the protecting veil around Garren that this evil had established.

Suddenly, Elsinore was seized with an intense buzzing feeling; a vibrating shook her body, as she grew aware of a fragment, a sliver, a very small break in the cloak of the person interfering with her. For a fraction of a second she was able to see a black robe, but the thick fog returned before she could see a face.

Elsinore commanded the Orb to show her the fate of Garren of Rimeal. Blackness. Deep inside the blood-red throbbing Orb, she saw only swirling, misty fingers of blackness. Someone knew secrets that were only supposed to be known only by herself, her grandmother and the Spirits of the Realm that created the Orb. Someone had discovered ways to interfere with the Orb. She would find out who that someone was! Angrily, she summoned all of her energies and touched the bare Orb. Bolts of light burst off of the Orb as it struggled to push her from its surface. It was an entity in itself . . . to be touched by the powers of the Enchantress of Isgor was to be drained of its knowledge. Defensively, it fought for its own preservation the same way the Enchantress would fight for hers if threatened.

"Ahgh!" Elsinore screamed as she was propelled backwards into the wall. She slumped to the floor. Her hands smoked, her skin was charred and hanging in fleshy pink and black strips. Dazed, she searched her brain for the remedy and then muttered something to her hands. She laid her head back against the cold stones and breathed deeply as her hands were restored.

When she opened her eyes, and looked upon the Orb, a chilled horror filled her. A deep crack ran down one side across half of the Orb's diameter. It glowed the same pulsating red, but where the crack was, mist seeped slowly outward, curling over the Orb and through the air.

"What have I done?" Elsinore cried out in mingled disbelief and horror. She had broken what could not be broken.

29

Elsinore watched the seeping mists crawl and spiral from the deep crevice in the crimson orb. Its gold stand glittered in the throbbing light; the foggy fingers swirled around the Orb, spreading out into the room, inching ever closer to Elsinore.

For the first time in her life, she feared the Orb. This sphere that she had danced around as a child, laughed into and talked to. She had been as one with the Orb; it was a part of her. The fear was all consuming. It surrounded her like the cold blanket of death and tried to draw her into its dark web. She raised her hand and chanted a Cantation of Protection. The smoke fingers recoiled backwards as if wounded by her words. Elsinore was transfixed, waiting to see what would happen.

She gasped as a gnarled hand grasped the outer edge of the Orb. She huddled against the wall, enveloped in her Cantation of Protection as the figure of a grotesque man stood up within the broken shell of the Orb, climbed out and over the jagged, shattered edges of the Orb and landed solidly on her stone floor.

He squinted in her direction, his dripping snout foul and dirty, twitching this way and that like a rabbit, as he sniffed the air for her scent. It seemed his eyes did not adjust well in the pulsating redness of the Orb's glow. He sniffed in her direction again. He reminded Elsinore of a dog sniffing for a hiding rodent, ready to pounce the moment the scent was located.

He stood there, his body bent and deformed due to his half-breeding, but when he finally saw her, he looked upon her with Human eyes. His eyes looked through her and into her very soul.

Elsinore stood up. She was amazed at the power contained within his eyes. From where did this power spring? Despite the shiver that ran down her spine, Elsinore fought to gather her strength. He might have been able to grip the hearts of Orcs and ordinary men and rattle them with feelings of fear and self-doubt with his piercing stares, but she was not an Orc nor was she an ordinary man. She was the Enchantress of Isgor, and he only had an inkling of the magic Isgor possessed. She would not cower before this stinking dog in fear. Elsinore summoned the courage of her mothers and the great and mighty Goddess and drew herself up straight and fierce. She was not just a girl nor was she just a cunning woman with a bag of herbs and some magic words.

She was the Enchantress of Isgor.

He was half a monster—half a man. He was Garren of Rimeal.

"You are the Enchantress? The powerful one?" Garren said in a gruff, snorting voice. He looked at her from head to toe as if he was inspecting her for purchase.

Elsinore watched him, studied him. "Yes. I am the Enchantress of Isgor and you are Garren of Rimeal. What purpose do you have here?" she demanded.

"Ah! So, you knew I was coming! I see Mother was wrong," Garren's lips twitched in a sort of smile.

Elsinore didn't know he was coming, but as long as he believed she had known, she would have an advantage. "What do you want?" Elsinore asked in a commanding tone.

"To kill you."

Elsinore laughed. At first it was a soft lilting laughter, but then it mounted in intensity. "You? Kill me? What powers do you possess that you believe this is possible?"

Her laughter confused and enraged him. He stared at her with his strange human eyes set in the animal-monster sockets of an Orc's face. "Enough!" he growled.

"Do not think that you can command me to be silent, Orc!" Elsinore raised her hands into the air and sent a fireball hurling towards Garren. He ducked the blazing ball and rolled across the stone floor at remarkable speed, avoiding the spell. He leapt to his feet and charged her. "I do not take kindly to intrusions of this sort!" Again she shot a fiery projectile in his direction. This one hit him in the leg and he collapsed, yelping like a wounded hound.

Garren's eyes flashed angrily and his face grew even more hideous with the rage that seethed and brewed in his heart. "You will pay for that witch!" he yelled, struggling to stand, clutching the charred and bleeding wound on his leg.

"No! You will pay. You and whatever dark master conjures for you. Your link to them is gone! You lost it when you destroyed the Orb with your coming! I hope you have enough power on your own

31

because you are beyond help now that you're behind the veil of Isgor!" Elsinore raised another hand, but Garren was quicker. He lunged for her wrist and grabbed it, knocking her onto her back, pinning her arms to the ground.

He looked at her face, his own features contorting and twitching with the disgust and contempt he held for her. "You are nothing more than a girl! Where is the Enchantress I seek? You cannot be her!" he spat the words through gnashing teeth. His hatred was apparent; his confidence was acted well, but not convincing. His words sounded powerful, but his body shook and quivered as she spoke. He had expected more power in the way of a physical being, and now, having been presented with this slight, wisp of a girl, found he had been shaken to his core. Her strength found its origins in the ancient power of Isgor. The realization of this dawned on Garren too late to have reversed his foolish plans.

Elsinore stared back into his eyes and knew in an instant what she saw. Hate. Loathing. But above all, his eyes reflected fear. He had no real powers. A few spells, a few potions—that was all. This one was all bark. Elsinore summoned her powers and at once shot to her feet. Garren flew across the room and crashed into the wall. He fell to the ground in a broken heap, dazed his head lolling.

"Is this the Enchantress that you seek?" she shouted. "Who sent you, pig?!"

Elsinore had never felt such rage before. She had never felt such power surge through her body. Her strength was incredible. She had never been challenged so defiantly before. If this was a test from the Spirits, she was passing it with flying colors.

Garren was silent. Elsinore flung back her hand, and at once, he rose to the high vaulted ceiling with ferocious speed. He held his hands above his head to stop himself from smashing into the hard stone. He screamed.

"Talk to me! I want to know who sent you!" she shouted.

Garren looked around frantically as if there was some way to escape.

Elsinore dropped her hand and Garren came crashing to the stone floor. He bellowed in pain and lay there writhing. Elsinore leaned over him and stared him in the face as he had done to her. "Where is Garren of Rimeal? The soldier? The warrior? You are but a dog—where is the one I sensed?" she laughed as she toyed with him. "Come now, use your powers. You do have some, do you not? Who would send you to do battle with The Enchantress without powers of your own?"

Garren grasped an amulet from around his neck. He yanked it off and threw it at Elsinore. She threw up her arms and a barrier formed around her—protecting her like a wall. The amulet exploded into a fiery cascade, sending smoke and sparks all around and catching the curtains on fire. Elsinore leaped out of the path of the falling sparks and protected her face with her hand. Casting a glance at the fire that consumed the curtains she snapped her fingers and shouted, "Extinguishet!" The flames disappeared in a pouf of black, acrid smoke.

"Is that what you've come to battle with? An amulet? Come now! Is this all?" Elsinore laughed again.

Garren struggled to his feet, reciting a low cantation. Elsinore listened closely to his spell and quickly chanted a counter spell before he could finish. Garren was knocked to the ground once again and lay struggling to breathe. Elsinore shook her head in disgust.

"What have I done to you, Orc, to make you come here—in this manner—under some dark power—to kill me? What have *I* done to *you*?"

Garren winced in pain and shouted, "I come to avenge my mother!"

"I know not your mother," Elsinore said simply. "What has she to do with me?"

"She is your aunt. My mother is Lisbeth of Raganor. Daughter of Lamrea of Isgor," Garren said while breathing jaggedly with pain.

"I did not know I had an aunt," Elsinore said.

"It is true. Lamrea of Isgor left my mother to the invading Orcs. Left her behind to suffer whatever fate lay in wait for her at the hands of my father's race. It is for her that I seek your head," he growled, dog-like, between his sharp yellow teeth.

Elsinore circled the beast. Why had her grandmother kept this

33

from her? Who was this Lisbeth of Raganor? Why had Grandmother deserted her to the Orcs—who deserved such a fate?

"I did not know this, Garren of Rimeal," Elsinore said in a quiet, even tone that revealed the truth in her statement.

"The rules of Isgor demand that blood bars you from killing me," he growled in between bouts of pain as he crawled about on the floor.

"Aye. That is the law. This must be the reason you are not dead yet. You should have been dead already. The Spirits have intervened," Elsinore sat down in a chair and shrugged.

"My mother will come for me!" Garren barked, sounding like a child attempting to reason with a bully.

"Will she now?" Elsinore looked doubtful. "If that is true, why then, did she not come for my head herself?"

Garren's face went blank as if he had not thought of that before.

"Why did she send you to do her dirty work?" Elsinore said softly. "I don't think she has any plans for coming here. For one, she cannot cross the barrier between the mortal world and Isgor unless invited, and she has destroyed the Orb so she cannot circumvent the barrier as you did. So, tell me, how will your mother come rescue you?"

Garren snorted. "Release me!"

"How did your mother transport you through the Orb?" Elsinore demanded.

"She knows secrets. There was a book. It was burned," Garren said between jolts of pain. "When she was a girl. In Lamrea's chambers."

"She memorized parts of the book?" Elsinore raised her eyebrows.

"She removed pages. The book was huge. Lamrea didn't even notice."

Elsinore's heart beat rapidly. Missing pages with secrets she did not know. What else was there that this aunt knew that Elsinore did not? "Where is your mother now?" she asked.

Garren began to laugh. "Do you think I'd betray my own

mother?"

Elsinore held up a finger and pain coursed through Garren's body once more. "She has betrayed you already, you fool," she knit her brows together in vexation.

"My army will destroy Aldaetan!" he yelled out, as if this gave him some bargaining leverage.

"Your army has already destroyed Aldaetan," Elsinore said sadly, but then a slight smile curled her lips. "And the Goblins, none too happy to discover Orcs crossing their territories, engaged your forces within the walls of Aldaetan, destroying whatever remnants of the city that your dogs missed, *and* your army as well. The Goblins have claimed Aldaetan as their own. So, you see, Garren, I'm afraid you have no army now."

Garren pounded the ground. "Defeated?" he shouted.

"To the very last Orc, I'm afraid," Elsinore said simply.

"Damn the Goblins!" Garren cursed.

"Now, cousin, *there* is something we agree upon," Elsinore said with a tilt of her head and a sarcastic chuckle.

Garren lay back on the floor and looked up at the ceiling. Elsinore waved a hand and the spell broke, leaving Garren breathing rapidly on the floor.

"Your mother, no doubt, will be angered by your failure," Elsinore said slowly.

"She should have done the job herself as you said."

Elsinore raised a brow. "Perhaps."

"What now, Enchantress, will you feed me to your dogs?"

"No. We are much more civilized than that. I don't know what I'm going to do with you actually," Elsinore frowned. "I don't appreciate you trying to kill me, but seeing how you failed miserably at that, what really irks me is that you've destroyed the Orb." Elsinore walked around the shattered glass that once was the Orb of Orion. "My life has always revolved around this Orb."

Garren rubbed his neck as he lay on the floor. "Seems to me you don't need that blasted ball of glass."

Elsinore sighed. Apparently, she hadn't. Well, she wasn't going to sit there and talk friendly with Garren of Rimeal. She pulled a long gold cord that was hanging from the ceiling and after a few minutes four guards burst into her chambers. "Take this beast and lock him up. He is a wily one, be alert." The four men yanked Garren up from the floor. He watched Elsinore as they dragged him away.

She crossed the room, which was now in shambles, and threw open the window. She sat down on the window seat and sighed deeply. She was exhausted. The Orb was broken, shattered, destroyed. She had long thought that it was the source of her power, but today she had learned that the power had come from her. She was the one that knew the magic, the charms, the spells, and the incantations. She was the one who could see through the veils and realms. The Orb was only an instrument. She knew that now.

Elsinore gathered her long legs up under her skirts and pushed a pillow behind her head. As soon as her grandmother returned from the Dwarven provinces of Karuth, where she was healing the wretched victims of a virulent plague, there would be much to talk about. Elsinore looked out over the green rolling hills of Isgor. Out there beyond the enchanted realm was a powerful, dark sorceress who wanted her head. Out there was an aunt who had been deprived of her birthright and was bent on punishing Elsinore for her loss. There were many questions in need of answers.

As for Garren, she had lied; she knew exactly what she would do with him. She would send word to Rowlfghorm that Garren of Rimeal was in her possession. Rowlfghorm would take care of that situation. For her, there were more pressing issues to resolve than dealing with a half-breed rogue Orc.

Elsinore sighed loudly. This was her calling. This was why she was here. She tried to see Lisbeth of Raganor with her seeing eye, but the fog was heavy as it had been within the Orb. Lisbeth had thought that destroying the Orb would destroy the Enchantress? How wrong she had been! Instead, Lisbeth's folly had made Elsinore aware of just how powerful she was and how she had been missing that point all along. She was not just a girl. She was the Enchantress of Isgor.

"Go on, hide, Lisbeth of Raganor, *Dark Witch*. Run and hide," Elsinore lightly touched the rippled glass of the open window and knit her brows. "But hear me now—I *will* find you."

Somewhere in a distant land far away from Isgor, a black robed figure abruptly halted her horse as Elsinore's words sliced through her like a knife. Lisbeth threw back her hood, searching for the source of the voice, before realizing that the words had broken through her magical barrier of protection and penetrated deep into her mind. She shuddered and spurred her horse into the fog of the uncharted Orc territories.

The Starred Sapphire

by Pamela Hearon Hodges

Domaia pressed her fingers to the hermit's scrawny neck and held them there, waiting for the pulse to stop. It didn't take long; the poison worked quickly. She kept her eyes averted from his glazed stare. Death was not something she feared, but she disliked looking it in the eye. It reminded her of the morning she found her mother, cold and staring. She wiped her fingers on her cloak, symbolically brushing away the memory. Such a pity. Having to dispose of Tilden, who trusted her, to gain Hein, who didn't.

She sighed. Hein, the handsome Llaholdran prince was best suited for her purpose. Arrogant . . . conceited—he would definitely have to be taught some lessons in behavior, but all men required some tutelage. Hein had potential—more than the other five in the lineage she had studied carefully for quite some time.

They were a vile race, these Llaholdrans, and their princes were the vilest of all. Prone to violence, they warred continuously amongst themselves. Hein and his five brothers had each claimed a portion of the country upon their father's death, ripping Llaholdra to small factions and rendering it easy prey. Domaia spat on the ground, discharging from her mouth the bile that rose when she thought of them. None of the whole lot was worthy of ruling a kingdom.

Garon, the eldest, was a barbarian who slashed his subjects into submission with his mighty sword. He was ruthless in his treatment of all and would be the first to be overthrown, Domaia knew. Winning his affection would have required cruel games of submission that she had no taste for. It would be a pleasure to watch him fall by his own power, much more fun than removing him from it.

The second-born was Ludane who had intrigued Domaia at first. His lust for battle and his lust for women were equally matched, or so the rumors said. She observed from a distance his apparent insatiable appetite as maiden after maiden was coaxed to his chamber, sometimes alone and sometimes in pairs or small groups. When at last she decided to be chosen, she soon found his speech was much more animated than his lovemaking. He was a boor . . . and a bore.

Domaia had moved on to Raier, whom she immediately recognized as having more interest in the stable boys than in her. Drawn by his brooding masculine countenance, she had hoped his obvious preference might digress for a time. She charmed him, cajoled him, and won his interest one night.

During their love play, as she lightly tickled his ribs with her tongue, Raier fell into a fit of high-pitched, uncontrollable giggling. That sound coming from that body was a nauseating combination, one she would be unable to tolerate for long. While he could fulfill her immediate purpose, she had her future and her own needs to think about. Would it not be better to have someone available to whom she was at least attracted?

Vyhym, the fourth-born was nearly as useless to her. The poor man was madly in love with his wife. They had known each other since childhood and had apparently been in love their whole lives. All of his campaigns were fought as homage to this woman he adored. She was the source of his power and would ultimately be

40

his undoing. Domaia understood what Vyhym did not: one must not divide loyalties between a kingdom and a spouse. Domaia considered removing the woman, and that was still a possibility, of course, if anything went wrong here. But nothing would go awry. Domaia would not allow it.

One son younger than Hein also remained, but he was little more than a boy. Domaia much preferred the company of men. She was sure the lad would be eager to please, most were. However, his campaigns were led by advisors and he would be guarded closely. She ascertained he would require more time and patience than she was willing to expend, unless all else failed.

Mentally scanning the group, it was understandable why her father chose to blame the Llaholdrans for her mother's death. Domaia might have even believed it had she not overheard her father's confession to his lover, who was now his wife.

Men. Such a nasty breed. Domaia had yet to meet one she trusted. The more powerful they became, the less trust one could place in them. Why had her mother not learned that lesson? Or had she merely chosen to ignore it?

Domaia's father was a king; Hein was a prince. Neither could be trusted, not with her life and certainly not with her kingdom. Both wielded great power. But power alone was merely brute strength waiting to be bested. Power must be infused with knowledge and reasoning and a sense of justice to develop into a prevailing force. Domaia would prevail in Garanthali as no man ever had.

Though never allowing herself to become enamored of a man, Domaia had allowed herself a physical attraction to Hein, especially to his eyes. Those eyes held a delightful gleam when he was pleased . . . and for a time, she had pleased him often, as it suited her purpose. That gleam was meant for her alone; it made her feel secure. She would not allow the gleam, or anything else, to be shared with anyone—especially not that mewling sop, Caralyn. Domaia felt her face flush at the thought of the woman.

A fly landed on the hermit's face. Domaia absently watched it crawl into the open mouth, perhaps already sensing a secure home for its larvae. She wrinkled her nose in disgust. Too bad Hein hadn't

41

been more cooperative. All of this nasty business of consorting with dirty hermits and lowly seneschals was distasteful—definitely beneath her.

Domaia checked Tilden's wound, stretching the neckline of his sackcloth garment to reveal a bit of shoulder. The nick hadn't festered, wouldn't even be noticed in an hour or so. Poor lonely Tilden the Hermit. His body probably wouldn't be found for days or weeks. Death by natural causes would be the assumption, for no one would care to assume anything different. By then, maggots would have destroyed any evidence.

Domaia closed the knife, being careful not to touch the tip. A tiny droplet of milky green liquid glimmered in the candlelight, enough for one more application. She tucked the knife into her sleeve, adjusting it to the perfect position to be withdrawn smoothly. It shouldn't be needed for a while, but one could never be too careful.

She rose and leaned over the table, admiring the hermit's handiwork. Three small vials lay atop a worn leather cloth, each tinged a slightly different hue with a colored stopper to match. Yellow. Blue. Red. How droll! Such wondrous magic contained in such simple wrapping. Tilden's wondrous magic by his own account. She chuckled derisively. Someone else's magic, not hers. The Prophecy must be fulfilled.

"She shall return to Garinthali with the Llaholdran Prince whose blood shall atone for that of my lost Queen. In this endeavor, she must employ none of her sorceress powers as true justice requires no magic." Domaia mimicked her father's voice, using her most sententious tone. "Only then, will I deem her worthy of my succession." Worthy indeed! He was terrified of her power, just as he had been terrified of her mother's. The scheme that saw her mother murdered, reputedly by a Llohaldran prince, would be revealed. "Justice!" her father had declared before the silent Oracle. Well, justice he would get.

Domaia coldly eyed the dead hermit. The only "magic" she had needed was her feminine wiles: a cooing voice and misty eyes had convinced both Tilden and Gir she truly cared for them. Then they fell all over themselves trying to please her and continually earn her favor. Fools!

"Exulted High Priestess Domaia, Queen of Garinthali!" She sounded the words, trying on the title as if it were the ermine cloak she wore. A perfect fit, she decided. "And in a fortnight, it shall be mine!" She gathered the vials, carefully wrapping them in the leather, tying the bundle securely with a strip of rawhide.

Then she turned her attention to the object remaining on the table: her beautiful blue sapphire, the last gift from her mother. Leaving it with the hermit so long had been difficult. The stone needed to soak up all the magic in the potion, he had explained, but Domaia understood his game as she had all the others. Tilden lived for her visits, wanted to prolong them as long as he could. She glanced at his crumpled body. Well, he didn't have to live any more; she wouldn't be returning. She secured the sapphire in her locket, then slipped the chain around her neck.

Leaving the candle to burn itself out, she started for the door, pausing at the hermit's gnarled body. "Primitive magic. Brews . . . potions," she nudged the corpse with her toe and sneered. "I could have shown you amazing feats, yet you were content with a simple kiss."

Domaia slipped quietly into the cover of darkness.

~~~~~

Impatiently, Gir patted the small bundle tucked into his vest. His freedom and his passage and the assurance of Domaia's love, all wrapped up in a strip of leather. He shuddered involuntarily at the thought of the seductive beauty, his Domaia. His body tightened at the thought of her touch. He never knew such ecstasy existed!

Gir laughed aloud, and his laugh echoed across the lake. Luckily for him, Hein hadn't known how to tame her! Gir had often secretly watched the two of them when they thought they were alone; it was obvious Hein was no match for a woman such as Domaia. Caralyn was more Hein's type. Docile. Subservient.

Gir rolled his eyes in amusement, remembering the scene when Hein had been confronted about his dalliance. Of course, Domaia was jealous when she learned of Caralyn. Any woman would be, but especially one as hot-blooded as the Garanthali seductress. Yes, she screamed . . . went so far as threatening him with heinous spells. What did Hein expect? She was a sorceress! But to punish her by banishment? Did he really think that would stop her if she were determined to have vengeance? Bah! Gir knew how he would have handled the situation. A few tender kisses, some whispered promises coupled with endearments, and Hein could have had both women! Stupid fool!

Gir loosened the amber flask from his belt and emptied its contents with one swig. The liquid burned its way to his core, reminding him of Domaia. That she was "forbidden fruit" made her more enticing. He licked his lips. Her banishment from the kingdom meant certain death if he was found with her. But he was Seneschal, most trusted of all Hein's servants, above suspicion. And Domaia always made their meetings worth any danger. His breathing quickened in anticipation.

The sound of light footsteps made him turn, and then she was there before him, a radiant vision with her white ermine hood gathered around her pale face. She rushed to him, dropping the hood to reveal golden tresses that caught the moonlight in their web. Her body pushed eagerly against his while their lips merged into an exquisite, fiery oneness.

"Do you have them?" Her warm breath scampered delicately across his neck sending delightful shivers up his spine.

"Yes, my lady. I have all you need."

Her smoldering eyes told him she caught his innuendo. "Show me."

Taking her by the arm, he guided Domaia to the coverlet he had spread upon the ground and instructed her to sit quietly. She folded her hands demurely in her lap and waited while he removed the leather bundle and unrolled it. Three small vials and an inked parchment were soon displayed.

He chose the parchment first, holding it up for her inspection. "Passage for one from Llaholdra to Prjeve."

"And I will secure it from there." Moonlight pooled in Domaia's black eyes, giving her an enticingly sinister look.

"When will that be done, my love?" Gir worried she was cutting time a bit close. She had said the spell would only last three or four hours . . . enough time for him to reach the harbor, but not so long as to make anyone suspicious.

Domaia's breath made soft clouds in the air. "As soon as our time here is done, I'll make straightway to finish the arrangements," she promised. "Now tell me how you accomplished the deed."

Gir picked up the vial with the yellow stopper. "Hein wanted his hair trimmed for the ceremony; I volunteered. One hair from his head delivered to you, Madam."

He sat beside her and picked up the vial with the blue stopper, tilting it to reveal a single droplet as its contents. "We engaged in a little friendly wrestling, as we have done since childhood. When we finished, I wiped his sweat with my cloth, and later, squeezed out this droplet."

"Very ingenious," Domaia leaned against his chest, giving his ear a playful nip. "And how did you get the drop of blood?"

"A tiny nick while shaving him. My jaw bore the brunt of his wrath!" Gir rubbed the spot, hoping to gain some sympathy.

Domaia kissed his hand. "A small price to pay for your freedom. Now," she removed the chain from around her neck, opening the locket to reveal a blue sapphire, "let us move quickly so I can hurry with the spell. Take each of the vials, and empty its contents onto the sapphire," she instructed. Gir did as he was told, taking care to blend the liquids so they would hold the fine-textured hair onto the blue stone.

"Now close the locket and replace it around my neck." Gir followed the directions, planting a kiss on her forehead as he settled the chain in its place.

"Has the spell started?" he asked, brushing her face with the back of his fingers. Surely, they would have some time before he had to return.

"No, it won't activate for awhile, Love." Domaia laughed at his eagerness. "But by the time you get back, Prince Hein should be feeling deliriously, uncontrollably happy. He will not understand it to be the effects of a spell, but will merely think he is excited over

45

the nuptials. You will find him ready to offer you anything you wish. Ask for your freedom from his service. That shall be granted—then leave quickly before the spell wears off and he realizes he has lost you forever." She kissed him passionately. "And I will have gained you forever!"

The combination of freedom and life with Domaia gave Gir a sense of urgency. He pushed her onto her back, eager to find release. His tongue probed her mouth as his hands started loosening her cloak. He buried his face in her soft tresses, breathing in her exciting aroma. An insect stung his neck. He swatted it away, catching the withdrawing knife blade across his hand. He made to raise himself up, but his strength left him and he fell forward.

"Whatever is the matter, Darling?" Domaia purred, rolling him off of her, onto his back.

He stared in horror, speech gurgling unintelligibly in his throat. A cool hand closed his eyes when the gurgling stopped.

Domaia worked quickly, slashing his wrist and dragging his arm across the coverlet to draw a bloody letter C, then closed his other hand around the hilt of her knife. She wouldn't need it any longer. A small crumpled note pulled from her bodice was placed in his other hand and carefully laid across his heart. No magic had been needed to mimic his scribbled penmanship.

Standing up, she eyed her handiwork with satisfaction. Who would imagine Gir capable of such strong emotion? The strong, faithful seneschal. To think that he would commit suicide rather than see his beloved Caralyn married this day to his master.

Domaia hurriedly gathered the contents of the leather wrapping, tossing them into the lake, then tucked the parchment promising passage for one into her bodice. There was much to do before the wedding.

~~~~~

"Can I help you to a seat, Viepere?" The youth addressed her as "Old Father". Domaia was pleased; obviously the disguise was a good one. She nodded and allowed herself to be led through the crowd and up a few steps to a bench.

She patted the young man's head, smiling. He turned quickly

away, repulsed by the sight of her blackened teeth and the stench of her breath. Ashes rubbed into her hair and skin turned both a dirty gray and gave an aura of imminent death. Clouded lenses allowed her to see, while giving the appearance of blindness.

Those already seated gave plenty of room to the blind beggar. All manner of disease could be caught from such a filthy creature. Domaia positioned herself for an unobstructed view of the proceedings.

Conversations flitting within earshot, focused on the pending nuptials: Caralyn's beauty, the perfection of the couple, Hein's good fortune of finding such a deserving mate. Some wondered if Domaia the Sorceress would try to stop the nuptials, perhaps by appearing on the back of a dragon. Others speculated she might be disguised, lurking somewhere in the crowd.

Domaia listened to the conversations with glee, biding her time patiently. Occasionally, she would draw her arm inside her tunic to finger her locket.

At last, the ceremony began with all the pomp necessary to marry off a member of the royal family. Bells pealed loudly as the handsome couple made their way to the dais in the center of the arena. Specially written choruses were played by the finest musicians and sung by the most beautiful voices in Hein's kingdom. Doves were released from cages, and finally, marriage vows were spoken. Caralyn's sweet voice captivated the audience. She stared directly into Prince Hein's eyes the entire time she spoke, obviously too enamored to know anyone else existed besides the two of them.

Hein's words were tinged with a huskiness that spoke volumes of his desire for the woman standing beside him. When the priest declared them husband and wife, the crowd sighed collectively, then hushed to hear the sealing kiss. They weren't disappointed. Hein claimed his bride with a lusty kiss whose endurance was so long several women swooned just from watching.

Reluctantly, the couple parted at last and turned to present themselves to the waiting crowd. A roar of approval filled the air. Caralyn bowed her head demurely, a gesture indicating her humbleness at being raised to such a station. Hein cupped his hand adoringly under her chin and raised her face to kiss her once more. The crowd cheered their prince and new princess. Hein smiled broadly, facing the crowd with their clutched hands held high. His eyes shone brightly with that special gleam Domaia knew should be meant only for her.

She pulled the locket from beneath her clothes and opened it with a smooth, unobtrusive gesture. Instantly, Hein disappeared. Domaia closed the locket, replacing it once again below her ragged garments.

The crowd sat silent for a moment, too stunned to speak or move. Princess Caralyn spun around, bewildered. A murmur arose, then crescendoed to a frantic cry of alarm: "Where is he? What has become of Prince Hein?" Guards rushed to the floor, prepared to do battle with the invisible enemy.

Someone shouted, "Where is he? What has happened to Prince Hein?" And from across the arena, an answering shout: "The Sorceress Domaia has done this!"

The crowd took up the suggestion. "Find Domaia! Find her! Let her burn for this treachery!"

The old beggar turned, making his voice heard above the chaos to those standing nearby. "It is the Princess Caralyn," he said calmly. "She is Domaia in disguise."

A few heard the declaration. The old beggar was blind . . . perhaps a seer? Surely he knew what others could not! "The Princess Caralyn is Domaia the Sorceress!" The section of audience surrounding the beggar spewed forth the words as a battle cry, soon gathering strength from the entire crowd. "Seize her!" they demanded.

Guards were upon the frightened girl in an instant. She hardly had time to protest before the mob spilled onto the floor, demanding justice for such a vicious deed.

No one noticed the old blind seer, hobbling his way out of the angry throng, smiling broadly with blackened teeth, clutching a locket beneath ragged clothing.

~~~~~

The journey from Llaholdra had been arduous. As the beggar, Domaia had to limp several miles to her waiting horse and the

48

second disguise. The warm spring-fed pool provided a luxurious bath which washed away all signs of the blind seer.

Binding her breasts, she donned the garb of a youth. A hat covered the golden tresses during the horseback ride to the coast and the entire voyage by ship to Prejve.

At Prejve, the black attire of a mourning widow had helped her secure the palfrey she needed from a farmer on the edge of town. A touch of yellow ointment to her cheeks and a bit of charcoal under the eyes had convinced the farmer her days were numbered. She would soon be joining her dear departed husband, but first wanted to spend a day saying good-bye to the countryside of her birth. He practically threw the reins at her in his haste to remove himself from certain contagion. He was even reluctant to touch the money she left. No doubt, his greed would overcome his logic eventually.

The palfrey had at last brought her to the secret shelter, a cave in the cliffs overlooking the Chandris Sea. Using the shrill whistle she had been taught as a child, Domaia summoned her magnificent winged horse, Megariff. Through her mother's sorcery, that sound reached the creature, anywhere.

Gliding her hands along the snow-white feathers of his outstretched wings, Domaia luxuriated in the feel of her faithful companion beneath her. She was safe at last.

Three days flew by as swiftly as the land beneath them. Domaia watched eagerly as the blue shades of sea gave way to the white of chalky cliffs and then the green of home.

"Land here, Megariff," she instructed. Her locket vibrated gently as the magic ebbed away; it wouldn't be long. Tilden had been quite precise in his timing after all. The pallid creature came to rest in a meadow of purple heather.

Domaia breathed deeply, intoxicated by the smell of home after her two-year absence. She wondered if the messengers had reported her return to her father. Though still several hours away from the capital city, even on the back of Megariff, her return would be sensed by the messengers. That would probably work to her advantage.

A crowd would be gathered at the Oracle to watch her father's reaction to her return. She would present Hein to the Oracle as fulfillment of her father's false prophecy. And then, her father would be exposed. The Oracle would break its long period of silence and denounce her father's treachery and she would be declared High Priestess, Queen of Garanthali. She had seen the events unfold through the Sight passed to her by her mother.

"My beloved Garanthali," she declared to the gentle breeze welcoming her, "by this evening, you shall truly be mine!"

Kneeling solemnly, she removed the chain from her neck and placed the locket on the ground. Gingerly, she opened it, hands shaking with anticipation.

There it lay. Her beautiful blue sapphire; the last gift from her mother. She understood now. Her mother had given her everything she would need to avenge her death.

The stone vibrated more strongly than before. She prepared herself for Hein's appearance. He would protest, perhaps fight or try to escape. But he was no match for her, never had been. Escape would be impossible. She nuzzled Megarif's neck lovingly.

Once the public presentation was made before the Oracle, the truth would be revealed. She would show her father the same mercy he had shown her mother.

Hein would soon be dispensable. His fate would depend on his willingness to give her pleasure. Surely, he would realize that one of his brothers would have laid claim to his kingdom by now. She doubted that anyone cared enough to look for him.

She laughed gaily. In a way, she had probably done Hein a favor. Of all his brothers, he alone would be raised to legend status. Troubadours would sing for generations to come of the gallant prince stolen away by the evil sorceress.

The sapphire shook violently, drawing Domaia's attention. Sunshine reflecting on the stone drew a star to its surface. The star radiated a special gleam, a delightful gleam meant just for her. Just looking at it made Domaia feel secure. She held her breath and waited.

The Moonstone of Kadre Maryn
by Bryan R. Durkin

Twilight lay over the earth, a soft blanket that promised the coming slumber of night and a brief respite from the heat of the day. The orange sun gradually sank below the distant, dark hills in the west, the fiery arms of its corona making one last futile effort to reach out and embrace the stars. To the southeast, like glowing gems in the deep blue vault, two moons rose, each surrounded by a gathering of a million stars. One was just a crescent, colored a deep red, and the other, nearly full, was a pale amethyst. Erenón Haldora and Amphissa Myara they were called, the Crimson Rider and the Lady of the Stars. As it had been for countless centuries, the lonely knight continued to pursue the enchantress across the heavens.

Bors Malik stepped into a small clearing, one of the few spots in the valley that was not covered by the green canopy of the forest. The skies were peaceful, he thought, and ordered—so unlike his life. He chuckled to himself as he regarded the Rider and the Lady, once again caught up in their eternal game of tag. Few people had the same interest in the skies and all that was within them as he did. It was easier to forget one's cares and to find peace when looking at something as beautiful as the stars and the moons. They were so far away from the harsh realities of life, and they spoke only of wonder and serenity.

But few people found interest in much of anything anymore, besides staying alive and trying to feed themselves. Bors tried to push the thought out of his mind as he started walking once again, but as he went, he had a feeling that, before long, he would end up the same way. One could avoid the repercussions of the past only so long, and he could not shake the growing suspicion that his past was about to catch up with him in some unforeseen manner.

The shadows cast by the trees began to lengthen as the evening drew on. Bors wanted to reach Kadre Maryn before nightfall, and if he continued to stop and look at the stars every few minutes, he was going to reach the city significantly later. He made sure his longsword was slung securely at his left hip and continued north. The walk was peaceful, as most of his journey had been; the woods were silent save for the sounds of the night animals waking and the occasional birdsong as the winged creatures flew back to their nests.

Bors traveled for another hour, following a narrow trail that twisted among the trunks of the dense forest. He came to an abrupt halt as a small noise caught his attention, a skittering among the undergrowth, the rustling of multiple *somethings* hurrying around him just out of sight. The sound was almost indistinguishable from the ordinary noises of the forest, and he had not heard it before. He remained motionless, his ears straining to hear the sound again, but whatever it was, if anything, was now gone. He was about to continue again when it dawned on him.

There was nothing to be heard; the forest had gone completely silent. The insects, the birds, the night animals, all had gone suddenly and utterly quiet. He shifted nervously where he stood, scanning the trees that now seemed to loom threateningly above him. Nothing moved among the undergrowth, no birds flitted through the canopy above. There wasn't even a wind to rustle the leaves. He swallowed hard, realizing that something was amiss, even though his eyes told him otherwise.

As soon as he took another step, the things attacked.

They came from everywhere, materializing out of the thick undergrowth and leaping from the canopy overhead, lurching up the trail and slithering down the trunks of the trees. Yowling and screeching in some language he had never heard before, the creatures swarmed toward him. Less than three feet tall, thin and wiry, they were hideous looking things, their rough skin colored black and their small, round eyes glinting with an odd light in the setting sun. Each of them sported rows of jagged teeth as they howled their war cries. Some were armed only with sharp claws, but others had spiked clubs, short-hafted battle-axes, or long knives.

Bors muttered a curse as he dropped his sack of provisions, holding his staff ready to meet the onslaught. He knew there was no way he could hold back so many of the little demons; there had to be scores of them, but there was nowhere to run. The first monster reached him, and Bors lashed out with his birch staff, catching it across the head. The thing dropped with a squawk, but it was immediately replaced by another. Bors brought his staff back around and obliged the second attacker with a swift blow across the throat. He ducked as he sensed one of the things leap at him from an overhanging branch, barely evading its reaching claws. His next swing caught it in midair, sending it flying into the undergrowth.

The next thing he knew, one of the vermin had latched itself onto his face, hissing and clawing madly. Bors yelled in pain, stumbling aimlessly about; the thing stuck to him like tree sap. His cries of agony turned into a roar of anger, and Bors dropped his staff and ripped the creature away from him with both hands. Ignoring the blood running down his face, he drew his sword, the long blade glittering like a tongue of fire in the light of the setting sun. He began carving a path through the black horde, pressing onward relentlessly, realizing he would have to keep moving if he hoped to have any chance of surviving. Suddenly, he felt clawed hands curl about his legs, but before he could do anything, his feet went out from underneath him, and he fell into the throng of creatures. They howled in glee, swarming about him, each one doing its best to land a solid blow with whatever weapon it wielded.

Even as he tried to bring it up to defend himself, Bors's sword was wrenched from his grasp. He felt one of the creatures bite into his left leg, and then a clawed fist caught him across the right side of his forehead.

This is it, he thought as his vision started to go blurry. In vain, he tried to fend them off with his bare hands. *Just like that.*

As if his thoughts had summoned them, a score of men burst onto the trail, yelling madly. Their plate-mail armor glittered in the red rays of the sunset, and their swords scythed a path through the throng of creatures. Their sudden onslaught scattered the black vermin, who fled yowling into the forest. Those few that were foolish enough to stay and snarl in defiance of the intruders were cut down.

Bors blinked in surprise, wiping thin rivulets of blood from his forehead as the men quickly made sure the surrounding area was safe. He lay there, the shock from the suddenness of the attack, and now the rescue, paralyzing him for a few moments. He looked up as a shadow fell across him.

It was one of the soldiers, clad in silver armor and a black and gold cloak. The man grinned as he leaned over Bors. "Come on, now, you'll live," he chuckled. "Not sure how pretty your face will be after that little melee, but 'tis nothing that will keep you down," he said, offering his hand.

Bors reached out and took the hand, groaning as he was pulled to his feet. Apparently, more than his face had been wounded; his left leg was afire with pain, and his left arm felt as if it had been bent the wrong way more than once. "Many thanks," he gasped, still trying to regain his breath. "I believe I am in your debt."

"No, it's her you should be thanking," the soldier replied, gesturing with one mailed hand over his right shoulder toward a tall, cloaked and hooded figure that had appeared on the path. "She's the one who heard the sounds of the fighting a mile away."

Bors looked to the shadowy figure standing quietly on the road, staring back at him from beneath the hood that concealed her face.

He started toward her, picking up his staff and what was left of his sack on the way. He stood before the tall form and tried to catch a glimpse of her face, but failed. "They tell me I owe my rescue to you," he said. "So I thank you."

The figure gave a curt nod. "You're welcome," came a woman's voice. Gloved hands came up to pull back the hood, revealing the face of a young woman, probably no more than twenty years in age. Raven-black hair, done in a single, tight braid, accented her fair, almost pale skin. Piercing green eyes peered back at him from beneath dark, sharply slanted brows. "I'm glad you're all right. I am Alexia, of Kadre Maryn. I assume that is where you are headed?"

Bors swallowed, forcing himself to meet the gaze of those beautiful, fiery eyes, and nodded curtly. "Yes. I am Bors Malik. I was summoned by High Lord Vessyn to come to the city as soon as I was able. I received his message a fortnight ago."

All at once, Alexia's demeanor seemed to change. Her eyes narrowed, her lips pressed into a line, and Bors felt as if an aura of ice had suddenly sprung up around her. "Oh, yes," she breathed softly. "I *would* be the one unfortunate enough to find you. You're the mercenary the Council sent for, aren't you?"

Bors straightened, squaring his shoulders, but his eyes were still a good two inches below Alexia's. "I *was* a mercenary," he replied. "That past is behind me now."

"The past is never behind us," Alexia replied shortly. "Especially one like yours. Vessyn must be even more desperate than I thought if he has sent for one such as you." She fell silent a moment, her cold gaze scrutinizing him once again, and Bors had the uncomfortable feeling that he was little more than a potentially dangerous insect being studied by something that would just as soon kill him as watch him go by. Finally, she beckoned sharply with one hand, and the soldiers hurried to gather around her. She raised her voice as she spoke. "It seems we've found what we're looking for. It's time we headed back to the city."

The men spread out in a circle around Bors and Alexia, and the group continued up the trail, heading north through the thick forest. There was no sign of further attack by the creatures, but the soldiers remained ready, blades bared.

Just by glancing at her, Bors could tell Alexia didn't want to speak with him; the young woman refused to look at him, and the way she walked—arms crossed within the folds of her cloak, her gait stiff—suggested that just being in his presence was distasteful to her. But there were a few things that he wanted to know, and the sooner the better. "I don't suppose you would have any idea as to why Vessyn needs my help, would you?" he finally got up the courage to ask. "I assume there is some sort of trouble, but his message did not reveal much."

Alexia looked at him for but a moment, then spoke. "Calling it 'trouble' would be an understatement." She paused, as if that was all she was going to tell him, but then added, "Kadre Maryn is under attack."

"By who?"

"The Red Triad. Their armies laid siege to the city two months ago. They have taken control of most of the countryside outside the walls. For a time, we were able to send out raiders to keep their ranks disorganized, but fielding men has become increasingly dangerous of late. We hardly dare to send out patrols or even scouts."

"I had heard that the Triad was making trouble again," Bors said, "but I did not realize they could amass such strength in such a short amount of time. What about those creatures that attacked me? I've never seen anything like them before."

"The creatures are the source of the Triad's new strength. They call themselves the Gathak. Under the employ of the Triad, they serve as proxy soldiers for armies with elite cores of the Red Knights. The Gathak are a communal species, operating under a tribal system that is highly superstitious and extremely fanatical. And that makes them particularly dangerous; they care nothing for themselves, so long as they perceive that the outcome will benefit the tribe." She paused to give him a little smirk. "As I'm sure you've noticed."

Bors ignored her expression. "What about the other cities? Have they not sent aid?"

She looked away and shrugged. "The other cities are apparently unwilling to send soldiers to help us."

"I thought the Order of White Cities was sworn to protect each other. Surely the other nine could come up with some sort of help."

"You ask a lot of questions, mercenary," Alexia growled at him. "Be patient. Even I do not know everything that is involved in this matter. All will be explained when you speak before the City Council."

Bors fell silent for a moment as Alexia pulled her hood back up, hiding her face in shadow. He started to ask another question, but the glare she gave him made him close his mouth with a snap.

She had a good reason for not liking him, he mused. His past was dark, mysterious, and less than reputable. He pushed it aside. For now, he had to worry about what lay ahead.

~~~~~

They reached their destination an hour later. They had left the path they were following, for fear that the enemy might be using it, and now approached the city through the forest. Kadre Maryn was a great sprawling mass of white stone buildings, surrounded by high walls of the same color. To the east and north, Bors could see smoke rising from the camps of the invaders. Atop the ramparts of the city walls, red glints marked where the last, fitful rays of the dying sun reflected from the helms, armor, and weapons of the defenders.

As they neared the last line of the trees, slowly making their way through the thick undergrowth, Bors saw that the main gate to the city was some distance to their right.

"The main gate is carefully watched by a large number of the enemy," Alexia said, noting the direction of his gaze. "We would not make it halfway there before we were swarmed and killed. The Gathak have the majority of their army camped on the far side of the gate, to the east, so we usually enter the city on the west side. There is a small guard gate there, made so that it cannot be seen from the outside."

Bors nodded in understanding. "But won't they have sentries in the area, patrols?" he asked.

She gave a curt nod. "They do, which is why we'll stay out of sight until the last possible moment."

They continued toward Kadre Maryn, now turning a bit to the

west. They kept their pace slow, sticking to the thickest patches of undergrowth, using ferns, brightly flowering bushes, and the tree trunks for cover. Every now and then, they would hear a rustle in the trees, the same skittering sound that Bors had heard just before he was attacked. Whenever that happened, the party would rush to find cover, and would not move until the sounds had faded.

"Gathak scouting parties," one of the soldiers muttered at Bors's questioning look.

It took them another half an hour to reach a spot that Alexia felt was safe to wait in. She gestured to four of the soldiers. "You know what to do," she said simply.

The soldiers readied short bows that had been strapped across their backs, then vanished into the forest, heading northeast, back toward the walls of the city and, Bors supposed, the hidden gate. They returned a few minutes later.

"A scouting party passed by," one man reported to Alexia, "but they do not have sentries posted in the vicinity. They do not yet know of the secret gate."

Alexia nodded in satisfaction. "Let's go," she said.

The young woman once again took the lead, with the rest of the group trailing behind. They went less than five hundred yards before the forest abruptly ended; an open space covered in grass, nearly two hundred feet wide, separated them from the massive white walls of Kadre Maryn.

"If we can't see the gate," Bors wondered aloud, "how are we going to get inside?"

Alexia gave him a baleful look. "Do you think that, after using it all this time, we do not have a way to find it? I have memorized its location."

Bors gave a small shrug as she started across the clearing. "Just thought it would be a good idea to know."

The spot that Alexia led them to was no different from any other section of the wall, at least as far as Bors could tell. The huge white face loomed above them, forbidding in the growing dark, sloping slightly inward as it rose. There were no seams, no joins, nothing that indicated the wall was not simply one solid piece of white rock.

60

The young woman set her left palm against the stone, sliding it about for a moment as she searched for something.

Bors and the soldiers crowded close about her, realizing that they were dangerously exposed on this open ground. Finally, though, Alexia found what she wanted. She pressed against a section of the wall, and two feet to her left, another, larger section of stone slid aside to reveal a metal latch. She pulled the latch to one side, and with a soft groan, a portion of the wall three feet wide and nearly six feet tall sank back and then slid to the right. Beyond, Bors could see a narrow, torch-lit alley. One by one they slipped inside, and then Alexia shut the secret gate behind them.

Once on the main streets, they hurried toward the center of the city, where tall, columned buildings of white towered over a huge plaza paved entirely in pale marble. The whole area was a seething mass of activity, full of squads of soldiers running about their business, most of them heading out toward the walls. Ballistae, siege weapons that could also be used for defense, were being pulled down the streets by teams of horses, also bound for the fortifications that surrounded Kadre Maryn.

It seemed that High Lord Vessyn was eager to get down to business; Alexia quickened her pace as she led the group in a weaving path through the throng of soldiers. Frankly, Bors could not blame Vessyn for his haste. The amount of smoke that hovered over the valley outside the walls indicated thousands of enemies.

They proceeded into a building that was taller and wider than any of the others that were on the plaza. Its pillars were far more ornate, carved in flowing patterns that were vaguely vine-like. The doors that opened to admit them were three times as tall as Bors, and were gilded in silver and gold. They made their way through wide, tall halls lined with stone statues of lords and ladies, knights and princes, dragons and mighty birds. Here, the soldiers that had rescued Bors disappeared, returning to their posts and leaving him with Alexia. Guards armed with tall pikes were positioned every twenty feet all along the corridor. Their silver chain mail and conical helms glittered in the light of torches, as did their pikes, which were crafted with double blades and a slightly curved hook at the top.

61

Bors was not particularly impressed, though a newcomer might have been overawed; even though his last visit here had been years ago, he remembered it well. He looked to Alexia, but the young woman was doing her best to ignore him, staring straight ahead as they walked.

They reached a set of giant double doors. They were made of some sort of lightly colored oak, and like the main entrance doors to the building, they were gilded in intricate, wandering patterns of gold and silver. Alexia nodded to the guards positioned on either side of the doors, and without a word, the soldiers stepped forward to open them. With a groan, the massive weight of the doors slowly shifted on their hinges, opening to reveal a huge chamber beyond.

As soon as the doors opened, the noise of hundreds of raised voices immediately flooded out to assail Bors's ears, shattering the silence that had pervaded the corridor. This was the great council hall of Kadre Maryn, where the City Council met to discuss all matters of importance. The room was completely filled with the nobles of the city, along with higher ranking military officers and the ambassadors from the other nine White Cities. People packed the seats that rose in a circle around the walls, and the Lords of Kadre Maryn, ten in all, sat behind the large table at the far side of the chamber, atop a raised dais.

"I guess they've been expecting me," Bors muttered.

Alexia did not respond, but led him through the doors, which the guards then closed. A deathly quiet descended upon the hall, and all eyes turned to look upon the two newcomers. Bors kept his eyes straight ahead as he followed Alexia down the center aisle toward the front of the room. They stopped before the dais and stood in front of the nobles, who sat behind a large table of dark wood. Whispers started to rise a second time, but one of the nobles behind the table held up a hand, and silence fell once again.

The noble, a tall man with long white hair, flowing white beard, and a grizzled face stood, his dim eyes fixed on Bors as he spoke. "It is imperative that we begin this meeting at once. Bors Malik, I am the High Lord Vessyn, ruler of Kadre Maryn. I would welcome you here, but I fear there is no time for pleasantries and I doubt you would feel very welcome at this point anyway."

Bors returned a polite nod, but did not speak.

"By now, I'm sure you know that our situation is quite desperate," Vessyn went on. His eyes turned to Alexia. "But unless my daughter has spoken of it, I doubt you know why you have been summoned."

Bors glanced to the woman next to him. *So, she's royalty*, he thought. *That might explain the cool behavior.* "All I know is that you need my assistance in some way," he replied in a level tone. "Bad enough that you were willing to track me down in my self-imposed exile to deliver the message."

Vessyn nodded. "I'll put it succinctly. The Red Triad has stated that their intent is the complete and utter conquest of the Order of White Cities, all ten of them. Kadre Maryn has not been sent aid because eight of the cities are under siege, and the ninth has already fallen." Vessyn paused as stunned whispers filled the chamber; even Alexia looked up in shock. The High Lord nodded, his gaze sweeping over the assembly. "I received word just before this Council convened that Kadre Mythia has succumbed to her invaders. No survivors, if there are any, have left the city. And so you see that our situation quickly grows even more desperate."

"And what am I to do about it?" Bors asked, trying not to look at the ambassador from Kadre Mythia, who was becoming quite ill.

Vessyn's gaze did not leave Bors as he replied. "Shortly after the founding of the Order of White Cities, nearly half a millennium ago, the creators of the Order gave to each city an ancient magic that would provide an almost impenetrable defense. The walls of the cities are made of no ordinary stone. When provided with a proper energy source, they channel it, much like the heat of a flame spreads through the metal of a cooking pot. With the walls emanating this energy, it is impossible for enemies to lay siege to them; they cannot be climbed, and anything brought into contact with them bursts into flames. Even boulders hurled by catapults shatter harmlessly upon them.

"But there are only two sources that have ever been able to provide enough energy to infuse them with the necessary power.

The first is lightning, and of course, that cannot be predicted, and lasts for but a moment even if it could be harnessed. The second are the moonstones."

Another murmur ran through the gathered diplomats, and Bors narrowed his eyes. Suddenly, he thought he was beginning to see where this conversation was headed.

"No one knows what the moonstones are," Vessyn continued. "When the cities of the Order were founded, they were each given a moonstone, which could give the walls enough power to withstand any assault. Roughly the size of large melons, the stones were each stored in the vaults beneath the cities' council halls until such time as they were required. They have never been needed, until now. When the Red Triad marched on the cities of the Order, it was decided that the moonstones had to be used. But the Triad's cunning went deeper than we could have known. It was discovered that several of the stones had been stolen, and others, like ours, had been shattered." Vessyn held up a sliver of deep purple stone. "Only Kadre Periath has been able to use theirs."

"Fantastic," Bors muttered. "But I seem to have missed where I come in." Alexia shot him an icy stare, but he ignored it.

"The moonstones must be replaced," Vessyn stated. "But now that those within the cities of the Order have been stolen or destroyed, there is only one place where they are known to exist."

At that moment, Bors knew for sure where this was going. "Oh, burning stars, man, you must be insane!" he said, raising his voice before better judgment could stop him. "The Moonstone Oracle is a deathtrap for anyone who sets foot within it. If you're asking me to take a quick stroll in there, grab a moonstone I probably won't be able to lift, and then walk back here and save your precious city, you've lost your mind!"

"There is no other way–" Vessyn began.

"I tell you it's impossible," Bors cut him off. "Entire expeditions have been lost trying to enter that Vale."

"It's not impossible," Alexia cut in.

Bors looked back to her sharply. "What do you mean?"

"It's not impossible. I've been to the Oracle. I've been inside the

Vale. I even reached the Barrier, but I dared not go past it to where the Guardian waited."

Bors crossed his arms and arched an eyebrow. "The Guardian," he breathed. "Is there anything else protecting this Oracle?"

"It can be done—" Alexia began again.

"We need that stone, Malik," Vessyn interrupted, resting his hands on the table's dark surface. "All the cities need one, but Kadre Maryn is in the most desperate situation. Now that Kadre Mythia has fallen, the Triad is concentrating its forces here. If you cannot get the moonstone for us, no one else will."

"And what makes you so sure that I am the one best suited for this suicidal task?" Bors asked again. "I'm no hero of old, and I'm certainly no mage."

"You were leader of the Crimson Fist," Vessyn said. He paused as the echoes of those words faded, letting their full import sink into the minds of the assembly. "The greatest mercenary band ever to fight from one end of the world to the other. You summoned warriors from every nation to fight under your banner, and like an army of light, the Crimson Fist swept across countless enemies, even ones far greater in numbers than they. You saved dozens of nations from ruin, not for wealth or power, but for honor. I think that would count you as a hero."

Bors was silent for a moment, lost in memories he would rather have forgotten. "Yes," he replied softly. "And in the end, all of them died. In the end, the Crimson Fist became just another tale about a catastrophe that should never have happened. I was the only one to survive. And you call me a hero?" He exhaled slowly. "Perhaps you should redefine the word."

"The fact remains," said Vessyn, his voice softer this time, "that you are the only man alive who possesses the courage, the personal strength, and the wits necessary to get into that Vale, past the Guardian, and to the moonstones. We *need* you."

Bors did not reply at first. Then, he shook his head in resignation. After all, he could not just let a city die. "It'll cost you," he said.

Alexia glared back at him. "You would make us pay for your

aid?" she hissed.

Bors shrugged, a grim smile threatening to break through his serious expression. "You're the one so fond of bringing up my mercenary past. Mercenaries don't fight unless there's payment to be had. You should know that." His polite, cool expression was gone now, replaced by a mask of determination.

Vessyn sighed and nodded, leaning wearily on the table. "How much do you want?"

Bors answered immediately. "Once I've finished saving your city for you, I want you to leave me alone." He paused for a moment to let the astonished murmurs that broke out from the gathered nobles die down. "I want you to leave me in peace, and never summon me again. Once, I may have been the hero you claim I am, but now I am just a man. All I want is to live the rest of my life the way an ordinary man does."

Out of the corner of his eye, he could see Alexia gaping at him.

Vessyn looked up in surprise. "That's it? That's all you want? No gold, no title of nobility . . . nothing of material worth?"

This time, Bors grinned openly. "I have no need of money," he said. "I earned more than enough during my time with Crimson Fist to live comfortably. And right now," he added, looking around at the room and its occupants distastefully, "money is the last thing I want."

~~~~~

It was early the next morning when a small party led by Bors and Alexia prepared to depart from Kadre Maryn. Bors would have preferred to have only five or six of the city's better soldiers along, but of course, Alexia insisted that she would be needed, though she would not say why. And instead of a handful of soldiers, there were fifteen, along with horses for all of them to ride and five more to carry their supplies. The former mercenary found himself doubting very much that such a large party would be able to escape detection by the Red Triad forces once they were outside the city walls.

Alexia, however, had planned ahead. When the group of travelers reached the hidden gate in the western wall, they found nearly fifty more soldiers already waiting. These men were clad in chain mail covered by cloaks of green and brown, and most of them carried bows while the others carried javelins.

"These soldiers will cover our exit from the city," Alexia explained to Bors. "They will attack a small encampment of enemy scouts that we have found to the north and east of here, as if they are making an attempt to break through the Red Triad's blockade. Once the Gathak have focused their attention there, we will move south as fast as we can."

Bors nodded, but looked doubtful. "Eventually, these soldiers will be outnumbered. If they stay in battle too long, they will have no hope of reaching the safety of the walls again."

Alexia nodded back. "Then we'll just have to make sure that we get away from the city quickly."

Moments later, everything was ready. The soldiers that would provide the distraction exited through the gate first, followed by the party that Bors led. They crossed the open space between the walls and the forest without incident, after which the two groups separated.

"Now we wait for the fight to begin," Alexia said.

They hid themselves carefully, using bushes, tree trunks, and the occasional dip in the ground. The horses they could only tether to the trees, and hope the animals didn't make too much noise as they grazed. The seconds turned into minutes, and as the silence grew ever deeper, Bors began to wonder if something had happened. He looked questioningly to Alexia. When she gave him a shrug and a helpless shake of her head, he knew that something *had* gone wrong. Terribly wrong.

But before any ideas as to what that something was could form in his mind, one of the horses screamed in terror, and chaos broke loose.

The Gathak dropped from the trees, shrieking and howling and snarling, some of them falling straight onto the backs of unsuspecting soldiers. Cries of pain filled the air as first one soldier, and then another, was cut down.

"Ambush!" Bors cried as he lunged to his feet and drew his sword.

He caught his first opponent as it was dropping from the trees, his blade scything through it before it hit the ground. He turned to aid one of the soldiers as the man was borne to the ground by three of the creatures. He skewered one beast on his sword and kicked another in its hideous face even as he drew his weapon from the body of the first. The downed soldier grabbed the third monster and hurled it from him, then drew a long dagger from his belt and lunged after it. Satisfied that the man was able to take care of himself, Bors looked for Alexia.

The young woman was on the far side of the melee from him, wielding a pair of long knives that flashed in the sunlight as she battled another trio of the Gathak. One died even as it leapt at her, its throat slit open by an expert twist of her knife. The second turned to face a soldier that had come up on Alexia's right, and the third fell with a shriek as the woman took advantage of its moment of distraction and planted her other knife in its chest.

Bors raised his sword to block a spiked club that was wielded by a creature coming up on his left. *What happened to the other soldiers?* he briefly wondered. *Were they ambushed as well?* The thought was banished from his mind as the dying cry of a third soldier echoed through the trees. Right now, he needed to worry about himself, and those who were with him.

He parried another attack from the Gathak with the spiked club, feinted with a lunge, then spun around into a move that brought his sword slashing in from his enemy's left. The creature barely had time to give a squawk of dismay before it was sliced in two.

He looked up just in time to see yet another soldier pulled to the ground by a screeching mob of the little demons. The man had lost his sword and was fighting with his bare hands. As he charged to the soldier's aid, Bors realized that must have been what he looked like when *he* had been attacked.

He reached the downed soldier too late. Even as Bors bulled into the group of attackers, he saw the man go limp, killed by a short sword to the chest. Bors howled in wrath, swinging his sword viciously as the creatures scattered from the body.

At that moment, a horn sounded in the forest to the east, and

68

with an angry hiss, a score of arrows and javelins slashed into the foray and cut down several of the Gathak. Bors barely had time to shout in triumph before the fifty soldiers they had left at the secret gate came charging through the trees, swords glittering in their hands. They yelled as they ran, each man screaming his own war cry as they flooded into the battle.

The Gathak were caught completely off guard; nearly a dozen fell as the two sides collided.

"To victory!" Bors roared, and with an answering shout, the soldiers of his party fought with renewed vigor.

Moments later, it was all over. The remaining Gathak fled into the forest, wailing in fear and frustration. The soldiers shouted after them, hurling oaths and taunts in their jubilation.

But as Bors took stock of the situation, he saw that although it wasn't as bad as it could have been, it wasn't good, either. His party alone had lost four soldiers, three of their horses were dead, two were nowhere to be seen, and the second group of soldiers had lost a man as well.

"What happened?" he demanded of no one in particular. The soldiers quieted down and turned to face him. "What happened?"

One of the men from the second group spoke up. "The enemy camp had been moved," he said. "We had just found signs that they had traveled in this direction when we heard the sounds of fighting."

"We walked right into them," Alexia finished, her voice heavy with disgust. "I can't believe they surprised us like that!"

"Well, we'd better not stand around and discuss it," Bors said. "I have no doubt that the Gathak that got away will be looking for some friends to bring back. We'd best be long gone by then."

The soldier that had spoken nodded. "I'd send some of my men with you to replace the ones you lost, but we don't have horses. The best we can do is cover your escape, make sure that none of the enemy pursue you."

"Then let's get out of here," Bors said as he mounted his horse. Alexia and the rest of their party followed suit, and then they were riding south through the trees at a fast trot.

"Good luck," the soldier called behind them.

Bors just raised a hand in farewell.

Moments later, they had disappeared into the forest like wisps of smoke. Five of the soldiers left the main group to scout ahead, and would occasionally return to guide the others around an enemy encampment or a patrol party. After three hours of riding like this, the soldiers announced that they had made it past the Red Triad picket lines, and Bors finally began to relax. Now all they had to do was get to the Moonstone Oracle, and get back to the city in one piece. That was no short order, he realized, but if what Alexia had said about her foray into the Vale was true, they just might have a chance.

"So where exactly is this Vale located?" Bors asked Alexia later that day. They were following a narrow dirt road that was hedged closely on both sides by dense pinewood, still heading south and a little west, ever wary of detection by Red Triad patrols.

Alexia did not look at him as she responded. "It is in a valley located at the eastern foot of the Mirmyra Range, nestled within the hills and surrounded by the Evewood. It is very hard to find unless one knows exactly where it is."

"Which is the reason you had to be along," Bors said.

The woman arched an eyebrow at him. "One of them," she replied. In his mind, Bors could hear the reason she had left unsaid: *The other is to keep an eye on you.*

"How long till we get there?" he asked.

"Three days, four at the most."

"Assuming we don't get caught by the Red Triad before then," Bors muttered.

Alexia shot him another of her icy glares. "We will not be caught. We must not be. If we are stopped, Kadre Maryn will fall."

"And I won't ever be left alone again," Bors couldn't resist muttering to himself.

He ignored the woman's venomous look and kept moving.

~~~~~

The sun set behind the Mirmyra Range to the west, and with the coming of night, the stars once again sprang into the sky. They formed constellations that spread across the sable vault, tracing intricate, majestic patterns that swirled about the rising moons. Bors looked up at their countless number, and felt the tension of the last two days melt away. The party stopped to make a quick camp, a few hundred feet away from the road they had been following. They chose a few of the soldiers as sentries, and settled themselves in for some much-needed sleep.

They were on the move again before the sun had fully risen in the east. They made good ground; their pace was steady rather than quick, gradually eating up the distance as the day wore on.

The next day was much the same, and finally, on the afternoon of their third day out from the city, Alexia guided the group off the narrow road, and took them west into the forest. The undergrowth was thick and stifling, choking off all smaller plant life and making it almost impossible to move between the trunks of the trees. They forced their way in for a few minutes, then Alexia signaled for them to halt. They carefully dismounted, trying not to get tangled in the briers and thorn thickets.

"The Evewood?" Bors asked casually.

Alexia shook her head. "Not yet," she replied, then lowered her voice to little more than a whisper. "You'll know it when we get there." She turned to the rest of the party. "We'll have to go on foot from here. If we move quickly, we should reach the Moonstone Oracle by mid-morning tomorrow."

Bors just arched an eyebrow at her cryptic comment about the Evewood, and pulled his supplies from his horse.

After all the horses had been tethered to tree trunks, the group readied their gear and started off, with Alexia in the lead. They pushed their way through the dense undergrowth, making slow progress. Bors soon realized that if Alexia had not remembered how to get to the Moonstone Oracle, they would have been hopelessly lost. The young woman followed a path that was not apparent to even his well-honed tracking skills, and she kept a course that was remarkably straight, despite the fact that the sun was hidden by the canopy of the trees, and there were no obvious landmarks to go by.

Time wore on, and hours passed. Then, just as Bors was about

71

to ask Alexia how much farther they had to go, the group suddenly pushed clear of the clinging bushes and thickets. They found themselves standing on open ground, the underbrush behind them forming a tangled, thorny wall that stretched out of sight on either side. Before them, the massive trunks of ancient trees rose toward the sapphire blue of the evening sky, their mighty branches arcing out to make a dense canopy. Stray rays from the setting sun shone through the branches, lighting the forest in red and gold and orange. The short, springy grass that covered the ground between the trunks seemed to glow, absorbing the last light of the day and casting it back. The constantly falling leaves caught the lonely rays and glittered like jewels as they drifted to the earth, creating a sort of magical rain through which the travelers walked.

"Evewood," Alexia said softly. "The Living Forest. Even the trees here are alive. They can see and hear everything that passes beneath their branches. And there are other, less pleasant things as well."

"It seems a nice enough place," Bors replied as he looked around.

"Its appearance is deceiving," one of the soldiers muttered, his eyes darting around the surrounding trunks nervously. "Many a traveler has wandered into these woods, and few have ever come out. Most of those that did make it back to civilization were never the same again."

Bors arched an eyebrow at him, but Alexia spoke before he could ask his question. "This will likely be our most dangerous challenge in getting to the Moonstone Oracle," she said. "Keep your eyes open and your weapons ready. If we let down our guard, we may never live to see the Vale. And whatever you do, do not harm the trees. Do not even touch them."

Bors nodded and kept a hand on the hilt of his sword as the woman started off. All too soon, the sun set behind the looming hills in the west, and night fell over the Evewood and the thirteen travelers. But the forest was by no means dark. Pale beams from the two moons above reached the ground, though they were few and far between. And they were not the only source of light.

The forest was alive, just as Alexia had said, a presence that rose all about them, emanating a sense of watchfulness. Tiny orbs of light materialized in the dark spaces between the trunks and flitted about, darting here and there, weaving intricate patterns with each other as they wandered through the air. They were like fireflies, but Bors could not see any substance to them, just spheres of light. Occasionally, one would dart into the midst of the group of travelers, circle about for a few moments, then streak away to disappear into the branches above or vanish among the trunks. It gave Bors the uneasy impression that the things were studying them.

"How soon till we reach the Vale?" he asked Alexia.

"Don't tell me you're frightened of some trees and a few flashes of light," she replied, the barest hints of a mocking smile playing about her lips.

"I'm not afraid of anything that's flesh and blood and carries a blade," he said back. "But this wood . . . it is something else entirely, something I can't quite put my finger on. And it is not of flesh and blood."

"No, it is not," the young woman agreed. "It is as old as the earth itself."

"What is it?"

"The Evewood," she replied mystically, ignoring Bors's puzzled look. "It *is* the forest. As for when we shall reach the Vale and the end of this wood, we should be there by dawn, if we keep this pace."

Bors nodded. The sooner, the better. Few things had frightened him in his life, but the Evewood was one of them. There was something about this forest that whispered of watching eyes. Something that reminded him of his own mortality, of his own insignificance when compared to the ancient forest in which he was the intruder. He shook the thought away, keeping his hand on his sword hilt as he kept close behind Alexia. As he looked at the trees looming over them, the solid weapon gave him a measure of comfort, and he began to doubt that the Evewood would prove to be any trouble.

~~~~~

73

They quickly lost all sense of time and distance. Alexia continued to surprise Bors. Never once did she pause to question her direction. She led the group ahead with confidence, keeping a steady pace, drawing on energy reserves that were surprising for one of her slender stature. Bors, though, felt himself growing tired; the last few days had been anything but easy.

His drowsiness was shattered when Alexia stopped, stiff and motionless as she peered into the darkness of the trunks around them. Her eyes narrowed, glittering in the light of the forest.

"What is it?" Bors asked. "Did you see something?"

She took a long while in responding. "No, I heard something."

"What?"

"Find cover!" she commanded as she started toward the nearest tree.

The men scattered, each headed for a different tree, their armor flashing in the light of the mysterious fireflies. But they hadn't moved more than half a dozen paces before they stopped cold in their tracks once again. Bors looked at them in puzzlement for a moment, then felt a chill run through him. He tried to shake it off and start moving, but he found that his body wouldn't obey. He was still out in the open, with his intended hiding spot only a few feet away.

"Don't bother," came the musical sound of a female voice, drifting about them eerily. "We can see you already. We've been watching you ever since you entered the Wood."

Another chill ran through him, and Bors found that he could move again. Gripping his sword tightly, he looked around for the source of the voice. But there was nothing to be seen. The wood appeared to be as empty as it had before. "Who are you?" he said quietly, somehow knowing that the speaker would have no trouble hearing his words.

"The question should not be *who* am I, but *what* am I." A figure stepped from the shadows of the trunks before them. It was a woman, tall, with shimmering, golden hair that flowed to her waist, accenting her fair, pale skin. Eyes of obsidian flashed beneath dark brows. She was clad in robes of green, and she wore bracelets made of gold and silver that were fashioned into the shapes of leaves.

Several more women appeared behind her, identical in appearance except for the varying colors of their eyes and hair.

"I am the Evewood," the first woman said, her voice soft and compelling.

"What do you want of us?" Bors heard himself asking. He realized that he was staring into her eyes, and only with considerable effort did he manage to tear his gaze away.

"You are trespassers here," the woman replied. "No mortal being is permitted to pass into the Evewood."

"I think you forgot to mention that," Bors hissed at Alexia.

Alexia ignored him, her eyes fixed on the Evewood. "We are simply passing through this place," she said. "We do not intend to stay."

"Your intentions do not matter," the Evewood said back sharply. "I know who you are, girl, I know of your kind. You have been here before, and others before you. You had no respect for the ancient life that resides here, no reverence for that which is as old as the world itself. You took of the living branches of Evewood, and set flame to them, destroying that which has been wrought over many centuries. And for that, you must pay. Even as those of your kind before you did." Her eyes narrowed, and the women behind her began to advance, their own faces masks of icy anger. "You would be dead already," the Evewood said, "if your skills in woodcraft had not allowed you to elude our snares. But there will be no subtly this time. This time, you will not escape me."

Alexia took a step back, looking from one figure to the other. "I didn't know," she blurted. "I didn't know that I had entered the Evewood. Believe me, if I had, I wouldn't have brought fire here. I was alone and lost, and it was dark. You must understand that."

The Evewood smiled, a rather unfriendly expression, and the women continued to advance on the wary soldiers, forming a half circle about them. "I understand. But it is too late. Any mortal that sets fire to this wood must be slain."

Then, before either Bors or Alexia could say otherwise, the soldiers sprang forward. They charged toward the advancing women, moving with trained precision. They gave a collective howl as they went, perhaps hoping to intimidate what they saw as only women.

"No!" Bors yelled, straining to be heard over their war cries, but it was far too late.

Moving with stunning speed, branches that had moments before only been twisted pieces of wood came alive and darted down at the attacking soldiers. Some of the men managed to throw themselves aside, but three of them were too slow. They were hefted into the air like rag dolls, wrapped tight in the branches, and were borne away from sight into the depths of the dark canopy. Only one had the time to yell. Moments later, pieces of their weaponry and armor fell back to the ground, clattering through the branches to land in the grass with sickening thuds.

The remaining men wailed in fear and immediately fell back, retreating behind Bors and Alexia.

The embodiment of the Evewood raised her hands, and more branches slithered down, poised to strike once again, twisting and writhing like enraged serpents. The woman narrowed her eyes, and the branches began to advance.

"Stop this!" Bors shouted desperately, angrily, his commanding voice halting the strange women in their tracks. "We are not here to fight! We have not come here to harm this forest. We only wish to pass through."

"And do what?" the Evewood retorted, her voice lowered to a scornful hiss. "There is nothing on the other side of the Evewood. Nothing but mountains and wilderness. You have no reason to be journeying through here."

"We are on a mission of great importance," Bors stated, not knowing where else to begin. "The Order of White Cities, ten human cities that are–"

"I know of your world, Man," the Evewood interrupted.

Bors nodded. "Then hear me out. The Red Triad is attempting to overthrow the Order. Even now their black armies are sweeping over the land scarce miles northeast of here. We are on our way to the Moonstone Oracle, where we hope to find a magic that will defend the cities. If we are not allowed to pass through here and reach the Oracle, the White Cities will all fall."

"That is none of my concern."

"It should be," Bors replied. "Once the cities fall, the armies of Gathak will come here. The Red Triad seeks the destruction of all resistance, and it will see the Evewood as nothing else. If you do not let us pass unharmed, in time, the Evewood will become nothing more than a wasteland, ravaged by the hordes of beasts that the Red Triad will unleash upon the world. If you do not want to see this happen, you will let us reach the Moonstone Oracle, so that the invasion may be averted and the Red Triad stopped."

"The Moonstone Oracle?" the woman repeated suspiciously. "Humans have not gone there in centuries. How do I know that you speak the truth? How do I know that you really intend to go *there*, after all this time? Your kind is notorious for lying."

Bors held up his hands. "Watch us, as you have been doing. If we in any way harm this wood, then deal with us as you see fit. But let us reach the Oracle and return, and we will not come here again."

"If you wish us to let you pass unharmed," the Evewood said, "then you must leave *her* with us." She raised a slender arm and pointed at Alexia. "I do not know you, or these others that follow you, but she has set fire to the branches of the Evewood, and for that she must die. Give her to me, and you may go."

Alexia breathed a soft curse, but Bors shook his head. "No," he said firmly. "Without her, we cannot succeed. She alone among us knows exactly where the Oracle is. If you take her, we will not be able to reach the moonstones, the cities will fall, and the Gathak will come for you, once they are finished with the Order. She comes with us."

The Evewood hesitated, then nodded; the other women relaxed, stepping back once again. "Very well," she said. "But be quick. The Evewood will not have compassion on you a second time."

Bors nodded, but before he could offer thanks, the woman turned on one heel, and in a swirl of green robes, disappeared into the darkness of the forest. The other women vanished with her. "Well, wasn't that entertaining?" he said, whirling on Alexia. "You didn't tell me this place would try to *kill* us!"

Alexia looked as if she wanted to be angry, but she couldn't quite manage it. "You didn't need to know beforehand," she snapped halfheartedly. "It wouldn't have done us any good, and I had hoped to get through the forest without encountering something like this." She lowered her voice a little. "Besides, you handled it just fine." With that, she whirled and continued on, drawing the nervous soldiers after her.

Bors stayed put for a moment, puzzled. Had she just given him a compliment?

~~~~~

They made the rest of the journey through the Evewood as fast as they could. Just as the new dawn was beginning to color the eastern horizon a brilliant yellow and red, tainting the land a deep orange, the group passed through the last line of trees, and stood at the edge of the Vale of the Moonstone Oracle. Just as Alexia had said, the valley would have been almost impossible to find, had she not known exactly where it was. There was no warning of its beginning; the ground dropped sharply away before them, the slopes of the valley clad in verdant grasses and tall pine trees. Its floor was still hidden in shadow, as yet untouched by the rays of the rising sun.

Bors paused before following the others down, his gaze scanning the entire valley. "No sign of the Oracle," he muttered.

"It's there," Alexia replied, pointing to an open clearing below. "In the exact center. You can't see it from up here. Some sort of magic hides it from sight."

The eight remaining soldiers spread out as they made their way down and Bors and Alexia stayed close behind them. They didn't expect any immediate trouble, but they didn't want to be caught by surprise either. It took them little more than half an hour to reach the bottom, and they did not see any signs of life, save for the first morning birds. The valley floor was forested in most places, and large gray boulders were scattered throughout the massive trunks of the trees. The ground rose and fell with gentle knolls and ridges. Still guided by Alexia, they made their way in the general direction of the center of the valley, careful to keep their guard up.

There was a mood about this Vale, something that did not take kindly to disturbances. The air was thick and heavy, a warm, humid blanket that lay like a shroud over them all. The entire valley was deathly silent; no birds sang, no insects hummed, and there was not even a breeze.

"We will reach the Barrier before long," Alexia whispered to him. "Your part in this journey will soon begin. And it will be the hardest of all."

Bors thought she sounded a little smug about that, but he ignored it. "What exactly is this Barrier?" he said, keeping his voice low as well.

"A snare," she replied. She saw his puzzled look and explained. "To the eye, it simply appears to be a wall of light. But it is more than that. When a person attempts to pass through it, it begins to affect the mind. It creates illusions, fantasies, images that distract him away from the Oracle. At first, they are harmless, but they gradually take over, until he no longer has any control over his actions. He will remain trapped in the Barrier, chasing whatever fantasy it puts before him, until he dies of hunger, thirst, or the Guardian, whichever finds him first. Only a person who has complete control over his mind can withstand its effects."

"And you think that I have that sort of control," he finished.

She nodded. "You were able to command one of the deadliest armies this world has ever known, and you were able to hold it together for several years. You employed tactics that puzzled even the most brilliant generals."

Bors just looked at her. Did she really think that meant he could get through the Barrier? He shook his head, but took a moment in answering. "And what about the Guardian?" he said. "What does it look like, what does it do?"

"No one knows what it looks like. None who may have seen it have lived to tell about it. But according to the legends and stories in Kadre Maryn, what it does is well-known: it kills to protect the Oracle, and the moonstones within."

Bors nodded, but did not reply. He had heard all the legends, of course, and even though most of those rang false, he would not be surprised to find what Alexia said to be the truth. At least he would be *earning* his reward . . . .

They stopped for a break a few hours later, which consisted of a quick meal and some rest, less than two miles from where the Oracle and the Barrier were supposed to be. The mood of the impromptu camp was rather oppressive; the soldiers were nervous, always glancing about. They were picking up most of it from Alexia. The woman's face was cool and composed, except for her eyes; they were distant and worried, preoccupied with what lay ahead. The few words she spoke grew increasingly curt.

Two hours later, she finally nodded to Bors, and, after gathering up their gear, they started off again, now on the final phase of their journey to the Moonstone Oracle. The soldiers spread out, weapons ready for action.

Not long after, they stopped just inside the last line of trees that surrounded the clearing, holding back cautiously. All was still and silent, but Bors did not relax.

Alexia raised an arm and pointed out into the clearing. "There lies the Barrier," she whispered. "The wall that separates us from the Oracle."

It rose up hardly a dozen yards from the last line of trees, its surface sloping up and back, forming something like a dome, though it did not meet at the top and left the ground within open to the sky above. It pulsated, as if alive, writhing and seething, murmuring with a whisper of power that was soft, and, Bors noted with alarm, oddly comforting. It changed color constantly, first white, then blue, then turning pale red and back again, all the while translucent enough for them to see through to the other side. But there was nothing to behold within save for a grassy clearing.

"And what of the Oracle itself?" Bors whispered back. "I can see through the Barrier, but there is only an empty clearing."

"It is there. The Barrier conceals it."

"Then how do you know it is there?" he prompted. "You said you had never crossed through the Barrier."

"It is there," Alexia said firmly. "It is there."

Bors took a deep breath. "Then lead the way. Let's get this over with."

The woman looked back to him for a moment, something like approval in her eyes. Then she nodded. "Stay close to me."

They moved slowly out of the trees and into the clearing, leaving the soldiers behind in a bristling line of steel to watch over their supplies. As they approached the Barrier, Bors studied the magical wall, wondering what sort of force it was that created and sustained it. It was unlike anything he had ever seen before, and he doubted that he would ever see anything like it again.

They stopped just outside the barrier, watching the ever-changing pattern of colors. It was so beautiful, Bors thought, unique . . . .

"Take my hand," Alexia's voice broke into his thoughts.

"What?" he asked.

"Take my hand. You'll go in first, with me behind you."

"You're not serious!" he exclaimed. "You said that I was the only person who had the mental strength to get through this barrier–"

"Which is precisely why you will be guiding me," she said. "I know that I will not be able to resist whatever it is I see in there. But you may need my help when it comes time to face the Guardian. So I must come. Whatever you do, keep walking to the other side; do not stop, do not pay attention to the illusions. And do not let go of me."

Bors opened his mouth to protest again, but as he saw the fire in her emerald eyes, he sighed. She would not be refused. "Well, in that case, we had better make sure we do not get separated." He slid his pack off his back, and with a dagger he pulled from his boot, he cut one of the leather straps. Then, taking Alexia's right hand, he bound her wrist to his left. "Ready?"

She nodded.

Bors turned back to face the Barrier, and stepped through.

As Alexia had instructed, he kept walking, taking in his surroundings as he moved. There was not much to see, which bothered him. He could see and feel the Barrier around him, pulsing, almost as if it were breathing; its touch was refreshingly cool to his skin, soothing away the weariness of his journey. The world he had left behind was a fuzzy blur as he cast a glance over his shoulder, as was the one ahead. He was about to ask Alexia where all the

81

illusions were, when she screamed.

"Bors! Look out!" She pointed ahead of them, her eyes wide with terror.

He followed her gaze, sword flashing out of its sheath . . . but there was nothing to be seen, save for a few dozen yards of empty space between the two of them and the other side of the Barrier. He looked back to her, ready to ask what it was she had seen, but she was already doing her best to pull away from him, desperately fumbling with the cord that bound them together as she sought to escape whatever horror it was she saw. Quickly, before she could free herself, Bors pulled her close, holding her to him, speaking firmly but softly into her ear. "Alexia, it's all right. Whatever it is you're seeing, it isn't real." He continued talking to her, gradually calming her with his gentle murmurs.

Finally, she shook her head, and her eyes cleared. She pulled away from him quickly, glaring at him. "Don't stop; keep moving!" she snapped. "We haven't even begun to experience the worst."

He nodded and started out again, quickening his pace as he sought to reach the other side as soon as possible. It appeared to be only a hundred or so feet in front of him; all he had to do was keep the woman with him, and he would be fine. He kept his sword ready, though, just in case.

That was when the voices began, calling out to him from every side, soft, whispering at first, then growing in volume until they were nearly shouts. At first, they were easy to ignore; he realized what was going on. But whatever force sustained the Barrier was not about to give him up so easily.

They're coming at us from all sides, Bors! We're surrounded!

Bors stopped short. He knew that voice. "Jaran," he breathed. Jaran had been his second in command when he had led Crimson Fist. He had spoken those words only moments before he was killed during the last battle the mercenary group had fought.

Our left flank is breaking! Everyone down there has been killed!

That was Velyears, his best friend. He had fallen as he led a pitifully small band of men in a desperate attempt to cut their way

82

out of the ambush.

Bors shook his head. As much as the memories pained him, he could not allow himself to be affected by them. That was in the past, and right now, he had something more important to do.

Don't leave us, Bors, a woman's voice screamed. *Don't let us die here! Please!*

He stopped again, the echoes of the voice still drifting about him. That had been Chelseaa's voice. His sister. She had died, too. "But you weren't there," he whispered. "You died a year after that!"

Help us, Bors! Help me!

He was breathing heavily, gasping for air as he tried to push the voices from his mind. Sweat ran down his forehead in rivulets. He took another step . . . .

And howled in dismay as the ground opened up before him, falling away to form a rocky valley that disappeared into the horizon on both sides. Smoke rose from the valley floor, and he could see the flash of steel, hear the screams of dying men as the battle raged below him like a maddened sea. He shook his head in disbelief. He was witnessing the downfall of Crimson Fist.

Again.

He closed his eyes, wiping sweat from his brow. *No, this is not happening. This took place five years ago.* He opened his eyes again, and, with a deep breath, continued on. Even as he would have stepped foot into open space, the image vanished, and he was once again walking on level ground, nearing the far side of the Barrier.

Alexia. He had forgotten to make sure Alexia was still with him. He whirled, only to find her gone. The cord he had used to tie her to him dangled from his wrist, its jagged ends testament to the raw terror that had given her the strength to tear away from him. "Alexia!" he called. "Alexia! Where are you?" He started back for the other side of the Barrier, desperate to find her before it was too late. But would the magic of the Barrier even let him see her? "Alexia!"

His initial shock of finding her gone quickly grew into panic. Where was she? How could he not have felt her trying to get free? With one swift attack, the Barrier had separated them, and now at least one of them was going to die. Alexia would never be able to find her way out of whatever fantasies she was caught in. But he could not give up, not yet. He had to find her. He kept moving, trying to catch sight of her.

Suddenly, he felt something pulling at his left wrist. He looked down in surprise to see the frayed ends of the cord jerking wildly. And then it hit him. It was another illusion. Alexia was still tied to him; it was just that he could not see her!

Breathing a sigh of relief, he turned back toward the other side of the Barrier, determined to get through without being stopped again. He closed the distance quickly, and with a triumphant shout, he stepped through to the open space beyond. As he had expected, Alexia materialized behind him, still bound to his wrist, her eyes wide with shock as she tried to shake off whatever it was she had seen inside the Barrier.

Bors saw that the clearing they had just entered was no longer empty. A hill rose in the middle of the clearing, several dozen feet above the surrounding ground. Huge chunks of white marble, great pieces of stone that looked as if they had been rent asunder by some massive blow, dotted its grass-clad slopes. A path, dug into the side of the slope, wound its way up the face of the hill, leading to what had once been a domed pavilion, open on all sides, its former majesty still evident in its tall, carved pillars of marble. But the roof had several holes in it now, and some of the pillars were cracked and scored with deep gashes.

Bors took a careful look around, but everything seemed deserted. Nothing stirred, save for the grass ruffling in a soft breeze from the west. He turned back to Alexia. "Are you all right?" When she nodded wearily, he went on. "Where is this Guardian that you mentioned? I don't see anything."

Alexia shook her head. "I don't know. But it's here. It must be."

Bors nodded, then began to untie the cord that bound the two of them together. "Well, let's not keep it waiting. I'm ready to get out of this place."

"Thanks for bringing me out," Alexia said. "I didn't think I was going to be able to stand it any longer. Thanks for keeping me with you."

Bors did not look up at her, but busied himself with wrapping the cord up and putting it into his pack. "Don't mention it. Come on, let's get up to that cursed Oracle and get out of here."

They started up the hill, following the winding path, their boots crunching bits of shattered stone beneath them. Bors kept his sword drawn, eyes constantly watching for danger; Alexia didn't carry anything larger than the two long knives at her belt, but Bors knew she could be quite deadly with them. They proceeded slowly, trying not to make noise. He didn't think it would help them against a magical being such as the Guardian, but he was willing to try anything that might give them an advantage.

Following the sinuous curves of the stone path, it took them nearly fifteen minutes to reach the crest of the hill. Bors gasped as he beheld the Moonstone Oracle, sitting beneath the shattered dome of the pavilion. The ground within the circle of pillars was paved in marble blocks, and from the center of the pavilion rose a pedestal, four feet tall, with four talons of the same white stone arcing out and up from it. Suspended in mid-air within the crook of the talons was a single moonstone, colored a deep amethyst that pulsed with a light of its own. The stone was slightly larger than a watermelon, just as Vessyn had said.

"That's not going to be easy to carry," Bors breathed. "Maybe we should have brought one of the horses with us."

"Bors," Alexia exclaimed softly, touching his arm.

He followed her gaze to the far side of the pavilion. A girl stood there, half hidden by one of the pillars. She regarded them warily with bright eyes, her hands nervously fingering her long braid of brown hair. *What is she doing here?* Bors wondered. She was only a child, perhaps fifteen years of age.

"Who are you?" she asked softly before he could speak. There was nothing threatening or demanding in her voice, only curiosity. "Why have you come here?"

Bors took a careful step forward. "I am Bors Malik," he said. "I have come for the moonstone. I presume you're the one called the

Guardian." But even as he said it, he had his doubts. Could this child really be the mighty defender of the Oracle?

But she ignored his question. "No one may take the moonstone. It must remain here, where it belongs."

"But we have desperate need of it–" began Alexia.

"That does not matter," the girl interrupted sharply, moving forward to stand on the other side of the pedestal. "The moonstones are not meant to be handled by mortals. Only the mages of old have any right to them, and they have not walked the earth for five hundred years. You may not have the moonstone."

Bors gave an exasperated sigh. "I am tired of this," he said. "I am tired of having to argue and debate and negotiate during every part of this blasted journey! I have come for the moonstone, girl, and I will have it. Without it, an entire city will die, and I will not let that happen!" His sword glittered in the light of the sun as he spun it in an experimental arc. "Now stand away."

Alexia drew back at the sudden vehemence in his tone, but the girl in front of him just lowered her brows, eyes glittering eerily. "You will not take the moonstone, human," she growled in reply, her voice dropping in pitch with every word she spoke. It was no longer that of a human female, but of some dark creature. "If you will not leave, then you will die."

Even as Bors took another step forward, the image of the young girl shimmered and shifted, darkening, growing in size until it stood head and shoulders over him. The youthful face and blue dress disappeared, replaced by a deep violet cloak and hood. Where the face had been, there was now only shadow. "Come and taste your death, mortal," the Guardian growled, raising a massive sword.

Despite his surprise, Bors did not hesitate. He launched himself forward with a shout, and the two combatants met in a clash of steel. The ferocity of the attack took the Guardian by surprise, putting it on the defensive. Bors brought his sword down from above, but the blow was parried with a jarring shock. The creature pushed him away with relative ease, then followed up with a slash from the right. Bors leapt back, blocked the next slash that came from the left, then lunged into the gap in the Guardian's defenses.

The Guardian avoided the blade with ease and lashed out with one armored fist, hitting Bors on the back of his head as he stumbled by and sending him sprawling onto his face. The mercenary rolled away from a downward stab, leaving his opponent's sword to strike the stone in a shower of sparks. He pushed himself onto his feet and waded back in, slashing his blade down and in from the right; the Guardian stepped back a split second too late, and Bors's sword opened up a gash in its purple robes. Bors took the opportunity his opponent's momentary loss of balance afforded and followed up the first attack with a vicious backhanded swing. The Guardian parried, but the force of the blow knocked its blade spinning away.

The creature howled in anger, reaching out with one hand to grab Bors by the collar of his tunic and lift him off his feet. Bors kicked and struggled as hard as he could, but the Guardian's grip did not lessen. His sword skittered out of his hand, flashing as it spun away across the stones. His breath left him in a rush of air as the Guardian slammed him against one of the pillars, keeping his feet well above the ground.

"Now you die, human," the cloaked form hissed.

Bors gasped as the Guardian began to crush him against the column, pushing harder and harder. No matter how he fought, he could not break free. His mind raced, seeking a solution. His eyes fell on Alexia, who was still standing on the far side of the moonstone, and suddenly he knew what to do.

"Alexia! No! Stay back!" he gasped.

The Guardian whirled, expecting an attack from behind, dropping Bors as it did. The mercenary dove away from the pillar in the split second that was given him, reaching for his sword as he did. He rolled to his feet, blade whirling in a deadly arc as the Guardian saw the deception and launched itself at him.

It realized its mistake too late.

The Guardian's howl of pain shook the hilltop as Bors's sword plunged into its shoulder, cutting through cloak and whatever passed for flesh with ease. Bors drove the blade to its hilt, bulling into the creature and pushing it over with his own weight. Even before the Guardian had completely fallen, he was standing over it, glittering sword raised high above his head for the killing stab, straight through the chest. The hooded figure lay motionless as it looked up, waiting for the end . . . .

But the blade did not fall.

Bors lowered his sword, took a deep breath, and stepped back. "I *will* have the stone," he repeated in a low voice.

"Why do you not destroy me?" the Guardian asked. "You have triumphed."

"And what says that I must kill you in order to take the moonstone?" Bors asked in return. "I don't want your blood on my blade. I just want the stone so that it can be used to save an innocent city under siege. And besides, if I killed you, who would keep the moonstones safe from those who would use them for evil? Give me this one moonstone, and I will let you live. I have no quarrel with you."

The Guardian got to its feet, clawed hands folded before it. For several moments, it was silent.

"You have honor, Bors Malik," it replied finally, its voice somehow less menacing. "Few men possess such mercy. You would not use the moonstone for your own gain, your own power?"

Bors shook his head. "The city of Kadre Maryn needs its magic to withstand an invading army. I have no intention to use it for anything else."

The Guardian hesitated, then nodded slowly. "Very well. You may take the stone. Your honor has proven you worthy."

Bors and Alexia watched in awe as the hooded form gestured with one hand, and the moonstone shrank until it was the size of a large egg. The Guardian reached out and plucked the stone from the air, then placed it in the mercenary's hand. "See that you use it wisely."

"Thank you," Bors muttered, not sure what else to say. He turned to Alexia and gave a wry smile. "Now we just have to make it out of here alive."

"That will not be a problem," the Guardian assured him. Even as it spoke, there came a brief flash of light, and the writhing, pulsating wall of the Barrier slipped downward into the earth, giving them a clear view of the forest and the distant figures of the soldiers just inside the last row of trees. "Go now," it said finally. "There are other forces that seek the Moonstone Oracle, and I must use the magic to conceal this place once again. See that you speak to no one of what you have seen here."

Bors nodded. "You have my word. And thank you once again."

With that, he slipped the moonstone into his pack, and, followed by Alexia, made his way quickly down the hill toward the distant edge of the clearing where the rest of their party waited. They had hardly reached the trees before the Barrier sprang up once again behind them, but Bors paid it no mind. Ignoring the babbling questions of the excited soldiers around him, he merely made sure his pack was secure and started off through the trees, headed northeast, toward Kadre Maryn.

What Lies Between
by Michael Penncavage

The bell above the wooden door made a faint *rinkle tinkle* as Harold and Kelly entered the bookstore. Then, as if to further announce the couple's presence, the ancient floorboards emitted a low groan.

"God!" Kelly quickly cupped her hand over her nose. "I think something died in here!"

Harold glared at her. "Be quiet!"

"Do we *have* to look around?" she asked.

"There's a perfectly good bench outside if you don't want to stay."

Kelly, seizing her opportunity, spun around and grabbed the doorknob. "In that case I'll be down the street in *Le Caché*."

"Don't forget to . . ." Harold began, but Kelly had already darted out the door. He sighed heavily as he turned back to the bookshelf.

"I suppose we can't all be book lovers now, can we?"

Harold was so startled by the voice that he took a step back, and in doing so, knocked over a stack of paperbacks atop a table.

"Oh, terribly sorry," said a short, elderly man who looked somewhere between ninety and a hundred years old. He was perched behind a large oak desk and till that seemed just as ancient. "I didn't mean to put such a fright into you."

"That's all right. I'm surprised I didn't see you when I walked in."

The old man smiled warmly in response.

Harold looked around the store. Oak bookshelves ran from floor to ceiling brimming with titles. In front of the bookcases were even more books, making those on the lower shelves impossible to see.

"Jerves. Allistar Jerves. And you would be?"

"Harold Bennect."

"Well, Mr. Bennect. Welcome to the *Cryptanthium*."

"You have quite a collection."

Jerves gazed around with pride. "Yes. I am quite proud of my collections."

"How many titles do you have?"

"I could only guess. The exact count was lost years ago."

"Do you specialize in any particular type of genre?"

"No. I'd like to think my selection caters to readers of *all* types." He looked at Harold with raised eyebrows. "Can I help you locate something?"

"No thanks. I'm just browsing."

Jerves nodded. "Very well. But I don't think you will find anything of interest."

"Excuse me?"

"Here at the *Cryptanthium*, you do not search for books. The book finds *you*."

"Uh, huh," replied Harold. "And how exactly does that happen?"

"I tell you what you like to read."

"Oh really?"

"I have been a purveyor of books for more than 50 years, Mr. Bennect. Just like a tailor, I can size you up and determine what your likes and dislikes are."

"Well . . . go right ahead."

He studied Harold for a moment. "Hmm . . . well, *that's* certainly a change from the norm. Not too many fellows come here looking for *those*."

"Excuse me?"

"Romance," he clarified. "Though, not the steamy kind. You prefer it with a bit of adventure."

Harold's eyebrows rose as his lips parted. "How did you . . ."

Jerves, with the aid of his wooden cane, rose from the seat and walked to the wall opposite Harold. "Now that we know what *type* of book you like, we need to find the *right* one. Anything less would be wasting your time."

From his jacket pocket, he removed a pair of chrome-wired spectacles. "Let's see. Which one, which one . . ." His eyes began to roam over the ocean of titles as he gently tapped his chin with his index finger.

Jerves pushed a small stepstool up to the shelves. The spines on the overflowing shelf seemed to blur into a collage of maroons, blues, and blacks. Very few appeared to even have writing on them.

"Ah—what do we have here?" Jerves gripped the edge of a thick, navy-bound book.

Harold watched as the bookseller removed it from the stack. On the cover, in bold, embossed ivory letters was inscribed, *Love's Journey*. Jerves removed the dust jacket and Harold could see that the book was bound in fine linen. He reminded himself to stay price conscious.

The bookseller's smile was quickly washed over with a concerned frown. "Oh dear." Jerves began feverishly flipping through the pages in the book. "Oh dear, oh dear, oh dear."

He's lost his mind, thought Harold.

Reaching the midpoint of the book, Jerves emitted a gasp of nervousness. "As I thought." He closed the book with a snap. "I'm sorry. This is not for sale."

"Excuse me?"

"I had assumed all of *these* books had been archived," Jerves said, as if trying to reassure himself. "To think it has been lying on

93

this shelf for all this time!"

"What's wrong? You just told me about how it was the perfect choice!"

Jerves shook his head. "No. The story is not what concerns me. It is the book itself!" The bookseller glanced at the door as if expecting someone to barge through the entrance. "This book . . . there are only a handful like it. Unfortunately, I receive so many titles, I do not have the time to examine them all with the proper care they deserve!" Jerves opened to the novel's midpoint. "This book was printed with the page between 333 and 334 sealed together."

"Just because there is a printing defect . . ." Harold stopped himself as he considered what Jerves had said. "Wait a minute. What do you mean *sealed*? How can you seal the same sheet of paper?"

"So you would think. But such is not the case for these. In all of my years of operation, I've come across only two others like it."

"You've only seen two books with printing problems?" questioned Harold. "Obviously, you haven't picked up too many newer books! These days, you're lucky to find a title that has the print set squarely on the page!"

"No, no, no. It's not the same. The flaw in this book is much more *unique*." Jerves held up the page in question.

"Can you see it?"

"See what?" To Harold it looked like a normal piece of paper.

Jerves snapped the book shut. "Your eye is untrained. But it is there."

"*What* is there?"

"The curse. They say if the pages are pried apart and the contents within revealed, a curse is bestowed."

"A curse." Harold stared at the old man for a moment before starting to chuckle. "I'm sorry. But that sounds ridiculous!"

Jerves looked at him with no hint of bemusement.

"This would make a great urban legend."

"An urban . . . what?"

"You know. Like the story about the boy having a pet dog that turns out to be a rat. Or the one about the guy finding himself in a bathtub, his kidneys missing."

94

"You take this to be some sort of joke?"

Harold pulled out his wallet. "How much do you want for it?"

"It's not for sale."

"You know, I don't want to sound rude, but I'm sure you can benefit from a sale. It's not like customers are banging down the door to come in!"

Jerves paused for a moment as he considered what Harold had said. "After all of my warnings, you are still insistent on purchasing it?"

"Would it make you feel any better if I promised not to pry the pages apart?"

"You . . . *swear*?" Jerves looked at him carefully for his answer.

Harold held up two fingers. "Scout's honor." He fished out a twenty-dollar bill. "So, how much are you asking?"

Jerves looked at the bill between his fingers. "My dear fellow. You are going to have to do better than that."

~~~~~

"You were in there an awfully long time," remarked Kelly as they walked out of the clothing store. "I was expecting you to show up earlier."

Harold looked at the large bag in each of her hands. "I almost wish I had."

"Well, at least you got a book," she said, noticing his parcel. "Was it something you were looking for?"

Harold didn't answer.

~~~~~

As he closed the book, the phone began to chirp.

"Hello? Hi, honey. No, not much. I was just finishing my book when you called. Yes, *that* one. What's that? Sure. I'll meet you *there* for dinner. No. I don't mind. What time? Six? All right. Bye."

Harold disconnected the line and placed the receiver back onto its cradle. *Why did I ever agree to go to her mother's for dinner?* He was perfectly comfortable staying home for the evening.

Sighing, he looked down at his book. "*Love's Journey*," he said, reading the title. It was a *journey* all right. *A journey into boredom.*

His conversation with Jerves's popped back into his head. On

95

the trip back home Harold examined the page carefully but found nothing out of place about it. He simply chalked up the extra money spent as a type of charitable donation to keep the bookstore in operation.

Now bored, he reopened the novel, and he leafed through the sheets until he reached the page in question.

His curiosity piqued, he ran his index finger along the edge of the page. It was so seamless that it simply felt like a thicker stock of paper had been used. *Crazy old goat.* He was about to close the novel when he noticed a small separation where the page was joined to the binding. Looking more carefully, he realized two pages *were* pasted together along the edges.

Using his pocketknife, he slid the blade carefully into the small gap.

The pages began to separate.

Removing the knife, he stared down at the book, unsure. A myriad of thoughts ran through his head. *Was there some truth to the old man's ramblings?* He placed the book down but his thoughts began to wander. *What if someone had placed something valuable like a rookie baseball card between the pages? Then again, what if there was something illegal like child pornography? What if Kelly opened the book and found them? How could he explain that?*

No. He definitely needed to know what was between the pages.

Firmly gripping the knife, he slipped it in and ran the blade down the length of the book. The glue holding the pages together was old and brittle. It broke easily.

Bringing the blade across the bottom of the page, he suddenly reconsidered if he was making a mistake.

Using his thumb as a marker, he closed the book again.

A trickle of sweat crept down his side.

Chicken.

Re-opening the book, he pulled the two pages apart and held his breath.

But there was nothing.

Nothing at all.

Two pristine and utterly blank pages greeted Harold.

For a moment he simply stared in disbelief.

Then, holding it up to the light, he studied the parchment more carefully, thinking there might be something written in an invisible ink.

But still he saw nothing.

He had been scammed.

Closing the book in frustration, Harold got up and walked into the kitchen. Being quite accustomed to his mother-in-law's cooking, he decided to make a quick sandwich. Odds were favorable that Martha was cooking up a vat of her special battery-acid spaghetti sauce.

In the kitchen he was greeted by a set of dirty dishes atop the table and a stack of blank, low-grade paper on the chair. He placed the dishware into the washer. Harold wondered where the papers had come from. For now they would go into the recycling bin. He made a mental note to ask Kathy if they were of any importance.

Fixing the sandwich, Harold walked back to his recliner.

Carefully balancing the sandwich on his lap, he reached for a periodical from the magazine rack.

Instead of grabbing the current issue of *Popular Mechanics*, he pulled out a small bundle of bound photocopy paper. Dropping it to the floor, Harold reached again.

"What the hell?" Harold mumbled as he produced another wad of photocopy paper, slightly thicker than the first and this time square bound.

Leaning over, he looked down into the bin. Leafing through the contents he was surprised to find it full of blank paper. *Was this some sort of joke?*

Putting down his sandwich, Harold sat up, annoyed with Kelly for what she had done with the magazines. She was always tossing them into the recycling bin before asking him if he had a chance to read them. But what was the deal with all of this blank paper?

Scanning over the titles in his bookcase, Harold pulled out *Heart's Desire*, one of the many titles he had been meaning to read. He opened it to the title page.

Or where the title page should have been.

Flipping over several more pages, he was faced with blank sheets of paper. Flipping a dozen more, the pages were still blank.

Tossing the novel onto the floor, he pulled out another, one he had read earlier in the year. Opening it yielded the same results.

Blank.

Harold began pulling titles at random off the bookcase, opening them in different spots.

Blank.

Blank.

Blank.

Again he thought back to his conversation with Jerves. *I swear I will not pry apart the pages.*

Grabbing his car keys, Harold bounded out the house, not even pausing to lock the front door.

~~~~~

The lights were on inside the Cryptanthium as Harold came screeching to a halt. He jumped from the car and swung the bookstore door open.

The smell of musty books was gone, replaced by a foul, acrid smell. There was a haze in the air as if something had been burning.

Harold called out for Jerves but the man did not reply. Thinking that he was in the rear of store, Harold made his way around the counter. His foot struck something and Harold gripped a nearby bookcase to prevent himself from stumbling forward. He glanced down to step over the object and saw the bookseller lying on his back, staring back at him with glassy eyes. A revolver was clutched in his right hand.

Harold screamed and stumbled out of the bookstore.

Outside on the street, a girl who seemed just old enough to be in kindergarten was standing with her mother. A book was clutched in her hand. Her eyes were scared, uncertain.

Harold's feet remained planted as he stared at the skinny bundle of paper the girl held. For a moment he considered offering her consolation.

But he had no words.

Lord of the Earth
by Michail Velichansky

Months before, a boy came to Tyr Oreheart's door. He was tall and thin—taller than Tyr, though he managed to look smaller. He had mangled black hair and wore cheap jeans.

"Are you Tyr Oreheart?" he asked, his voice trembling.

"What do you want?"

The boy swallowed hard. "I . . . I heard you were here . . ."

"Out with it."

"I'd like to apprentice with you." He took a deep breath and let it out; it made the statement seem final, done. Tyr stared at him for a second, then slowly began to laugh.

"And what exactly do you hope to learn from me, boy?"

The boy stammered, then finally, "I want to be a . . . a hero . . . like you . . ."

Tyr smiled kindly. "Go home kid. The age of heroes is past." He closed the door. "Long past . . ."

~~~~~

Tyr napped on a soft chair facing the fire, legs stretched out and propped on a stool to keep his bare and callused feet warm, head resting on the side of the chair. The firelight played shadow games on his face, and caused a small bead of drool to flash prettily.

He was a big man, though not a tall one. He took up the entire chair, his arms and legs were thick and wide. Strands of thin, broken hair fell to his shoulder, the color of faded rainbow, an oilslick catching the sun. It was not an even pigmentation, but splotches of color: swirls, uneven streaks, fractal patterns. There were similar bursts of color on his face and chest, though they were not as bright. The most visible was an orange marking that ran over his right eye and down his face, curving around his neck and down his back—signs of too many lifetimes around magic.

His left hand rested on his lap; the other hung down over the side of the chair. A small glass, half-filled with a deep-red wine sat on one of the chair's handles, a tiny reflection of the fire dancing within.

Tyr snored: a deep, rolling sound like gentle thunder.

There came a series of three knocks on the door, clear and sharp. Tyr's breathing jumped and skipped; he squirmed in the chair, then settled back down. Again, three knocks. Tyr sputtered and opened his eyes. He yawned and stretched, both actions very large, seeming as though any second the house would be too small to contain him.

"Who is it?" Tyr asked, his voice deep and thick with waking.

"Lieutenant Stokes," said a muffled voice.

"One second," Tyr said, and stood with exaggerated slowness, stretching and yawning.

Barefoot, he walked to the door. It was a short walk, the house was little more than a hut. But it was a comfortable, homey hut, a warm hut. And it was Tyr's hut; he'd been there for a long time.

He opened the door. Standing at ease with his hands behind his back was a man in uniform, a black leather trench coat hung from his shoulders, straight and tight before widening at the man's hips. The top three buttons were undone. Tyr could smell the magic, and a small part of his mind—dusty and rusted—insisted there were symbols burned into the coat. The army's equivalent of mage's

102

robes.

A small crystal pentagram was pinned to the coat over the man's heart. There were no other identifying insignia—there was no need: along with the coat, everybody would know what this man was.

"What do you want, Vincent?" Tyr asked, holding the door open with his left hand, leaning on it.

"Mind if I come in?" the man asked, running a gloved hand through dirty-blond hair.

The gesture was a sham. The man's face was a glamour to hide how the magic had warped his features. Tyr shrugged and stepped aside. Vincent walked in, and the coat melted away into the air. Tyr gestured at the stool he had moments ago been using to hold up his feet. "Sit down if you want," he said. "Only other chair I have." He sat down in his chair and stretched his legs out again.

"So what was it you wanted?"

The man stared down at Tyr, holding his chin with a gloved hand. "I've got a job for you," he said.

Tyr snorted. "I don't do public appearances, and I don't give pep talks about the glory of dying for one's country."

"Don't be difficult, Oreheart. A real job. Suitable for your . . ." he smiled translucent teeth, "*highly specialized* abilities."

"And just which ones are those? Surely you haven't come to ask my help with your gardening? Though, I admit I've gotten pretty good lately—"

"I'm *offering* to hire you as an adventurer, Oreheart. As a hero."

"Nobody hires heroes anymore. There's no need."

"I'm hiring you now. Don't be thick."

Tyr smiled and shook a flattened index finger with no nail. "*Trying* to hire, Vince, *trying* to hire. What exactly are you talking about? What do you want me to do? And why?"

Vincent began to pace back and forth, his boots making a dull thud on the wooden floor, the third board from the fireplace creaking slightly. He fingered the crystal pentagram, now attached to a plain white shirt.

"There's been a disturbance of sorts. Not too far from here, half-a-day's flight. Out in Keldor Forest." Vincent waited; Tyr remained pointedly silent. "Someone's taken up residence there."

"So what's wrong with that? Assuming someone would *want* to live there . . . there's no law or anything, is there?"

"No, not as such. But whoever it is, he's using some pretty nasty magic. Powerful stuff; leaking all over the place. He's got a castle built up, must be twice the height of the trees, and Keldor's got some skyscraper oaks. Not only that, but there've been some . . . strange reports. Creatures gathering. The farmers near the forest are getting nervous—they've had crops stolen and torn up, animals butchered. And with Kell Town only five miles down the road now … Anyway, that's the job. Go up there, investigate, and if someone's toying about with illegal magic, trying to play sorcerer—take care of them."

"No trial?"

Vincent smiled with only half his mouth, a look entirely devoid of humor. "Use your own discretion." His full smile managed to look worse. "We trust you."

Tyr stared at Vincent thoughtfully. His fingers twitched as he brought them close to his face. "Why don't you just go in and get whoever this person is yourself?"

Vincent spread his arms, turned his palms up and shrugged. "We could do that. But I think this way is better. After all, this is your kind of thing, isn't it? Climb the magic tower, slay the evil sorcerer. Right, Oreheart?" Tyr snorted. "Besides, it would be good for this place. Raise everyone's self-esteem a little. People like to see heroes, Oreheart, even when they don't need them anymore. The nation's having it tough; people want something to look up to, a reason to remember the Good Old Days." Vincent smiled again. "Half the runts who sign up want to be heroes. We beat that out of them pretty quick, sure—but they sign up, don't they? And they *are* heroes, in a way. That's the image the populace needs: the gallant warrior, fighting evil for the good of his nation."

"People aren't going to buy that kind of sap, Vince. Your war's going badly, even I know that—people are sick of it. My sticking some half-crazed mage who's probably doped out of his mind isn't

104

going to make things any better."

"People will believe what they want to believe. And in times like this, people want to believe."

With his index finger, Tyr slowly traced the orange discoloration down his jaw.

"Besides," Vincent went on, "we can't spare the troops or the weaponry. Too dangerous anyway: hellfire and salamanders don't stop easily—they'd burn the forest and everything in it, tear through half the surrounding farms, and if they hit a city . . . . My mages might be able to collapse it, depending how strong this sorcerer is, but collapsing a magic field like that isn't pretty—lots of energy tied up inside—and it's unpredictable."

"That's enough," Tyr said. He continued to trace the pattern on his neck.

"There're good reasons for you to do this, Tyr. Not the least of which, I'm sure you must miss the old days. It'll be just like old times for you. Maybe we can even arrange for a damsel to be—"

"Shut up, Vincent," Tyr said. Vincent chuckled. It was not a nice chuckle—his eyes and smile were too wide, his teeth were too prominent in his mouth. It reminded Tyr that Vincent's true face was hidden, that something alien hid behind the magic.

"What will you do with this tower once it's in your hands?" Tyr asked.

"Take it apart, of course. Dissipate the magic, nice and slow, completely harmless." Vincent paused. "You'll be well paid."

Tyr said nothing. Vincent settled back against the wall, all of his weight on one foot; he returned Tyr's silence with his own.

Finally, Tyr said, "I'll think it over. Come back tomorrow."

Vincent smiled and hummed a laugh. "Excellent," he said. "Tomorrow, then." And he walked out with long, military strides. His coat reappeared as he stepped out; he didn't bother closing the door.

~~~~

As he did every night that it didn't storm—and sometimes even then—Tyr slept outside, behind his house, a few meters from his small, struggling garden. Staring up at the sky, his gaze slid lazily from one star to another without really seeing them. It had been so long since he'd had a quest, even a small one . . . how many hundreds of years? He'd lost count. After the first hundred, they went by so fast, and there was so much in between. So many friends . . . lovers . . . so many places called home . . . .

He knew he would take the job. All that was left was to *decide* to take the job. Boredom was always the chief enemy of those with all the time in the world, but he'd managed to keep busy. There were innumerable skills to learn—and more often than not, fail to learn. Knowledge to gain, bread and clean water to work for.

So not boredom. Curiosity, maybe? Find out about the castle's maker. Something else? Find out if he still had it, if he was still the great hero of the last age. The last hero of the last age . . . . Or maybe just to feel useful and good again. Feel like a hero. Were they all reasons to go? Or none of them?

The thoughts moved through his mind like slow glass birds, seen through and idly examined. Trinkets. On any grand scale, it did not matter so much whether he stayed or went, and he liked it that way. Still, it would be interesting.

He knew that Vincent lied: if it was of any use to them, they'd keep the tower. But the world's affairs were no longer his concern. He wanted to live the old days one last time. He wanted days fresh and new, not just dusty memories. After that, he could go back to his hut and his garden, and leave the world outside.

But now Tyr felt that he'd slept on the same patch of grass for too long, and the old wanderlust tugged at his heart like an old lover. Happily not knowing what the next day would bring, he turned over and went to sleep.

Tyr woke at dawn. Usually, he would lie awake and watch the sun rise, the sky shimmering as pockets of magic caught fire in the sky, but today there was reason to be up early. He sat up, let the bedroll drop to his lap; the cold morning air hit him, forced him to draw breath, freezing his lungs along with his skin. He held the cold air for a second, then exhaled and breathed in quicker to warm himself.

With concentrated relaxation, he worked through slow,

methodical dances that brought a quiet, reassuring burn to the muscles. The sweat on his body dried quickly in the wind. Ready, he walked to the garden. At one end of it, several wooden planks— roughly carved, resembling crosses—stuck out of the ground. Tyr paced in front of them for a brief time, working his fingers, clenching and unclenching them. Then he picked one and pulled it out. A wooden sword.

For half an hour, he sparred with air and memories, moving the sword to a rhythm only he could hear. Then he pulled out other swords, each shaped differently, and danced with them in various combinations. His eyes saw nothing, mind lost in the movement of muscles. And when his meditations were complete, and he set the swords back into their grooves, Tyr had decided.

When he went inside, he was tired, out of breath, and covered with a cold sweat. He felt like he had been asleep for years, and only now did the sand fall from his eyes.

He put on simple clothes and walked to the room which was meant to be the bedroom. The rusted hinges stuck slightly. Inside, the air was dusty, thick with the smell of age, of mildew and old magic, like something gently rotting, like damp earth after the rain. The smell wriggled in his mind like worms in a puddle. Even locked away and covered in dust the magic was never quite still.

Carefully, Tyr unwrapped bundles of cotton and leather, opened wood-and-iron chests. Then he dressed:

He took out old chain mail wrapped in a dusty, oil-soaked rag. He wiped it carefully, the metal rings shining, reflecting more light than was in the room. He ran his fingers across it, and it moved like a wave, clinking like chimes. Tyr's fingers found a small hole in its left side—a flash of fire and steel in his mind; his hand shot under his shirt, touched his side to trace an old scar . . . .

He wrapped strips of leather over his legs—soft inside, hard outside.

Put a bracer over his left arm: dull green, covered with scrawls unreadable even in his younger days. A wide, curving blade protruded from it past his hand. It was stained brown, and nothing had ever managed to clean it. When he moved his fingers the right way, the edge vanished.

Around his neck he laid a small chain of tarnished silver. On it, a small blue stone, translucent and cloudy; inside it, something writhed.

He unwrapped a cloak and slung it over his shoulders. It shone brilliantly, and then darkened until he was wearing shadow.

And he slid on dark, skin-tight gloves. He moved his index finger in a circle on the palm of the right hand: he could feel where the fabric had been burned, though it was impossible to see.

Then, on his knees, Tyr moved junk and fabric to the side; he pulled out a long flat chest. Gently, he ran his fingertips along its wooden top. It seemed to him that he felt every grain, every hole and imperfection.

Tyr breathed deeply before opening the final chest.

Inside was a sword, its blade long and wide, small spider-etchings on its gleaming surface. The handle was long, meant for two hands, twisted for a comfortable grip; from it, three metal prongs curved out and then back in, fusing together at a point just inside the apex of a small glass prism.

Tyr stared at the sword for a long time, tracing the symbols on its blade, allowing his gaze to move with the twisted handle. He watched the prism play with the light—flickering, reflecting, breaking it up into deformed and stunted rainbows, blots of color writhing in place, one color flowing into another like a dog chasing its own tail.

And then he touched the handle, slipped his hand around it carefully. The blade hummed; the prism turned dark and clouded over.

Tyr whispered, "Hello, old friend . . ."

~~~~

Vincent stood in the doorway. "You look like a walking museum, Oreheart. I assume this means you've decided to accept the job?"

"I'll do it," Tyr said. The sword hung on his back, next to a pack. He stepped past Vincent and closed the door then hooked his thumbs into the straps of the pack, breathed deep, and started walking.

Behind him, Vincent said, "You know, I could just Gate us there.

Or we could fly, if you really want to see the scenery . . ."

"Thanks," Tyr said without looking back. "I think I'll walk. It's been too long since I had a nice walk." He did not bother to see how Vincent reacted.

~~~~~~

The road was overgrown with weeds and sickly roses the color of mud; off the road, they wrapped themselves around the rusted husks of derelict machinery, drawn by the leaking magic. Sometimes the roses hissed as though rustled by the wind, though the air was thick and still.

Though it had been a long time since Tyr had journeyed, he found his stride quickly; he'd learned early on that with the right rhythm, you could walk all day. There was a familiar tinge in the muscles of his legs as he kicked up thin clouds of dust around his feet.

A faint smell of magic, full of paradoxes, filled the air: pleasant sweetness and noxious rot, it called sleep to his eyes and anxiety to his muscles; it left his nose and throat tingling. Soon, his mind grew used to it, and the smell of magic faded to the background.

It was noon when he saw a small group of people walking in the same direction, travelers dressed in rags.

All around were only hills and mazes of prickly bushes that spawned no flowers, with only a few farms and struggling oak trees in the distance.

When Tyr was close enough to the travelers to make out individual features, they stopped and turned around, heads turned this way and that, children scuttled behind their mothers, peeking around to see.

"Hello," Tyr said.

One of the ragged figures, stooped and leaning on a stick, stepped forward. "We have nothing of value, sir. Leave us in peace." His voice was rough and shaky.

"I mean you no harm."

The man eyed Tyr's sword and armor. "In that case, move on."

Tyr looked at the ragged troupe and shrugged. He kept walking, and they parted for him. Staring ahead, he felt their eyes on him, tracking him as he moved past. He felt movement in the air behind him, the whisper of moving fabric. The back of his neck tingled. He did not stop. He felt more than heard the soft thud of each step and the swish of dust.

Behind him, hushed voices, hard and earnest.

A shout.

For a second, ozone and magic—an impact like a hammer on his back, the flaring amulet around his neck—then the taste of dust.

Tyr came to a moment later, his face raw and aching. Riding instinct and adrenaline, he rolled onto his back—there were shadows over him, surrounding him, touching with greedy hands. Tyr screamed and spit out dirt, threw himself up and forward, through the shades surrounding him, slashing out with his left hand. Barely any resistance. A scream turning to a choking gurgle. Something heavy on top of him and the familiar warmth of blood running down his arm.

Next moment he was standing up, knees bent, sword ready, flashing dimly with the last light of the day. The shades receded. One lay on the ground, and then Tyr remembered. He bent down carefully, trying to examine the body without taking his eyes off of the others. They twitched like rabbits who'd met the wolf's eyes. Hovering nearby, so like the shades Tyr had mistaken them for, they neither fled nor came closer.

The body on the ground was not an aged man, but his skin was ashen, wrinkled, covered with scars and calluses. He was not dead, but life seeped out of him.

Tyr stepped back, stumbling a little. "I'm sorry," he said. He couldn't hold up his sword. The point fell to the ground, and he followed its lead. He sat on the dirt and did not move when the travelers scurried forward to drag the body away.

He sat, not looking at the stars, or the glowing horizon. Not listening to the hiss of the roses.

A thought, a whisper in his head, again and again: "He didn't deserve to die."

There was silence. Then the old man came, leaning heavily on his walking stick, looking weary as though he had walked far, though the travelers were only a few yards away. Tyr said nothing, watched him walk up the path. Illuminated by moonlight, the man looked grayer still.

"I came to say that I—that *we*—are sorry. The boy who shot you, our William, he is young, brash . . ." The man squatted down, hugging his knees. Tyr saw his eyes, streaked with faded red and orange. The man went on: "I know he will leave us soon . . . sooner now, I think. Those like him, they always leave—to make their way, joining the Black-coats or becoming one of the bandits they spent their childhood fearing, and a thousand things in between." He laughed, and it was an old, crooked laugh, which broke down to a wheeze, a cough, a fit—into something spit up, dark and wet.

"Anything," he said, still wheezing, "anything but poor migrant workers." He took a few deep breaths. The smile on his face melted away. "And . . . and maybe it's *better* that they leave. Otherwise they get someone killed. And they probably will anyway, as you can see, only . . . better it's not here."

The sound of the man's voice faded, and he sat in silence next to Tyr for a few minutes. Then, he sighed; something thudded on the ground in front of Tyr.

"That's what he got you with. Don't know where he got it from, but it's not hard to guess. They're pretty common, now."

Tyr reached forward and picked up the object. It was a simple thing: a glass rod with something fuzzy at its core, attached to a splintered wooden handle. At the base of the rod, just before it met the handle, was a smooth, rounded stone; it seemed to contain an aurora within itself. Tyr was sure the stone was artificial, a worthless piece of shaped glass molded by a golem somewhere, imbued with magic—along with hundreds of others like it—by some industrial mage. He figured it was probably made by the military, the 'Black-coats' as the farmers called them.

"I . . . I'm sorry we tried to rob you . . ." the old man said, chuckling, a sound like gears grinding through. "We would have punished him anyway, of course. But why let it go to waste entirely, eh?" And then he sighed, "But I guess we got ours for that, didn't we?"

"What was the man's name?" Tyr asked.

The old man shrugged. "Does it really matter now? He didn't talk much; he was a mouth and a hand. Now he's dead. He died trying to rob a stranger dressed like a rich man's fool; he could have died of exhaustion, starvation, highwaymen, or practice for the Black-coats. He'd have died somehow sooner or later."

He sighed deeply. "Do you know how we survive out here, traveler?" He pointed at one of the rose bushes. "The stems bleed if you cut them. It tastes of the worst foulness imaginable, and it only fills your belly—you just starve slower. And they twist you slowly, some of the children are born . . .

"Well. The first time you try them, they make you vomit, but after that you can keep them in. They keep us going when we have nothing else.

"When someone dies, we leave them by the side of the road. 'They're feeding the roses' we say. That's who he is now—a corpse, feeding the roses."

"Can't you tell me his name?" Tyr asked again.

"We didn't know his name. Knowing your own name and your family's is enough of a burden—and he was alone. Anyway, don't think too much of it," the old man said, clapping Tyr on the shoulder. "It can't be much worse for him than life, eh?" The man smiled, hacked up more lung.

"If you want William, there's nothing we can do to stop you."

Tyr looked, and saw a young man watching him defiantly, an old woman hanging on to him and crying. He looked back at the old man and shook his head.

The old man shrugged and walked away. The group walked past Tyr and soon vanished into the night. Tyr stayed where he was. He looked at the stars, then at the faint swirls of magic inside the glass weapon; idly, his left hand rubbed the still-warm amulet around his neck.

He pounded the ground with his fist.

He laughed softly, clutching the naked blade to his chest.

And for his loneliness and pain, only the voice of wind howling in the night, a few cold, blue stars and clouds of magic dust like pale auroras drifting through the sky.

In the morning, Tyr stood and stared at the rising sun. Then down at the weapon and its squirming magic. He blinked and smashed it with his sword. A liquid like hot animal fat drained out of the stone, bands of color running through it, tying around each other. The dry earth sucked it up.

Tyr walked on, wondering vaguely what kind of plant would be growing there when he came back. (And always, always the question: "*Will* I come back?" He remembered a time when he had worn that question like a badge of honor.)

A naked corpse lay a few steps away from the road, entwined by rose bushes. From withered hands grew delicate pink flowers, while the rest of the body was stripped of flesh. Hands were the proverbial seat of magic.

Tyr saw no one else on the roads, for few used them anymore. There were Gates between the major cities, and people seldom left small towns. Sometimes military men flew overhead, steel masks covering magic-ravaged faces, dark leather fluttering behind them. With their coats billowing in the wind, they were like great bats, shadows in the sky. They held staffs of metal and crystal, and they carried larger versions of the weapon Tyr had smashed, lightning rods and hand dragons. But these were mere toys compared with the great magics the armed forces summoned in far off battle fields. Not that distance mattered—there was enough magic being thrown around to affect everyone. No wonder the earth was sucked dry and spawned things that bled and looked like roses.

On the third day of his journey, Tyr was surrounded by bandits. They were as ragged as the farmers, and threatened him with rusty knives. His muscles remembered. Killing them was easy.

On the fourth day, he could see Keldor Forest, and the spire that jutted out of it. Even in the day, the tower was dark, its edges blurred as though the light avoided it as much as it could. It weaved slightly, like a mirage. As he got closer, Tyr thought the air around it shimmered.

The weather turned bad: lightning split the sky behind him,

thunder rolled.

There were farms encroaching on the forest, and Tyr decided he would stop at one for shelter, information, and provisions. One of them still had a shimmering dome of magic over it to keep in heat and moisture, keep out insects, and force work from the soil and its farmers—but even it flickered unsteadily, and Tyr thought he could see roses growing on it like fungus. Tyr picked a simple farm to approach, just a few worn-down buildings and fields that gasped for the coming rain. A tractor stood abandoned, strangled by plant life; its lights flickered weakly and sometimes its frame quivered.

Tyr knocked on the door of the house, and after a few seconds, a tall, thin man opened it.

"Yes?" the man said in a mouse's voice. He was holding a rod; Tyr didn't think his amulet would be able to handle that much force.

"I'm here to take care of *that*," Tyr said, pointing toward the forest and its shimmering tower. "I'm working for the army. Please, I'd like to talk to you—"

The man stared at Tyr, fingering his weapon, his eyes darting down to Tyr's sword and over his antique dress.

"All right," he said, opening the door and waving Tyr inside with one hand, the other still pointing the rod at Tyr's chest. "It's about time they sent someone to take care of that damn thing, it's been scaring everyone around here to death. Bad enough the army's had to raise taxes again, and we keep getting this flash rain—crops need nice and steady water, you know." He moved slowly within the room's haphazard emptiness, his face blank and guarded even as he chatted. His voice did not modulate in any way.

"Can you tell me anything about it?" Tyr asked.

"I haven't been up there myself or anything . . . have to run the farm, barely getting by as it is. But there are strange things going on over there. Sometimes, there're footprints around the forest or on the road—two feet, you see, but not *human* feet. And I'm not talking about those dirty longears, either—I mean some kind of animal's feet, 'cept it's not any normal animal. Deformed.

"And Murry—mile down the road—he's had some cattle torn

up. Wasn't even eaten, most of it—just torn open. I haven't had nothing like that happen, thank God, I can't spare the stock. If you require help of me . . ." His face jerked briefly with the force it took to say the words.

Tyr said, "There's a storm coming, and I could use a place indoors to spend the night. And if you can spare any food . . ."

The thin man clutched at his weapon, his shoulders scrunched in. Tyr could see the battle being fought on his face: need or greed against the chance of retribution from the Black-coats.

"Well, I—I suppose . . . since you're doing us a service and all. But I don't have room here. You'll have to sleep with the migrants."

"That's fine," Tyr said.

The man led him out back, past the barn, to an old chicken shack of moldy, rotting boards.

The thunder grew closer and more palpable. It rained harder.

"You can have some of their food," the man said and tried to smile. Then he walked back to his small house, just as the rain began to fall.

Tyr entered the shack. Faded, empty eyes stared at him. It was packed. Several people were trying to sleep standing up against the wall, others spooned together on the floor. It smelled of rot. It smelled of unwashed, sweaty people all packed into one place. It smelled of urine, and the roof leaked. The only food Tyr could see were a few pieces of biscuit being passed around among the children; they nibbled on their pieces like rodents, then passed it on. Tyr put his pack down on the floor and dumped out the food inside. Then he turned and walked out.

"Don't sleep in the roses," said a voice from the barn, cracking, parched and almost too exhausted to care. "Not if you want to wake up again."

The rain was beating down, small, hard tears falling from the sky. Angry tears making mud out of the road and feeding the ever-wilting roses. Tyr stumbled away from the farm, the mire sucking at his feet.

Flash! and blue fire split and seared the sky ahead of him.

Crash! and the thunder was like a derailed locomotive.

There was a tree not to far away, and he ran to it, holding his cloak over his head, the wind hissing in his ear, the air thick and humid. Tyr slipped in the sudden muck and crawled to the side of the road, the mud threatening to swallow him. Among the plants, the ground was firmer.

There were roses. It sickened him to use that word for them, he remembered what 'roses' referred to in his youth. These were something else, thick and swollen like tumors, quivering on their stalks as the rain beat down.

Hunger assaulted Tyr. He had nothing with him, and he had to eat; but it was more than that—he had to know, to understand.

He grabbed a rose and sliced it off with his bracer. A thick reddish-brown sap oozed out of it; petals opened, then fell off. Tyr breathed heavily and wiped at his eyes with the fingers of his left hand. Then he stuck the stalk into his mouth and sucked.

It was rancid milk and spoiled cabbage. Brackish water, pus, rot from an infection.

He spit the stalk out and tried to be free of the taste, the *feeling*. He heaved and heaved until there was nothing in him. Then, with a shaking hand, he reached over and cut another stalk.

Once he was sated, he crawled through the roses and ivy— slashing through the thickness, leaving behind a path of rose blood and milkweed—until he reached a rocky hill. Half-buried in it was the metal husk of an abandoned vehicle. It held to the soil like a tree. Metal spokes rose high into the air. Rose bushes tried to reach it, but only a few had managed to get their roots into the shallow ground.

The rain drove him down, water ran down his face, he could barely see. He stumbled to the other side of the hill; covered with mud and splattered with rose-filth, he hugged his knees and wrapped his cloak about him, held it over his head. He drank rainwater from cupped hands.

Then, shivering, Tyr forced open the derelict's rusted door and climbed inside. He lay down on the rotten cushions. He clamped both hands over his ears to muffle back the thunder, closed his eyes tight to shut out the lightning, and wished for sleep.

The next morning, Tyr scraped the mud off himself. He did not eat. He made his way to the road, and from there entered the forest.

It was not a particularly thick forest, but it was a large one, and it was still possible to get lost. He found that he could sometimes look through the canopy above him and see the tower, and was grateful for the good luck. He walked along a small path which led him in the general direction, hoping that he would not be forced to leave it—he didn't want to find himself lost after the job was done.

After half-a-day's travel, he was once again surrounded. They were mostly naked—the clothes they did wear were wolf and fox-fur, the hides of deer. They had crude longbows and wooden arrows; they wielded knives of horn and bone. They were tall and thin, with very long arms; faces that looked stretched sideways, their eye sockets small circles on opposite sides of their heads. Their skin was pale and translucent, though tinted by the greens and browns of the forest. Three of them blocking the path: one with silver hair falling loosely over his shoulders; another, with green dreadlocks; the final, blue hair tied in ponytails.

Green hissed and said, "What should we do with it?"

"How about we cut out those funny eyes of his?" Blue said as they circled round. Under the blue hair, one ear slanted back like an arrow point, while the other was a dangling lump of flesh.

Silver said, "We could carve a tree on his back. Maybe draw a leaf on his nasty larvae holds, tickle his tool." They laughed and smiled, like the glint of steel in a dark alley. He was missing several fingers, and a pig-brand showed on his forehead; someone had tried to cut and shave it off, but only partially succeeded.

"Who are you?" Green asked, his one remaining eye burning with hatred spawned of fear and pain. "What are you doing here? It was stupid of you to come along. Why didn't you bring a posse with you, human trash? Answer fast—my friends have short tempers, especially for *you*."

Tyr tried to keep his voice neutral, tried not to move. "My name is Tyr Oreheart—"

"Oreheart?" Blue said. "What kind of name is that?"

117

Silver said, "I hope you're not lying to us."

And Blue, "I hope you *are*."

"It's not the name I was born with. It was an honorarium; I did something for a dwarven clan a . . . a very long time ago."

"Dwarves?" Silver said, his tone answering his question. He spit on the ground.

"Black-coat bitches," Blue said.

"Hold on," Green said, "there haven't been any dwarven clans for hundreds of years . . ."

Tyr tried to smile. "A very long time ago."

"What's it trying to tell us, Vess?" Blue asked.

Green said, "I think he's claiming to be hundreds of years old."

Silver asked, "What're we going to do with the little liar?"

"It's not a lie—merely a curse. I was there when the clans held a third of the world. I was there when an army of elves and men marched on the City of Lights, burning and pillaging—"

Blue: "Shut up—let's shut it up, Kronos."

Silver: "Cut its meat off."

"—I was there when men and elves broke rank. When their council broke their own laws and built machines for war to use against each other, tearing up the land, spilling as much magic as blood." Tyr's voice sounded strange to him. It had been a long time since he'd thought about any of it; with time, the memories had blurred together like fine noise, but now they separated out.

The green-haired elf with dreadlocks said nothing, merely stared and sweated heavily from the glands in his neck.

Blue: "Cut it," and Silver: "Die!" They sprang at him with horn and bone. Tyr slashed out with his arm-guard, forced them to keep back. Then he ducked past Green and ran toward the tower, weaving between the trees.

Thuck, thuck, arrows struck near him, quivering in the trees. For a while there was only the sound of his feet cracking twigs and thudding on soft earth. He became aware of movement around him, fast and fleeting. Arrows whistled by. The elves were faster than he was.

Tyr stopped and drew his sword in one motion; just as fast he

118

was surrounded.

Blue and Green had their knives in each hand, while Silver had an arrow knocked in his bow and pointed at Tyr: he wouldn't be able to run again.

"It doesn't have to go like this," Tyr said.

"No," Silver said, "It doesn't. You can cut yourself for us, instead." He grinned widely, showing teeth that had been sharpened to points and capped with steel.

Tyr no longer recognized these creatures. They had looked like elves, but they were something else, something feral. Old memories clawed their way from in his brain, crying out in indignation.

Something in Tyr snapped, like rusted metal beneath the weight of rose bushes. He sprang at Silver. The elf loosed his arrow, but Tyr had not taken a straight line, and it shot past the side of his head. He cut his sword across, through the bow just above the elf's hand, sending splinters flying through the air. As the hairs on the back of Tyr's neck told him the other two were moving, he turned his momentum so that it sent him toward Silver, his knee rising up into the elf's gut. The elf bent over, and Tyr knocked him on the side of the head with his armguard; Silver fell to the ground with a grunt.

"Back!" Tyr yelled, the tip of his sword on Silver's back.

They were very close, just out of knife's reach.

"Cut him and you die," Green said, while Blue ground his teeth and glared as though he could cut Tyr with his eyes.

The fury waned as quick as it had ebbed, but Tyr could still feel it deep down, frothing against the world he saw around him. Most of him wished he were at home, but memories of dead friends still pawed at him like beggars and starving children.

Green said, "Seems we're at an impasse. Either way, someone's going to die."

"You weren't like this before," Tyr said.

Blue said, "You touch him again . . . . You know how long we can keep you alive? Can't wait to cut you . . ." It was like watching a starving animal snarl at meat just out of its reach, and it made Tyr sick.

"Is your memory failing, old one?" Green said. "Forget us

already? Think we're meeting for the first time?"

"No!" Tyr said. "No, I remember. Elves weren't like this. You must be something else . . . something the Black-coats made . . ."

"I think he's mad," Green said, smiling.

"Kill him anyway," Blue hissed. "He'll still scream like a human."

"You're abominations," Tyr whispered.

And Green answered, "We're what we are."

With a shriek Blue leapt at Tyr. The fury was there again, spilling over—with a speed he hadn't felt in ages, Tyr impaled the elf. Momentum carried Blue down to the hilt, his knives just within reach of Tyr, but he slumped down, quivering. Somewhere in the background, Green cried, "Sol!"

Tyr kicked Blue off his sword and stumbled back, away from the body. Blood filled his vision.

"Please," he whispered. "Please leave. I don't want to fight."

Green stared at him. His hands jerked slightly, as though any second he would follow Blue's lead. Instead, he moved around to his friends, knelt down to touch silver hair stained with blood.

"He's still alive," Tyr said. "I didn't hit him that hard. Only . . . only the other one . . ."

The green-haired elf wrapped one hand around Silver and slung the elf onto his shoulder, then did the same with Blue. He spat on the ground. "I'll leave," he said. "A thousand of your kind isn't worth one of mine. And there are worse things in the forest than us, madman, worse deaths than we could give. The world will see that there is blood and justice done." For a second he gnashed his teeth, and Tyr feared that he would still attack. But then the green-haired elf stalked away into the forest.

As soon as he was gone, Tyr collapsed to the ground. He tried to clean the blood off his sword. But even then, it was on the moss, on the ground, on his clothes—

Where had this world come from? It betrayed everything he'd known, everything he'd fought for in his youth. The fury left him, seeped back into the sick earth. He *felt* crazed, then. How could such a world have come about from the one he remembered? It seemed impossible, an evil joke . . . everything sick, even the elves . . . it hadn't been like this . . . .

But it had. Another memory that for too long had had no voice suddenly screamed inside his head. It *had* been like this. He'd told them: about the City, about the nations and races breaking their pacts. The wars didn't stop, one serpent giving birth to another even as it died. And soon, Tyr turned away from the world, the last hero from the great ages that was still alive. He hadn't been able to stand watching their great works perish before his eyes—it betrayed everything they'd been.

So he turned away. He'd heard about the wars, heard about the elves, only it wasn't real anymore, not in his garden, not with his sword safely locked away.

And now he was in the world again, and it was so much worse, and he wanted to be gone again. He felt tired and empty and *old*. But there was the quest. He had that much, and he'd finish it.

Tyr thrust the memories away, back into their dark, wet caves. He let the single goal crystallize in his brain to keep him in the present, and walked toward the sorcerer's tower.

~~~~~

As Tyr made his way through it, the forest grew thicker. Then it opened onto a small glade from the center of which rose the tower that had brought him. He stared up at his destination and didn't know how to feel.

Time crept by: It didn't seem right to just walk right in, without some preparation, so Tyr wasted time straightening his clothes, trying to clear off all the dirt. Then he entered the glade. The ground was soft and spongy, giving slightly under his weight. The tower looked as if it was made of marble. When he was close enough, Tyr reached out and ran his fingers over it: hard and rough, like sandstone. He withdrew his hand and stared at the wall; the sensation in his fingertips faded, and he could not believe that something which looked so smooth could feel otherwise. The two contradicting sensations plied for control in his head even as he turned away.

Tyr drew his sword and walked around the tower. It had a great many sides, none of them the same width, and though the tower had not looked large, it took a few minutes to reach the entrance: a gate wide and tall, the same color as the rest of the tower. But it wasn't stone: veins pulsed and bulged without rhythm; tendrils hung away from it, twisting slowly, looking like the unfinished arms of a child born early; eyes blinked, and oddly shaped mouths gaped and shut.

Out of one mouth hung what looked and smelled like a piece of rotting meat, flies swarming around it. As Tyr watched, it was dragged back into the mouth. It smiled, and toothless gums chewed on the mass with wet and happy gurgles. Then it opened, and the bait slithered out again, glistening, porous and fetid. Rot gland.

Further along, two human mouths with dark-red lips were fixed on thin stalks, kissing slowly, gently biting; when they tried to separate, Tyr saw that they were fused together with tiny membranes running from one mouth to the other—only the tongues were loose and free. The mouths returned to their affections.

Tyr did not touch the gate, carefully avoiding the curious gropings of stubs and mangled, deformed hands.

Loudly, he said, "You will open for me. I will see your master."

The wall shifted slightly, countless miniscule rhythms changed. A small part of the wall spread open near Tyr—a rodent's eye, pool of oily darkness, huge black pearl. A slit appeared above it, leaking sparkling fluid, and formed into a mouth.

"Who are you?" it said. Half of the mouth didn't move, and it dribbled ichor as it spoke.

"My name is Tyr Oreheart. I wish to speak with the master of this place."

Jaws protruded from the wall in front of Tyr, a forked tongue flicking out from it. "Why would Father-master speak with *yoooou?*" The mouth itself had not moved, the sound came from somewhere within.

"The mages sent me to investigate. But nothing is set in stone," Tyr added. "There are many ways this can end, we can work something out."

The eyeball split open, spilled black ooze. A small puckered mouth within it whispered, "Yes yes, the Oreheart speaks wise. Open, open, let it *in* . . ." The gate separated at the center and swung inwards, slimy membranes stretching and tearing, trailing on the ground as the gate made its slow and jerking way.

Tyr heard something above him, a mad, gibbering screech that tore the air. In Tyr's mind flashed images of drooling smiles and tortured puppies. He looked up quickly, his hands jerked to his sword—but for a second he didn't draw. He'd almost managed to forget moments like this.

Then the sound multiplied, and Tyr's sword came up, both hands white-knuckled on the handle. There was a fleshy thud behind him. He spun around to look—a pink something on the ground like a lump of ground meat. Vines entwined it and ran through it. Where an arm should have been, raw bone jutted out, cracked on the end: a twitching rose-stem grew from the bilish marrow. The other arm was a tentacle of mouths and fingers, fungus and mushrooms grew from out of its short, still-wriggling neck. The thing's legs had spattered under it, a pool of rotting blood and rainbow oil sucked at by the mossy ground, masses of pink and black meat, cracked bone. Roots began to inch out of it like spider's legs, trying to dig into the ground.

Screams above him. Tyr looked up and saw two more creatures: one sliding down the wall, sparks flying, while the other glided down on two pairs of wings, one as from a vulture, the other of a many-colored beetle. It rocked in the air, each set of wings beating differently, yet it approached quickly.

Blade vibrating in his hand, Tyr slashed at the thing on the ground and split it like a ripe melon. It twitched, squirted blood. Tyr cut again, across and up, blood and moss flying up into the air, until the thing stopped moving.

The others landed.

"No!" the door screamed in a flesh-and-metal voice. "Father-master does not wish this! Bad children! Naughty naughty, to slash and tear at Father-master's guest!"

Tyr ran forward, chopping down; the winged beast's carapace cracked, and its insides oozed like jelly. A mouth above its udder choked on blood. Then something hit Tyr on his right side, the sword was wrenched from his hand as he tumbled to the moss

123

and rolled—something on him, his nose filled with the smell of dead things, his mouth choked with too-soft fur. Claws raked his side, he felt himself bruising beneath the clinking armor. Sharp teeth in slobbering mouths sought neck-flesh beneath his gorget. Tyr stabbed the blade on his left hand into the thing's side while his right grabbed at flesh and hair, tried to pull back its head. They struggled, their yells mixing together, the door's voices protesting in the background.

The thing's head was a mound of eyes and toothy suckers on a thin neck. Tyr cut through the neck with the bracer—the thing jerked and spit, its eyes rolled up, blood spurted from its neck. Tyr struggled out from under it and ran from the flying thing. He grabbed his sword and wrenched it free of the soil. It hummed softly in his hands.

Tyr turned on the headless thing quivering on the ground and with a feral scream hacked at it until the only sound was his own ragged breath and the pounding of his heart. He lowered his sword until the tip touched the blood-fed moss. He stood with hunched shoulders, his clothes sparkling with gore. He wiped his sword and armguard on the ground, and then stood up. He faced the gate.

"Hurry, Oreheart," boomed the door. "Father-master with the Caretaker fights!"

Tyr walked in. Behind him, insect and animal legs protruding from the back of the door began to push it closed again. There was a crystal stair ahead of him, and up Tyr went, sword drawn.

~~~~~~

Up and up.

Up stairs of crystal.

Up, and up, the sound of his footsteps reverberating in the halls.

Smashing through a hall of mirrors.

Through a room of sharp steel and chaotic machinery; past a room choked with greenery, away from the call of lotus-flowers.

His sword jerked and cut through flesh, shattered twisted bone.

Through hall after shifting hall—halls of stone and living tissue, walls which told the past and present. He looked into the silk room, past the layers of curtains, and saw a huge clam which opened invitingly, a naked woman lying suggestively inside—but her eyes were empty and gray, the color of the meat she lay on, a part of the hungry, waiting mass. She sat up and beckoned to Tyr with motions at once smooth and artificial.

Up until he reached a large chamber with no walls, the floor covered with vines and bushes. Set unevenly around the floor were pulsing sphincters. One had a large, discolored egg halfway out of it, while another had closed tightly over the foot of a thing still covered in black and yellow birthing jelly—a madman's parody of the races.

A few creatures already born slunk about, emitting squeaks and guttural moans.

Suspended twenty feet above the floor was a room made of a stone like green storm clouds. A door was set within it, and at the opposite end of the chamber was a staircase of shimmering oil leading up to it. He'd reached the top.

Tyr walked forward, and a deep voice rang out, "Look! He's already here! Quick, release me! Let the children tear him to shreds! The Black-coats will do nothing, I tell you! They are too busy fighting their wars—we are not *important* enough! Quick, *quick*!" The voice left an after-sound like the buzzing of flies.

A man was bound in metallic ivy near the stairs. He was easily ten feet tall. Long, looping horns grew from his bald head, and Tyr could see a rat's tail whipping back and forth. The demon appeared to be wearing a gentleman's dress suit, but Tyr knew it was merely the skin the demon chose to wear.

The sword in Tyr's hand turned dark; it hummed and throbbed, became a shaft of nothingness, of void.

Tyr approached the demon slowly, fearing a trap; yet it squirmed slightly, muscles quivering against its bonds. Then it stopped and sighed.

"Too late," the demon said matter-of-factly, and turned to Tyr. It had no eyes. "Well, well—Oreheart. You're still alive. Curse holding up, is it?"

Tyr stopped, held his sword in front of him. He squinted. "Who

125

are you?"

"Tsk tsk. Can't even remember who you've killed. Now what am I supposed to make of that?"

But Tyr didn't want to remember. He didn't want to hear the memories again, crying out at the world around him—without them, it was just another quest, just another job. Without them it wasn't his world that was sick.

"I would hate to think I was such an easy foe that you cannot remember me. We stood face to face and the world groaned beneath us." The demon's voice rose in grandiose self-mockery, "Up there, alone, it all pivoted on us. For a few seconds, we were lords of the Earth." He smiled bitterly. "I'm surprised you'd forget."

He hadn't forgotten; the memory was there. But the implications of it bothered him. A part of him wanted to kill the demon then, keep it from talking anymore, but he couldn't. There was too much he had to know. Tyr lowered his sword slightly.

"I remember," he said. "I killed you before. I knew your true name, once, but have not taken means to remember it throughout the years."

"Wonderful, wonderful! on both accounts," the demon said, smiling sardonically. "My name is, of course, best left to myself. You may call me Demon, though, if you wish to call me anything. It would remind me of younger days."

"Yes. Demon. Why are you here?"

"I'm here because I was summoned. The person currently in, ah, charge of this area summoned me. Performed the ancient rites and everything."

"Another sorcerer buying power with his soul?"

The demon shifted slightly, as much as the vines allowed. "Actually . . . I didn't manage to obtain that particular . . . item."

"He's bound you to him against your will?"

"Well, in a way . . . the *ritual* was the same . . ." The demon cleared its throat.

"But?"

"Not really against my will."

Tyr said nothing.

126

The demon whistled tunelessly for a second. Then he sighed heavily, the sound like an avalanche. "I missed the old days, Tyr. Working for some madman, wreaking havoc, creating chaos, fighting the likes of you. But things have gotten so muddled up now, with the wars . . . too much magic. It's leaking through everything, warping reality. Without order to ground it, chaos is just vacuum.

"Hell's become a very different place. It's sensitive, linked up to this world's magical field . . . . Now it's large, and dark, and empty. Most of the dead have left, and no one knows where—only those who really hate themselves seem to remain, and even then, they don't create punishments anymore. Demons are vanishing too—only a few of us left now." He sighed again and looked up. "No word from Heaven. We think it's gone. A few of the bosses went to check and never came back . . . . It was just nostalgia, Tyr. I didn't want you spoiling things, so I had the children attack. I didn't want it to end yet."

He chuckled. "That's why I'm bound up like this, see. He didn't want you hurt. I think having you here is all he really wanted, in the end. Still, it was damnable fun. Might be the last time I get to do this before *I* disappear. Now send me home."

"And what will you do there, Demon?"

"What else? Wait for the world to rot away and the tapestry of fate to fray and turn to dust. I might miss the world, but I'm not responsible for it." The demon jerked his head forward and snapped at Tyr's face. "It's not in my nature, and I wouldn't want it to be," the demon said, laughing.

Its words stirred up the memories again, stirred up all the voices that had died down in Tyr's world. He couldn't push them back anymore. They wanted him to act. Not fury, but something else now, at once weighing him down and tightening him like a spring. The demon was talking again, but Tyr didn't listen, there were too many distractions, he couldn't sort them out.

Like a shaft of icy light, he realized he had to finish his quest. He looked up at the top of the tower hanging overhead, then turned to the demon.

With hardly a thought, knowing he'd done it before, Tyr cut off the demon's head: it screamed, and the sword whined; red blood fell to the floor, steaming and boiling; the body burned to ash.

His mind pulsing and whirring like a great machine, Tyr climbed the shimmering stairs up to the end.

~~~~

It was a small room, unfurnished except for a single wooden chair in the center. Tyr stared at the person sitting in it, the great sorcerer he was supposed to 'take care of'. Who had summoned a lonely demon and created a tower of horrors.

The sorcerer stared back.

Mangled black hair and cheap jeans.

Tyr stared and remembered the boy who had come to him hoping to become a hero.

"Hi," the boy said. He was very pale, and small bands of color played in his eyes.

"We don't have to fight," Tyr said.

"Let's not, then."

Tyr lowered his sword until it scraped the floor.

"Where did these horrors come from? Why'd you create all this?"

The boy shrugged. "I didn't really create it—I just helped it be born. It was a possibility within the land made manifest. The land is choking, it has to do something with all the magic spilling over—that's why you get the roses on the side of the road. Some kind of balance has to be maintained. The world can't really keep up, though. What with the wars and all. I just helped it . . . consolidate its efforts. It wasn't very hard. I'm pretty good at magic.

"But I didn't think up any of this. Believe me—some of the things here I couldn't imagine in my worst nightmares, though they've certainly become that since I saw them." The boy's voice was strained, an exhausted monotone.

Tyr had seen more in the past few days than he had in many decades. Something in him yearned to understand. "Why do even that much?" he asked.

"Because I had nothing else to do. What kind of future do I have, with all my fine talent? Magic is all I'm good at, and what can I do

128

with it?" He breathed heavily and sweated profusely; his face had turned a pale red.

"Sure, I could do menial crap at some factory, fixing the golems that glued these crappy jeans together, which should keep me occupied for all of ten seconds. I could tinker with textiles or metals, trying to find new ways to do this or that—which is great, until the army guilds get a sniff of my abilities. You think they'd let me keep on doing commercial research? You know how paranoid those fuckers are. And if they can't have me, they'll make sure nobody else does.

"So either I spend the rest of my useful days designing things to kill people in new and improved ways, or they . . ." He sighed, "Or they do whatever it is they do. Cut off my fingers, slice up my brain, whatever."

"Can you take it apart? Destroy it?"

The boy shook his head. "It's too much. I'd be fighting the earth itself."

In Tyr's mind, he saw the Black-coats descend on the tower, saw it come to life again—it was too much, he pushed the thoughts away. Desperate, he whispered, "Why'd you come to me?"

The boy was silent for a while, staring down at the stone floor. "I . . . it was stupid. That's why, because I was stupid. I thought there would be something to do if I was a hero. Like in the stories my mom used to tell me. There seemed so few chances, and this one was just far-fetched enough, so I grabbed at it.

"I think in my head I saw myself traveling the world with you, doing good with my magic . . . . In a dream that fantastic, there's little room for reality, especially when you don't want any.

"I'm sorry about all of this. We didn't harm anyone. Just . . . played around with the magic some. Pretended we were making an army or something. The demon, he was just as desperate for a dream to cling to.

"And besides," the boy said, smiling wanly, "isn't it fitting? I mean, I can't become a hero—so I become the last hero's villain. Isn't that right, Tyr?" The boy smiled and drew shallow, ragged breath. "I always did . . . enjoy . . . irony . . ."

129

Smiling, the boy fainted.

Tyr put his sword away, picked up the boy, and carried him down the many steps. Along the way he took the demon's head.

~~~~~

The boy was awake; the water had helped. Tyr still carried him, though he had protested weakly. There was no strength left in the boy—controlling the tower had drained him. Behind them, the tower stood silent, brooding and waiting.

"What's your name?" Tyr asked.

"Philip."

"Family?"

"The war."

A silence descended. The boy closed his eyes; Tyr kept on walking, staring at the road ahead. Fueled on by the quiet, by the emptiness ahead of him, images of the tower came again. The back of his neck tingled—he could feel it behind him. Again he imagined it alive, heard its mouths speak to him. Imagined disfigured armies walking over tortured battlefields, led by battle mages floating overhead.

The boy's breath wheezed, weak and shallow. In an instant, Tyr became aware of the smell of magic again—the boy reeked of it; it was in the feverish sweat leaking from his pores, it tainted the air he let out of his lungs. Roses hissed loud around them and quivered on their stalks.

And from all Tyr had seen, from a slowly growing despair, came unbidden the thought of escape: he need only lay the boy down on the side of the road, and the roses would consume him. Need only do the task he'd been given, and he could return to his hut and his garden and shut out the dying world until it was ready to go and take him with it.

But he couldn't do that. The demon's head was heavy in his pack, a reminder of intent—he had what he needed to prove he'd defeated the master of the tower.

Tyr knew he could return home, but it was too late for him to keep out the world; going out, he'd let it in. To block it out now would be to betray the memories he'd tried to relive, and let the ones he'd tried to exorcise win out.

"When you save a life," he said, "you become responsible for it. If you want, you can come live with me. It's not much, but it's something."

Philip opened his eyes and smiled weakly, "Thank you, Tyr."

"And, who knows, maybe your dream isn't so foolish."

"What?"

"I was wrong, Philip. When I said that the age of heroes is past. Maybe . . . maybe the kind of hero I used to be. But this world needs heroes. Desperately. The *people* need heroes. Even the mage who sent me here understood that."

"It's . . . a *nice* dream."

"Dreams are important," Tyr said.

Silence.

"Where to now?" Philip asked.

"There's a town not too far away." He spread his arms out, and the clink of metal could be heard. "I can sell one of these trinkets and buy enough for us to eat till we get home."

The whisper of the forest. The slow cracking of twigs underfoot.

"Did you mean it about my dream?"

"Yes. And . . . I think it's my dream, too. It's just been so long since I really believed in it. I forgot I had to. It's like saving a life— you can't turn your back on the world you helped create."

Let Sleeping Dragons Lie
by Christine E. Ricketts

Jobe Lavel had never had any intention of becoming a hero. Certainly as a boy he had imagined himself vanquishing evil and saving villages, but he had never actually considered it as anything other than play. Heroes, his father always said, had an unsettling tendency to turn up dead. And at a rather alarming rate. Nasty business, being a hero.

Right at that moment, Jobe couldn't have agreed with his father more. With frigid winds blasting at his back, he rode his stocky, Vendarian war horse, Denga, across the wide emptiness of the Dead. The barren plains had been affectionately named for those who had marched across it not so long ago. If he stared out at the empty terrain for long enough, the memory of milky white faces and half-rotted corpses slowly trudging forward in uneven lines would creep into his mind. With it came echoes of shuddering terror. For the most part, he kept his eyes fixed on the well worn road as it disappeared beneath Denga's galloping hooves.

Above him, the sky rumbled and darkened with the beginnings of an encroaching storm. The few stunted trees that grew in the open land were spread far apart and offered him no protection from the weather. Sighing, he bent his head further and pressed his heels into Denga's flanks; the steed responded with an increase in pace. Nasty business, being a hero.

The rain came not long afterwards, crashing down in cold, heavy waves. The wind shifted direction and swept it sideways into his eyes. Jobe pulled his cloak closer in a vain attempt to shield himself. Ragged from months of rough wear and torn in a dozen places, the article was weak cover and within minutes he was soaked through and through. With another sigh, he brushed wet brown hair from lake-blue eyes and peered through the rain that ran down his strong face. The dirty, bulky wall of Tora loomed teasingly in the distance. After sledging half a mile through a muddy river that had started out as a packed dirt lane, Denga's hooves clapped soundly against the solid stone of the road leading into the city's eastern gate. The heavy, wooden doors were barred against entry. As he drew closer, water stinging his eyes like stone pellets, he saw but one guard standing vigilantly near the wall. A sign of the troubled times. Years before there would have been as many as half a dozen well-armed men standing tall. The war had claimed the lives of too many of them.

The guard stood beneath a tent-like contraption that looked as if one strong gust of wind could knock it over. There were three long support poles jammed into the ground and tied to the shelter in a manner that looked haphazard to Jobe's eyes. But the guard did not seem to be at all worried that his protection might collapse on him and it did seem to do an excellent job of keeping out the driving rain. The guard himself was bundled up in a heavy fur-lined cloak. One hand was fisted around the long handle of a halberd, and the two-foot, double-sided blade rose like a guillotine in the gloominess brought on by the weather. He remained silent as he watched Jobe's steady approach. When Denga came close enough, the guard shifted his grip on the weapon, lowering the blade half an inch in a gesture that Jobe took to mean he was to dismount. As he did so, the guard reached up with his free hand and took down a lantern that hung from one of the poles. With it, he took a closer inspection of the traveler.

Jobe left his hands at his sides, restraining the urge to wipe the water from his face, and made a study of the man before him. The guardsman was human, perhaps forty or so winters past. Grey pushed back from the edge of his temples into thin red hair. His posture was rigid, both from years of service and bones stiffened by the cold. Deep lines ran over his slightly slackened face, most of them taking residence in the folds of skin around his narrowed brown eyes. He was a man who had seen battle, for his face was marred by the souvenirs of violence. Scars marked his upper lip and the bottom of his square chin. An ugly purple line ran from his right cheek up into his hair.

"Hold traveler. State thy name and purpose," the guard requested in a scratchy voice that betrayed nothing and yet still managed to sound suspicious. In response, Jobe, who had no desire to be paraded through a lengthy gate procedure while standing in the pouring rain, held his hand up into the light, palm facing out.

A picture of an eye surrounded by flickering blue flames, tinged with white, was tattooed there. Recognition, followed by a hint of awe, flashed in the guard's eyes. Still, the suspicion had not faded from his gaze when he looked back to Jobe. Nonetheless he said, "Bane of the gods, thou mayest pass, if thou wilt bind thy weapon."

Accustomed to the new necessity, Jobe removed a long ribbon from a pouch on his belt and wrapped it about the hilt of his sword. At one time if had been rare for one to wear his sword within the walls of Tora, or any other city on the continent. Now only fools and those with no use for their lives went without.

Once the peace knot had been secured, the guard moved from his shelter to the right side of the massive gate. On the wall at chest level there was a red circle a foot in diameter. Curling his hand into a fist, the guard pressed his bare knuckles against the center. As soon as his skin made contact with the stone, a rapidly blinking glow emanated from the heart of the circle and the white outline of a door appeared within the gate. A moment later the light blinked out, leaving behind a door just large enough for a man and horse to pass through. With a low grunt, the guard motioned for Jobe to move on. He then returned to his post without a word.

Grabbing hold of Denga's reins, Jobe led the mare through the gate and into what once had been the great trading city of Tora. The bleakness of the storm combined with the shadows of uninterrupted warfare did much to diminish the splendor of the richest city built by human hands. The streets were empty and bare now, but there were ghosts in Jobe's mind of merchants and traders standing shoulder to shoulder, selling wares and services to any who passed. What had made Tora so appealing to traders was the fact that it lay in-between the two largest trade routes on the continent; the brutal north-south road known as the Merchant's Burden and the east-west route that cut through the heart of the Endless Forest. But those merchants and traders had donned armor and hoisted swords as soldiers. Precious few had returned.

That thought rooted itself firmly in Jobe's head as he passed by empty warehouses and inns with plenty of rooms to spare. But he had a unique destination in mind, though he was not certain what he would find when he got there. His memories were jumbled enough to have him wondering if he had simply dreamed up the battered old meeting place. Beyond that, the war had forced him to bury so many friends. He turned to glance over his shoulder at the bundle tied to Denga's saddle and, as result, did not see the figure in front of him until he collided with it.

Denga whinnied and snorted irritably as Jobe unintentionally tugged on her reins to steady himself. He found himself facing a city beggar bundled in clothes more tattered and ill-mended than his own. The beggar's face was hidden behind scarves, most likely to hide whatever disease he suffered from. There was only a thin slit for him to see through.

Jobe reached underneath his tunic and dipped his fingers into the money purse he kept strapped near his breast. From the small amount that was contained there, he removed several coins and held them out. "Here friend. Find some place that is out of this abysmal rain," he advised.

With a critical eye, the beggar accepted and then inspected the coins. A snicker of derision escaped from him. "Four coppers? I could have lifted your entire purse without you knowing it and you think I would be satisfied with four coppers?"

Taken back by the sarcasm that rolled off the street rat, Jobe's eyebrows rose and he took a closer look at the bedraggled fellow. His face remained obscured by bandages and the rain, but there was something familiar in the way he held himself. Slightly hunched in the shoulders and balanced on the balls of his feet. There was no trace of a limp or any other kind of hitch that beggars often used to inspire sympathy.

"It will grant you a night off the streets and a hot meal to sleep on," Jobe replied slowly, thinking that perhaps this was some bandit attempting to catch him off guard. He flexed his rain-stiffened fingers and slid his feet a few more inches apart. Fist-fighting was not something he enjoyed as a pastime, but he certainly was not going to let some stranger relieve him of the few coins he had left in his possession. And there were a number of other things about him far more precious than mere coins.

"I would not think it very comfortable or practical to sleep on a hot meal. Honestly Jobe, people like you are the reason thieving is such a necessary trade," came a pained, musical voice.

Hope rose like the sun inside of Jobe. Not daring to believe that he recognized the speaker, he wiped rain from his eyes and questioned, "Is that you Lott?"

With two fingers the figure tugged down the scarves hiding his face. The visage that was revealed was a roguish one, with sharp lines and almond-shaped eyes that crinkled at the corners.

"Who else could it be?"

"A beggar truthfully, judging by the state of your clothes. Thus the coins I offered."

Lott did not answer immediately and Jobe could feel himself being carefully scrutinized.

"Hmph. I would hardly say that the state of your dress is much better," the elf huffed, sounding vaguely insulted. But then elves always seemed to sound vaguely insulted when they were speaking to humans, or any other "lower" race for that matter.

Then the mocking humor fled from his voice and the elf held out his left hand, palm up, thumb curled in.

"Long has been the sun in rising."

For a moment Jobe could not speak. Somehow, even when he had struggled to remember their names, he had known that those he cared most about were alive, somewhere beyond his reach. But actually seeing one of them, hearing his voice again, flooded his throat with a dizzying mixture of relief and joy. And he was not a man of strong emotions.

Taking a deep breath and meeting his companion's steady gaze, Jobe placed his right hand over Lott's, palm down and thumb out. The traditional response was on his lips before he even thought about it.

"Glad is the sun to return to the sky." After a beat, he added, "Can't you do something about this weather?"

Lott dropped his arm to his side and arched one thin golden eyebrow. "What would you have me do? Steal the rain from the clouds? I have had enough trouble with the gods to last me all my remaining years."

Jobe chuckled and, feeling lighter than he had in many months, began walking again.

"What about the others? Are they well? Have you heard from them?"

"If you keep walking that way, you will never find out." Placing a hand on his friend's shoulder, Lott grinned and pointed to a street off to the right.

"The inn is this way."

Squinting through the rain, Jobe looked down the street he had been walking on, and then over to the right. Neither road stood out in his memory.

"Oh. Of course."

He fell into step behind the elf, Denga plodding along steadily behind him. Every so often she would bump his shoulder with her nose, and he got the impression that at least she recognized the route they were taking.

Not more than ten minutes later they stood outside what looked to be little more than a crack in a wall. Fifteen feet up a weather-beaten sign squeaked back and forth in the wind. Painted on it was a faded and chipped picture of a jester's cap and the name *The Tumbling Jester*, both nearly illegible with age. The two companions paused in front of the inn's broken cobblestone steps and looked up at it. It had looked exactly the same two years before. Built of sturdy, but non-descript grey stone, it looked more like a warehouse than a place of comfort for weary travelers. It had never been the kind of inn that catered to regular folk and even in the best of times true adventurers were few. Jobe felt his lips curve.

"You need a new sign."

"But then people might start showing up, looking for rooms and such," Lott replied.

"Isn't that the purpose of an inn?"

"Not my inn."

At the sounds of the voices, a pint-sized boy appeared from underneath a pile of blankets off to the left of the steps. He looked a little rough, with coarse skin and hair that was long enough to be plastered down into his mud-colored eyes. With the ease of one well-trained with horses, he took Denga's reins from Jobe's hands and grinned cheerfully at the two, proudly displaying a large gap in his front teeth.

"Welc'm back Mista Lott. I ben waitin' out 'ere all day. Dat fella yous was waitin' fer come in dis mornin'," he proclaimed enthusiastically. The boy's exuberance brought a smile to both of their faces, and Lott handed over two of Jobe's coppers, much to Jobe's amusement.

"He did not give you any trouble, did he Powl?"

Powl shook his head and went on talking as he slipped the coins into his tunic.

"Naw. Gave me a real shock when he took off his cloak. Thought he was you. Den he tip me a gold piece so I knows it wadn't you."

While Jobe gave a hoot of laughter, Lott started up the steps, inquiring over his shoulder, "And the others are still all here?"

The boy bobbed his head and began to lead Denga down the side street that led to the back of the inn where the stables were located.

"Yessir. Shelly an' dat dwarf ben goin' at it all mornin'. He say somethin' 'bout her cookin' and she wholloped him on de nose. Thought me'be he storm out afta dat but dat purty lady give him a look an' he settle right down. Dat of course got de big man laughin' an' I thought dat . . ." he was still talking as he disappeared around the corner.

"Maron, Raven, Silver, and Elkins. Your brother always was free with his gold," Jobe stated wryly, feeling the happiness of knowing his friends were all alive and safe settle into him.

Up ahead of him Lott gave a low "hmph" and led him through the narrow doorway into a small room used to store wet cloaks. Light and warmth spilled in from the inn's common room, chasing away the gloominess of the rain outside. "Conjured gold, most likely," the thief said as he unwound the scarves covering his face.

Jobe did not respond. He was shocked to see that in two years, his friend had changed. His golden hair—a trademark of the Gildenis family—remained scandalously short, falling just above his cobalt colored eyes. But there were lines on his delicate face, signs of age and care that Jobe thought he would never live to see.

"I had a devil of a time finding them. After I remembered them," Lott continued, hanging his dripping cloak over a peg and turning to meet Jobe's surprised expression. "When you pierced Belc's gem with your sword, there was this blinding flash and a terrible scream that sometimes still rings in my ears. I shut my eyes against the light and when I opened them again, I was just outside of Jordiche, in a tent belonging to a priest. Imagine me, in a tent with a priest. Besides feeling like someone had just dumped a boulder on me, I could not remember anything. It took me a year to recover my memories and another to hunt down the rest of our companions. I came back here about two months ago. Silver came a few weeks after that. Then Maron. Then Raven. And now Elkins and you." Those piercing blue eyes narrowed curiously at Jobe. "Where have you been these past years?"

Mimicking Lott's movements, Jobe removed his own cloak and hung it up. Rubbing his hands together, he tried to ignore the sudden

140

tugging in his gut. He did not want to recall the event that his friend had mentioned. There were too many blank spaces regarding it, along with the feeling that after the aforementioned deed, that white light had taken him somewhere he had not wanted to go.

"In a village up north, in a similar condition," he replied somewhat curtly, avoiding his friend's gaze. There was a brief moment of silence and then Jobe felt a hand upon his shoulder.

"I have a feeling we will find it is a condition we all shared," Lott said quietly. Then, in a louder tone, he asked, "I do not suppose that you happened to pass Dimes on your way in?"

The simple question had the effect of dampening the joy Jobe felt at having been reunited with his companions. He bit back a heavy sigh as he contemplated the grief he was now going to deliver to them. A weight settled over his chest; he rubbed his coin purse absently through his tunic.

"Dimes won't be coming," he began, his mind flipping back through all the ways he had thought of to break this news.

"So it is true then."

A voice as low and grave as the strumming of a cello greeted them as they stepped from the dim front room into the warmth of the common area. Half a dozen tables were scattered about; all but one were empty. An elf draped in long flowing robes of dark blue was sitting on a simple chair as if it were throne. On the table before him, a simple wooden goblet filled with clear wine sat untouched.

His face was a mirror image of Lott's and the eyes that gazed steadily at Jobe were the exact same vivid color. However, his gilded hair lay about his shoulders in silky waves and his perfectly sculpted lips were set in a thin line. He folded his slender hands on the table and completed his statement.

"The Prince did indeed fall."

Lott's head turned sharply in search of confirmation, but before Jobe could say anything, a door in the back of the room swung open, letting in the heavy scents from the kitchen. Powl slipped through it, whistling, and in his hands he carried the carefully wrapped bundle that had been tied to Denga's saddle. Across his slim shoulders he had slung Jobe's travel pack.

141

"Shall I place these in your room, sir?" he asked, without any hint of his former accent. Jobe reached out for the bundle, feeling the weight above his heart double. Here was one of his last links to a dear friend.

"Just the pack, friend. Please, if you would, call the others here as well." Bowing his head slightly, Powl left through another door off to the left and Jobe could hear his footsteps as he ascended stairs. Releasing a sigh that had been caught in his chest, Jobe approached the table at which the second elf sat and laid the bundle down upon it. Lott pulled a chair out across from his twin and flipped it so that the back rested against the table. The two stared at each other with the kind of tension that comes from being relatives who lead different lives with different sets of morals.

"Lott."

"Elkins."

Any further exchange of pleasantries was interrupted by a ruckus that originated in the kitchen. There was a great deal of banging and clanging followed by the expulsion of a dwarf with a long black beard just starting to grey at the edges and skin the color of stone. He landed in the room with an "oomph" and leapt to his feet all but spiting fire.

"By Bandger's Hammer that woman is a devil! I oughta send her straight back to the nine hells where she belongs!"

There came a deep rumbling chuckle and a giant of a man entered through the same door the dwarf had come sailing through. Not even the devil herself would have been able to throw that man anywhere. He stood no less than seven-and-a-half feet tall and must have weighed somewhere over three hundred pounds. His skin was a dusty gold color that came from years of life lived on the plains to the southwest. The only hairs on his body were in the form of two bushy eyebrows and a long, carefully braided beard of red that trailed off of his chin. Crisscrossing his massive chest were two thick leather straps that held up a mammoth sword that ran along his back. The hilt was nearly as broad as his shoulders and the blade reached just above the floor.

"Many times heard this I have. Still, done it is not," the barbarian said, his speech surprisingly soft.

The dwarf brushed himself off and glared up at the man, seemingly unimpressed by his size.

"Bidin' me time boyo. Can't well go after her when she's wieldin' that blasted spoon o' hers, can I? And I don't be seein' you doin' much to spite the wicked beast yerself."

The voice that answered him was not the barbarian's. It was much more delicate, filled with layers of both amusement and mild exasperation.

"That, Silver Stonecrusher, is because Maron's head is not nearly as thick as yours."

Entering the room was a smiling woman dressed simply in a dress of spun wool. The hair that cascaded down her back in waves was pitch black interrupted by thick streaks of snowy white that had little to do with age. Lady Raven of Armore had yet to pass the age of thirty. The use of magic had a way of bleaching color from humans, as they were not naturally magical creatures. As soon as he saw her, Lott rose from his chair and dropped his head. But not before Jobe saw the pain and longing in his vivid eyes.

Raven came forward with her arms outstretched and wrapped them around Jobe, resting her head on his shoulder for a moment. Then she drew back and smiled brilliantly at him. At her throat hung her only ornamentation in the form of a beautifully carved wooden tree. Roughly the diameter of a fist, the trunk curved up into seven branches that formed a knotted circle. It was what marked her as a Seeker, a priestess of the nature god Jada who was said to take the form of a magnificent oak tree.

"It is comforting to see you again Jobe. You were beginning to worry us. Have you brought Prince Dimes with you?" she asked, unconsciously lifting a hand to her talisman and stepping back to stand beside Maron.

Dropping his eyes from her hopeful gaze, Jobe felt his shoulders slump a bit and he turned his eyes to the parcel on the table. Because he could find no words in him, he reached out and unfolded the cloth bundle. Beneath the layers was housed an exquisitely crafted longsword of elven make. Its hilt and crosspiece were of delicately twisting gold and silver. In the center, a large emerald was snuggly set. Elven runes ran down the length of the blade. The six companions looked upon it with recognition and sadness.

"It grieves me to say that our brother, Prince Dimes, has fallen."

"Where?" Elkins inquired, voicing the question that had immediately popped into each of their heads. Jobe flipped the cloth back over the sword, for looking at it made him ache.

"At Astar's Keep. There was a nearby settlement of survivors who told me he had been overwhelmed while trying to hold back the army of the dead."

Silver shook his head, his beady black eyes glossy and wet. "Just like the boy, to be takin' on an army by 'imself. Stupid foolish boy," he muttered fondly.

Raven reached out to touch Jobe's arm comfortingly. "And his body? You buried it there?"

"There was no body. Only the sword."

Silence followed, heavy with grief. Six companions lost themselves in their own thoughts. Thoughts of life and death and the fleetingness of it all. In Jobe's mind he saw the sword as it had lain upon the blackened stone of the crumbling keep, gleaming still. Then the scene changed and the sword was buckled on the waist of a reckless elven warrior standing full against the rising sun.

"They come."

Jobe looked out at the horizon, squinting against the morning light. Though he could see nothing but the vast and endless plains, he had every reason to believe his friend. Elven eyes can see across distances ten times greater than an average human.

"How many?" he asked, feeling the tension rise in his stomach. There was so little time and still so much that needed to be done. Dimes continued to stare out at the steadily approaching doom.

"Fifteen, perhaps twenty thousand march. Perhaps more. I do not see the end to the line."

"How far?" Jobe asked, feeling his throat go dry at the size of the force marching towards them. The total number of men now within the keep was less than half the number the elven prince had

given. Jobe fervently hoped his friend would mark them at least twenty, even thirty miles off.

"Ten miles. They move slowly, but they will be here before nightfall. They need not stop for food or rest." Dimes turned and watched the bleakness settle into Jobe's face as he digested the news of death's approach. When he failed to make any comment, Dimes reached out and took hold of his arm.

"You and the others must ride for the tower. If you can slay Belc, the dead will fall," he stated precisely, wanting to snap his friend out of his daze. Jobe blinked and met his eyes.

"But what if I can't?"

"Then we will all fall." He paused and looked down at his left hand, sheathed in a metal gauntlet. After a moment, he tugged the glove off and let it fall. As Jobe watched uncomprehendingly, he slid a ring off his middle finger and held it out to his companion, his sword-brother.

"Should I fall, you must return this to my father."

Lott banged his fist against the table and the sudden noise returned Jobe abruptly to the present. Likewise, the others stared at the inn's proprietor. Instead of speaking to them, he called out, "Powl!"

From seemingly nowhere, the sandy-haired youth appeared near his elbow. "Sir?"

"Bring us the bottles of *quath'art* and six cups," Lott said, naming a traditional strong elven wine. Giving a quick nod, Powl dashed off into the kitchen. Once the boy had left the room, Lott leaned forward and folded his arms over the back of his chair. His eyebrows were drawn close together and his lips had lost their curve.

"We all sacrificed much to bring an end to the war. Dimes gave his life to halt the malignant spread of evil. Never has there been a finer swordsman or a more noble spirit."

Powl slipped back in silently and placed six cups in a circle on the table. Then he offered a beautiful blue bottle to Lott, who motioned with one hand towards Elkins. The mage took the bottle from the boy and, closing his eyes, slid his right hand up the side to the top of the neck. When he reached the glass cap, he snapped his fingers and it disappeared in a shower of bright sparks.

Wide-eyed with amazement, Powl took the bottle back and poured what looked like liquid starlight into the cups. Lifting his goblet, Lott cleared his throat and declared,

"To Dimes!"

The others followed suit, "To Dimes!"

Quiet drifted in as sips were taken of the sweet, apple-spiced wine and as the drink flowed over their tongues, a touch of their sorrow faded. Only a touch. But it gave enough room for memory to creep in. Settling more comfortably in his chair, Lott smiled and his eyes misted as he drifted backwards in time.

"I can recall one particularly nasty scrap that Dimes had happily dragged us into . . ."

~~~~~~

When Jobe cracked an eye open the next morning, he had no idea where he was or why his head was pounding as if a dwarven battle drummer had taken up residence in his skull. He felt the cushion of a bed beneath his face and lifted his head up half an inch so he could cast a bleary glance around, just in case his condition was the result of some fearsome battle. From what he could see though, there weren't any other bodies or any other sign of violence and struggle. *That leaves only quath'art.* The night came back to him in blurry images and he realized he was lying face down in one of the inn's rooms. Someone must have put him there because he couldn't recall making the trip himself. *No more elven spirits for you,* Jobe vowed to himself as he always did.

Gingerly, because his head felt as if it might fall off if he moved too suddenly, he rolled over and sat up. He brought his hands to his forehead just as the door to his room opened and Powl poked his head in.

"Oh, you're up. There's a messenger from the Lord Protector's guards here who wishes to speak with you. The others as well," the boy said, careful to speak quietly.

Pressing his fingertips against his eyelids, Jobe took his first deep breath of the morning air and looked up.

146

"Thank you Powl," he said. His voice sounded gruff to his own ears and he coughed to clear his throat before he added, "I see you've managed to overcome your lisp already."

Powl's grin was sharp and clever. "There's a play being staged this month for the spring festival. The first one this year. I ain't nuttin' but a po' farma's boy," he voiced, slipping easily into a drawl.

"And that gap between your teeth?"

The boy ran his tongue over his front teeth. "A couple of raisins did the trick."

Jobe smiled slightly and rolled his shoulders. "Clever. I'll be down shortly."

Nodding once, Powl ducked out and closed the door gently behind him, leaving Jobe to push himself up onto shaky legs. He half-walked, half-bumbled over to the foot of the bed and poured water into a wash bin from a pitcher that sat next to it. Closing his eyes, he dipped his hands in and splashed the liquid over his face, the coldness shocking him awake. Refreshed and dripping, he glanced around and saw that his pack was settled on the floor near the door and a fresh pair of clothes had been laid out for him. Thankfully, he exchanged his road-tattered breeches and tunic for warm woolen leggings and a clean linen shirt. Both bagged on him slightly, but were still comfortable.

He snatched up his pack and set it on the bed so he could rifle through it. Stuffed inside was his brigandine armor. For several moments he debated about whether or not he should put it on. One of the straps on the side had broken several weeks before and as he had not had the time or inclination to mend it, he had gone without it. Foolish of him really, he thought, fingering the hard leather. He was lucky some wandering bandit hadn't decided to put an arrow in his back simply for target practice.

"The world is going to hell, Dimes. And after we gave so much to save it."

Sighing, he dried his face with the bottom of his shirt, slung the pack over his shoulder and headed out the door. Perhaps he could mend the armor while he listened to whatever request it was the messenger was bringing to them. Something in his gut told him

147

it would not be an invitation to a welcome home festival. As he descended the stairs and entered the common room, he could see the guard standing stiffly near the front entrance. Elkins had already claimed his former table. Beside him sat Raven, looking older than she had the night before. There were spider web wrinkles near her eyes that he had not noticed before. Maron stood in his customary place behind her left shoulder and Lott was stretched out along the bar. The only companion missing was Silver.

"He will not be up any time soon," Lott answered, seeing Jobe's questioning glance. His delicate lips curved smugly. "You should never give elven spirits to a dwarf. They just cannot seem to handle it."

"They're not the only ones," Jobe replied, lifting one hand to his own aching head.

"If the two of you are finished with your inane banter, perhaps we might find out what deed we are going to be asked to perform?" Elkins interjected, sounding both bored and annoyed. That had always been his tone when speaking to his roguish twin. Lott was not at all offended by it.

"You sound as if you are not at all intrigued by the possibility of a mysterious adventure, brother," he mocked, teasingly. Elkins folded his long, slender fingers and raised one pale eyebrow.

"I am a mage, *brother*. My entire life has been a mysterious adventure. Beyond that, we have struck blows with the undead, battled sorcererous fiends, faced a power-mad god, and *still* I have no small country of my own to show for all my work. Forgive me if I seem less than interested in another foray into danger."

Lott frowned at his twin for a moment in silence, and then shook his head.

"You frighten me sometimes."

"Keeps you out of my pockets, does it not?"

Shifting his focus away from the brotherly exchange, Jobe zeroed in on the guard still waiting in the doorway. He was dressed in the formal steel grey uniform of the city guard. Beardless and with a face that had yet to lose the fullness of youth, the lad had his gaze fixed on Maron. Or, more specifically, the enormous sword strapped

148

to the barbarian's back. Jobe cleared his throat in an attempt to gain the boy's attention.

"You have a message for us?" he ventured when the guard remained silent. The youth nodded his head slowly but neither spoke nor lifted his eyes. Maron returned his gaze steadily, accustomed yet not comfortable with being the object of scrutiny. Shaking his head, Jobe stepped forward until he was directly in the center of the lad's vision, cutting off the boy's view. He could see both terror and awe swimming in the young guard's eyes and it nearly made him smile; he had felt a similar mixture the first time *he* had met the giant man.

"I can assure you friend, he'll not eat, nor slice you into ribbons," Jobe promised, trying his best to suppress his humor.

As if seeking confirmation of the statement, the guard lifted his head up and peeked over Jobe's shoulder. Maron drew back his lips, displaying his full set of white teeth in a wide smile.

Swallowing, the guard quickly dropped his gaze back to Jobe, apparently not at all reassured by the grin.

"I'm sent by Lord Declan, Lord Protector of the city of Tora and surrounding settlements. His Lordship has received word that an outpost and a village near the Pass have been ravaged by an unknown beast these past few weeks. His Lordship asks for your help in removing this dangerous creature," he exploded in one breath, wanting to get his duty over with.

Frowning slightly, Jobe folded his arms across his chest and mulled his way through the speedily delivered message.

"What do you mean by, 'unknown beast'?"

"The report was brought by a scout who was grievously wounded in battle with the beast. He died before he could give an accurate description or an exact location," the guard replied, staring down at his feet, almost as if he were embarrassed by his lack of knowledge.

"Wait. Let me see if I have this right," Elkins began, placing one hand to his temple. "Your Lord Delany wishes us to dispose of a dangerous beast, yet he neither knows what it is nor where it can be found?" The guard nodded and Elkins shook his head with amazed

149

disbelief. "Well this sounds like a marvelous idea!"

Lott hopped down from his perch on the bar and landed lightly on his feet.

"Sounds like a bit of fun to me," he declared glibly. Holding out his hands, he grinned cheerfully and asked,

"Who wants to go vanquish evil once more?"

His brother snickered. "The way you vanquished that banshee at Faerl's Crossing? Count me out."

Maron let out a booming chuckle and Raven lifted a hand to her mouth to cover her smile. Even Jobe had to laugh at the memory of the cocky thief bolting away from the lake's edge; his blue eyes the size of saucers and his blonde hair standing on end.

Narrowing those eyes, Lott glared at his twin. "I thought I told you to never—"

"Enough already!" Raven's voice was soft but it had the effect of silencing the thief mid-sentence. Lott crossed his arms over his chest and moved to the corner of the room to sulk. Not bothering to hide her amusement any longer, Raven sighed and turned her smile on the very nervous youth.

"Now, child. Where is this settlement?" she asked gently. The guard blinked slowly and relaxed without even knowing he was doing so. "To the east ma'am. A mile or so above the Pass. The outpost is at the mouth of the valley."

She smiled at him again, and then turned her violet eyes to Jobe. One by one the others did the same. It was their way of letting him know that the decision to go was in his hands. He had always hated being the leader, having that added pressure of being the one who drove the party to their doom. But now he found that it wasn't so burdensome of a responsibility. One might even say he missed it. Though a sense of duty to the people he had given so much to save tugged at him, he still was wary of rushing into battle against an unnamed foe.

Sensing his friend's hesitation, Lott stepped forward, his face as drawn and serious as it had been the night before as he toasted their departed comrade. "The lives of humans are so short. They pass before me as little more than a blur of motion. I wish I could tell you

150

all how much you have changed in only two years," he said softly. "It saddens me to know that too soon the only face I will have left to look upon is my own." His gaze shifted to Elkins who met his eyes squarely. "I will take any excuse to ride with you all again."

Silence followed and some of the grief from the night before returned. Last night they had remembered the mortality of a dear friend. That morning they were reminded of their own. How quickly the minutes, the hours, the days slip past. Death was an uncomfortably close companion.

Shaking the thought from his head, Jobe shifted his pack and clasped the thief on the shoulder. Death would come when it came. He turned to the guard.

"Tell your Lord that we will leave within the hour."

~~~~~

The journey to the lair of the beast took just over two days on horseback. Willing to cooperate, the weather remained cool, but dry for that duration. Perhaps the weather gods had as much to gain from the quest as the surrounding settlements. The companions had left Silver back at the inn for it was obvious the dwarf would be in no condition to travel. That is, if he managed to wake up at all.

After an internal debate, Jobe had rustled up an old, worn scabbard back at the inn and strapped Dimes's sword to his back. Undoubtedly a second sword could come in handy, though it felt somewhat awkward resting between his shoulder blades. Still, it had felt twice as uncomfortable resting on his other hip. He had been unwilling to leave it in Tora for two reasons; one being that it would be foolish to return to the city when the elven kingdom for which he was bound, lay in the opposite direction. And secondly because Tora was well known as a haven for those who were interested in taking things that did not belong to them.

Not long after they had started out, Jobe realized that though they had done similar things countless times in the past, the journey felt very different. There was no Dimes riding at his side filling the air with his acrid remarks. Several times Jobe unconsciously turned to his right, his mouth already forming the beginning of a conversation before he remembered his friend was not there. But there was something else missing. Something did not feel right. He distanced himself slightly from the group and mulled over what it could be.

After some time he became aware of a presence looming just off to his left. Lifting his head he blinked at the sight of Maron riding silently beside him, his eyes focused on the road ahead. The barbarian sat astride a mountain of a horse, a swarthy brown-colored animal with white hair spilling down in a long mane. Jobe couldn't imagine where the man had found the beast but it suited him perfectly, having nearly the same sky blue eyes as its rider.

Sensing the study, Maron turned his head and Jobe noticed something he had not noticed the night before; a long thin scar ran from the bottom of his face to his chin. The white line stood out starkly against his golden skin.

"Deep thoughts you have."

Jobe smiled, intrigued as he had always been by the large man's curious manner of speech. "I was thinking that this feels different than past journeys," he answered.

Maron nodded gravely his agreement. "Yes. Much time since last we traveled has passed. Much have we seen. Much have we done."

"I suppose that could be it. But why should it feel so different? Why should I? I don't feel . . ." Jobe frowned as he searched for the word he wanted. It came to him abruptly and his face lost its intenseness. "I don't feel afraid. We could be going to our deaths and I don't feel afraid. Why?" Turning his eyes forward he stared at the others who rode some ten to fifteen feet in front of them. Beside him, he felt Maron shift.

"No need for fear, has the phoenix. Only love for life."

At that Jobe opened his mouth, an unknown question on his lips, but Maron had already moved to rejoin the others. Jobe was left to stare at his broad back while he contemplated what he could have meant.

Hours passed and day slipped into night, then back to day again. There was no sight of a beast though there were the telltale markings of a vicious creature as they moved steadily east. Huge paths of flattened grass, trees broken in half, patches of churned earth.

On the morning of the third day, Lott led them past the outpost that the guard had mentioned and through the Pass; a stretch of land that cut through the imposing mountains that otherwise formed a wall separating the eastern side of the continent from the west. After a league or so they came upon an unnatural looking cave in the left side of the cliffs. The edges of it were tinged with black, as if black powder had been ignited nearby. Jobe tugged his armor out of his pack and pulled it over his head. He hadn't managed to fix the strap.

Well, as Dimes would say, "With any luck the beast won't know to stick a sword in your side."

Leaving their horses a short distance away, in the off chance a retreat was necessary, the five companions entered into darkness. The scent of rotten eggs stung their noses. A moment later the silence that filled the cave was broken by a clack and a hiss, followed by the flash of a spark and the crackle of flame as Lott lit a torch. The light was poor, but better than nothing. There was the sound of murmuring and a moment later a small green orb appeared over Elkins' left shoulder, providing a much more ample light source. Lott scowled a bit and kept his torch.

They had gone perhaps seventy feet into the cavern before Lott signaled for them to halt. A hole, perhaps thirty feet in diameter was like a giant eye staring up from the floor. It seemed to go down forever.

"I would wager this is where the beast emerges from. With a bit of luck, this is the only exit," Lott stated with a strange sort of cheerfulness. Jobe glanced over at him briefly and wondered if the thief was feeling the same almost euphoric absence of fear. Were they all feeling it?

Curious, he bent down on one knee and peered into absolute darkness. The light could not push back the blackness even three feet. But something interesting caught his eye and he leaned forward slightly to take a closer look. The outer rim of the hole had been blackened in the same manner as the outside of the cave had been. He reached down and rubbed against the rock. It crumbled against his skin; he brought his fingers to his nose, and then touched them to the tip of his tongue. Limestone. There must have been a large pool or vein of the mineral where the hole was now. Something had blasted it away.

While Jobe was inspecting the floor, Elkins sniffed experimentally at the air. "What is that smell?" he asked after a moment. Jobe shifted his attention briefly.

"Sulfur," he deducted and Lott nodded his agreement.

"Some type of explosion is what caused this hole," the thief stated, motioning to the scorch marks. But Elkins shook his head.

"There is something else besides the sulfur. Heavier," he insisted, sniffing once more. Uncertain, Jobe followed suit, taking several longer inhalations. Underneath the rancid smell of sulfur he thought he could detect another, muskier scent. Somehow familiar. He could not identify it.

Reaching up with one of his long arms, Maron grabbed hold of one of several hanging stalactites protruding from the ceiling and leaned further out over the pit. Positioned so, he took a deep breath through his nostrils, exhaled, and then breathed in again. The other four waited patiently.

"Dragon," he announced calmly, pulling himself back.

There was a full minute or so of silence.

"Oh, how wonderfully surprising," Elkins hissed. "As if battling a god was not enough, now we are given the opportunity to be eaten by a dragon."

Raven gave him an arched look. "Oh, hush Elkins. Your sarcasm certainly isn't helping anything."

The mage sneered a bit. "My apologies, but if you have forgotten, we have all lost two years of our lives. I would much rather not lose the rest of mine."

Jobe felt his own anger kick in at the elf's words. "At least you're still here. Think of those that sacrificed as much as we did and didn't make it!"

Elkins' eyes flashed and he tightened his grip on his long staff while Jobe curled his own fist around the pommel of his sword. The air in the small room vibrated with enough tension to shake the very

154

rocks surrounding them.

"Now, now children. Are we going to play or are we going to best ourselves a dragon?" Lott's voice was low and dry.

"I suppose you have some clever idea for doing just that, brother?" Elkins queried, his gaze still fixed on Jobe.

With something like a smirk twisting his lips, Lott sauntered forward until he was between his brother and his friend. Though his movements were casual, inside the thief was a mass of tension. Having his brother, perhaps the most powerful mage in the world, battle with Jobe, one of the finest swordsman in history, was not something he wanted to see happen.

"I was thinking something along the lines of a trap."

"Really. You know of a trap that is both large enough and strong enough to hold a dragon?" Jobe asked bitingly, letting his doubts slip into his tone. Without realizing it, he relaxed his stance and lowered his hand away from his sword. Lott returned his steady gaze.

"How about a mountain?" the thief suggested slyly. Their heads tilted up toward the ceiling where several thousand tons of rock loomed. Lott continued, letting the idea settle in their minds. "A dragon cannot burn his way through rock and even if he should claw his way out, it will take him far longer than any of our lifetimes. Now, unless you do wish to fight the beast, I suggest we figure out how best to bring down the roof."

Frowning, Jobe and Elkins stared at each other, their argument of moments ago forgotten as they both pondered the idea.

"It could work. But how do we cave the ceiling?" Jobe asked.

"I could cast an earthquake, but it would be impossible to target it specifically to this area of the mountain," Elkins replied.

Seeing the fight between her companions had been averted, Raven stepped in neatly to the conversation.

"What we could do is find a fault in the overhead stone and trigger it. That would give us the kind of cave-in we're looking for," she stated. Elkins mulled over the thought for a second, then lifted one eyebrow.

"That would require quite an extensive knowledge of the surrounding rock layers," he said.

155

"And a steady arcane hand. I'm ready if you are."

"Ladies first."

The two exchanged wide smiles.

Jobe watched as Maron took hold of Raven's waist and lifted her as if she were the most delicate of flowers so that she could press her small hands against the rock ceiling. A light murmuring drifted down, and through the darkness Jobe could see that glow from her pendant. He had seen her do such a thing before and tried to recall how she had explained it to him. In return for their services, the goddess Jada blessed her priestesses with the ability to "communicate" with nature. When she pressed her hands to a stone for instance, the stone "told" her about all the things it had come in contact with.

The ground it sat on, the air that swirled around it, the little boy who had thrown it. It did not make very much sense to Jobe, who had a bit of trouble imagining a rock "speaking."

While she searched for the fault they needed, he stood beside Lott. The thief's eyes were riveted on her though he made a show of pretending to look elsewhere.

"What kind of dragon do you suppose it is?" Jobe inquired.

After a brief hesitation, Lott replied, "A red most likely. Judging by the size of the hole, a female."

Why naturally, Jobe thought wryly. *Only the very worst would do.*

"I certainly hope that we don't wake her up," he commented. "I'd rather not have to face an angry red whose four-thousand-year nap has been disturbed.

"I hope that she is down there," Lott countered. "I would rather not be doing this all for nothing."

Just then the murmuring stopped and Raven's hands fell to her sides. She tapped Maron once on his broad shoulder and he gently brought her down. Once her feet touched upon the ground she brushed at her long shirt and turned to Elkins.

"There's one about thirty feet up. It's small, but if you can trigger it, it will do nicely."

Elkins held his hands out about a foot apart from each other and

156

blue lightning jumped from each finger on one hand to its opposite digit.

"I will trigger it," he promised, with a swagger reminiscent of his twin's. With that, he moved to Maron who lifted him in a manner similar to Raven's. Jobe thought he heard Lott mutter "show off."

Coming to stand beside Lott, Raven gave him a sweet smile. For the first time, and much to his surprise, Jobe realized that what had always been in the elf's eyes was also in hers.

"You've always had a knack for squirming around danger, Lott," she stated with bemusement, leaning a bit over the edge of the pit. As she did so, her pendant became untied and slipped from around her neck. It fell through the air towards the never-ending darkness and would have been lost forever had Lott's hand not reached out to grab it at the last moment. He flashed her a charming grin as he closed his hand around it and at the same time, the bit of limestone he had stepped forward onto gave way beneath him. For half a second he was caught in a free fall into empty space. But ever nimble, he managed to twist himself and grab hold of the edge before he had fallen very far. A fair amount of rock clattered down, but no elves. Jobe reached down and hooked his hands underneath Lott's arms and hauled him back up to safety while Raven fluttered nearby. Taking a deep breath and brushing dust off of his clothes, Lott handed the necklace back to its owner with another grin.

"That was close," he stated, almost casually.

A snicker came from Elkins' direction, followed by, "Not nearly close enough."

And that was when the rumbling began.

The three nearest the pit looked at each other as it gradually grew louder. Both Maron and Elkins were focused entirely on their own activities. Jobe felt a blast of hot air hit his back and, as he turned around to look down into the pit, he saw a pillar of brilliant red flame rushing up towards him. He managed to get his head back around as it burst up through the opening like a catapult, sending him, Lott, and Raven flying towards the mouth of the cave.

At the same time, Elkins released his spell up into the ceiling of rock, unleashing a quake into the overhead bedrock. True to his

157

word, it triggered the fault along with a number of others that had been close by. The stone over the pit gave way in a tremendous rock fall that overwhelmed the rushing fire. Large cracks appeared in the rest of the cavern's walls and chunks of rocks began falling at an alarming rate. Jobe, Lott, and Raven dragged each other up and out towards the entrance, doing their best to dodge falling boulders as they went. Maron simply slung the elf mage over his shoulder and pushed the rocks out of his way as they fell towards him.

The cave gave a great shudder and spit them all out in a cloud of thick dirt and stone that rose up into the air like smoke. Coughing, dirtied, a bit bruised, but still very much alive, they all sat where they had landed and surveyed their handiwork. It may not have been a god, but they sure had blasted the hell out of the side of the mountain. Where there had once been an opening almost forty feet high, there was now just a jagged side of a cliff. And with the number of faults Elkins had inadvertently triggered, it was likely the mountain would continue to shake for hours. If there were any other entrances, hopefully they would be sealed as well.

Shaking dirt out of his hair, Lott frowned at his brother a few feet away.

"Show off."

Jobe chuckled, and that chuckle turned into a laugh, and before he knew it he was nearly choking he was laughing so hard. The others joined in and for a while it was the only sound that could be heard. Then Lady Raven noticed something that made her laughter cease abruptly.

"Jobe."

He glanced over at her and wiped dirty tears from his eyes so that he could see her better. She pointed down at his chest. Not knowing what she meant, he looked down at himself, half-expecting to see blood oozing out from some wound. But there was nothing. Nothing. The strap that had crossed his chest was gone. Quickly he turned to look over his shoulder, even felt behind his back with his hand, but he knew it was gone. His eyes wandered back to the cave-in.

Dimes's sword. Lost forever.

"Oh, he's not going to be happy about that."

~~~~~

In the cave, where a red dragon angrily found herself covered in heavy rocks, a beautifully crafted longsword lay on the floor, its scabbard split by the fall. She had little use for it as a weapon, but the bright gem would go nicely with the others. Pushing her stony blanket off of her back, the dragon awkwardly picked up the sword with her talons and carted it away to join the rest of her various treasures. She would admire it while she devised a way to free herself from what had been turned into a tomb. While in her claws, the dim emerald flashed as the soul inside of it struggled awake.

Jobe, of all the places to drop me . . . .

VOTE ZEUS

Olympic Politics
by Kimberly Eldredge

"By thunder!" Zeus exclaimed, sitting up in bed, clutching the silk sheets around his nakedness, white hair and beard in disarray. "What is that racket? Hera!" He stumbled from the bed, trailing the sheets down the marble hallways, yelling for his wife and the guards and his breakfast. Bursting into one of the larger throne rooms in the Olympian palace, Zeus allowed the sheet to puddle at his ankles. The sudden banging of the door interrupted the band "practice" that had been going on.

"Apollo!" Zeus yelled, waiting for his son to disentangle himself from the three women wrapped around him and from the drum set he was perched behind. Zeus ran a hand across his forehead, causing his eyebrows to stick up as much as his hair.

"Yes, father?" Apollo asked, joining Zeus in the hallway just outside the throne room. He was finger combing his hair into place with one hand while trying to button the fly of his Levis with the other. "Problems, sir?"

161

"Problems? Of course there is a problem. What are these mortals doing here and what is all that noise? You do realize that you woke me up, don't you?" Zeus glared at his son, trying to muster all the dignity a naked, crazy-haired, middle-aged former deity could come up with. Zeus was suddenly very aware of the fact he wasn't wearing any clothes and that the gaggle of women giggling at Apollo were standing in the doorway and staring. His hands twitched at his sides, wanting to cover his private parts or reach for the sheet or both. He forced them to be still.

"It's just band practice, Father," Apollo answered, twitching at his pants and grinning over his shoulder at the women. "This is Fuchsia's Daughters," Apollo said, waiving his hand at the band members, who giggled.

"Fuchsia? Who's Fuchsia? I've never heard of a god by that name."

"They aren't named after a god, Father. That's the name of their band. Their very big in the State right now."

Apollo was taking that annoying condescending tone that all teen-agers seem to acquire the moment they think they know more than their parents. To the eternal annoyance of the Olympian Gods, Apollo would never get out of the terrible teens. It was his nature to be a teenager who had trouble with women; meaning that he wasn't supposed to be having relationships, let alone a whole pack of women dangling all over him. Well, teenage know-it-all aside, Apollo looked like he has gotten over his women problems.

"Send them home," Zeus said flatly. "Now."

"But Father," Apollo began, whining. Zeus made a throwing motion with his hand, wishing he had a thunderbolt, or at least a stiff drink. Apollo turned and slunk back into the room, muttering to the women that they had to go home now. He was the picture of a pouting sixteen-year-old who hadn't been allowed to drive the car. Zeus collected his discarded sheet, throwing it pointedly over one shoulder and not wrapping it around the sensitive bits of his anatomy that were beginning to get cold, and strode back to his room.

Hours later, Zeus emerged from his room: washed, oiled and with a solid meal of nectar and ambrosia in his belly. The strange creatures Hephaestus created attended him. There were no slaves anymore in Olympus to attend to the gods; Hera had thrown the last of them from the mountain some years back. Zeus hadn't wanted to interfere with his wife's rage as she muttered darkly something about all men being free and equal under god. Zeus hadn't been sure which god she'd been referring to, but certainly it wasn't him. He had the sinking feeling that she was talking about that upstart, bearded grinning idiot who thought he should be omnipotent and omniscient just because he was the Lamb of God. The Olympian Gods were stuck rinsing goblets and making their own beds for a few weeks because of it.

Now, these strange creatures of Hephaestus', Zeus thought as he strode around the halls of Olympus. They were a piece of work: not really alive and certainly not mortal. They had too pale skin and no hair and gold under their fingernails. Every night they stood on the balconies, not moving. Hephaestus called them androids and said they were collecting starlight—their power source. Zeus didn't like it at all.

"Hera!" Zeus called, startling an android that had been busy polishing a brass shield hanging in the hall. The creature jumped and sped away on silent feet. Zeus called it back again before it reached the end of the hall. "Where is my wife?" he demanded of it, staring over its head. The android raised a hand and pointed with one gold-tipped nail down the hall.

"Like that was a lot of help," Zeus muttered as he strode down the hall. "Why couldn't Hephaestus have made those things so they could talk? Hera!" He yelled again. Zeus finally found his wife in the south solar, preening in front of one of the new mirrors Hermes had brought back on one of his voyages to the mortal realm.

"Hera, my beauty, why do you bother with this mortal nonsense? This new silvered mirror, why don't you use the brass one I gave you?" Zeus sprawled in a low chair, upholstered in blue leather, kicking one leg over the back. He felt a breeze swirl around his nether regions; he'd never give up the old style of dressing like Apollo and most of the court.

"Do you like my earrings?" Hera asked, turning from the

free-standing, guilt-framed mirror. Zeus stared at her curvy body snuggled into a tight red something or other, accentuating her breasts and hips. "Well?" She asked again. When Zeus didn't answer, she swayed over to him, peering at him from under lowered brows, her tongue moving against her lips suggestively. She flung one leg over his hips, her skirt rising up her thighs. Zeus braced one leg on the floor and moved the other one so she was supported firmly. His wife began moving her hips against him, moving the material wrapped around his body up, and just when she was about to do something delicious, Zeus sat up. Hera slid off his lap and landed in a rumpled heap on the floor.

"I've been thinking," Zeus began, ignoring Hera's angry squawk. He rubbed his hand over his ears while he waited for Hera to get up and tug her dress back into order. "Why do we continue to let that One God and his son rule the world? It was ours for millennia, long before that peace-loving bearded boy was born. I say that we Olympians take it back!"

Hera stopped smoothing the dress over her hips and took Zeus' chin in her hand, tilting his face to look up into hers. "I think you should cut your hair," she said, pulling the soft curls away from his face and staring at him intently. "If you did—shaved off your beard—you'd look like Ralph Lauren. Very sexy." Hera turned back to the mirror, running a finger under her earring, leaving Zeus perched on the chair, openmouthed, staring at his wife. He got up, blood rushing to his head and howling in his ears. He said nothing, simply stalked from the room.

Zeus strode out to his favorite balcony and peered down at the mortal world below. He could see the dim shapes of mountains and sluggish brown rivers cutting through valleys but the details, once so sharp, were fuzzy and indistinct. He felt the presence of another god join him at the railing. Turning, he saw Hephaestus leaning on the rail, sucking on something that left a white stick poking out of his mouth. Hephaestus had a set of serious-looking metal braces wrapped around his legs. Zeus could see where the metal bands cut into the flesh of Hephaestus' thighs, raising the skin in red strips.

"What brings you to my lookout point, Son of Hera?" Zeus

164

asked, half turning to face his companion.

"Son of yourself, also, my honored lord, although you'd never admit it." Hephaestus shrugged heavy shoulders, giving Zeus half a grin. "Perhaps the question is, what brings great Zeus, the Thunder Thrower, to this balcony to peer through the mists at the mortals who have forgotten you?"

"You call this mist?" Zeus asked, waving a thick-fingered hand at the layers of brown clouds that separated Olympus from the mortals' earth. He ignored the jabbing reference to his lost stature among the humans.

"They call it smog."

"Who calls it smog?" Zeus glared at the offending cloud and at the smear of grime Hephaestus left on the pristine railing of the balcony, as he turned to fully face Zeus.

"Them. The mortals. It is good they gave it such a pleasing name, since they caused it."

"Have you nothing that will pierce its veil and allow me to see the mortals scurrying?" Zeus asked. He remembered when the rest of that statement went: "the mortals scurrying before my greatness and wrath." Now, he was lucky if he got a token mention in a college mythology class.

"Of course, honored lord." From somewhere in the dirty leather bag Hephaestus wore at his belt, he produced a tube. It was narrower at one end than the other and Zeus found that it was surprisingly light. "Put the smaller end to your eye, lord Zeus, and train the larger end on the mortal world."

"You truly can accomplish wonders, Hephaestus," Zeus said as he brought the end to his eye and looked. Features on the earth below suddenly jumped into focus and clarity like Zeus hadn't seen in more years than he cared to think about.

"I didn't build this thing," Hephaestus said. Zeus brought the tube away from his eye and turned to stare at Hera's son.

"It is called a telescope. An Italian named Galileo first built it. I merely brought it here and made modifications that would allow it to pierce the smog and not simply magnify light." Hephaestus turned and leaned against the railing, hooking both elbows over it. His half

165

smile was back and Zeus wasn't sure if he was mocking him or not. With a heaving sigh, Zeus handed the tube—the telescope—back to Hephaestus and scrubbed his hands over his ears.

"Must I surrender so easily then?" he asked. "Must I accede defeat to the One God and his nasty little bearded son?"

"Defeat, great lord?" Hephaestus said, the half-grin slipping from his face and returning almost at one, like one of the androids given two orders at once; Hephaestus' smile could decide to go or stay so it tried to do both. "You gave up on that battle two thousand years ago. The One God had taken your place as King of the Gods as you took the place of your father before you."

"The One God is no child of mine!" Zeus said angrily.

"Be that as it may, the mortals worship him now, not us. It seems that most of the Olympians have accepted that."

"I see that every day," Zeus said, suddenly tired. "Hera has a new silvered mirror and only dresses in clothes Hermes brings her from the runway." Zeus said runway like it was a word that didn't fit comfortably in his mouth. "You have this contraption built by a mortal and even Hermes prefers his Nike sneakers to his winged sandals. I've even heard that some of the gods don't drink nectar anymore. They drink this new mortal stuff called Coke! What is happening to us, Hephaestus?"

"We have been replaced," the god said softly, laying a dirty hand of Zeus' arm. Zeus' shoulders slumped and he nearly sank to the balcony floor in defeat. "But," Hephaestus continued in a voice that made Zeus raise his head and look at him. "There is always an option." He let the end of the sentence hang in the air between them, unsaid and full of potential.

"An option?" Zeus repeated, drawing closer to Hephaestus, for once not noticing that the other god was filthy from his work at the forge or the scent of sweat that always hung about him.

Hephaestus wagged his eyebrows at Zeus before continuing.

"Religions come and they go," Hephaestus began, throwing an arm around the former King of the Gods and drawing him close. "But what's to say that we don't encourage this one to go sooner rather than later. I have a plan to overthrow the One God and to put the Olympians—to put you—back into power."

Zeus' eyes glittered as he leaned into Hephaestus' smoky embrace to hear the plan. Soon, the one-time Thunder Thrower and soon-to-be re-crowned King of the Gods was nodding to Hephaestus' words and rubbing his bicep eagerly as he thought about once more flinging lightning bolts onto the heads of mortals from the great height of Olympus.

~~~~~

Zeus left Olympus early the next day, hitching a ride in the flatbed trailer attached to the John Deere tractor Apollo used these days instead of his solar chariot and team of horses.

"Have you forgiven me then, Father, for having Fuchsia's Daughters here yesterday?" Apollo asked as they were cruising easily over the eastern coast of Brazil.

"Huh?" Zeus asked, breaking his gaze from the frothy waves and staring at his son. He always felt very un-godly when a question such as this caught him unawares. Zeus hated to admit it, but it happened more often than he liked. Like the storms he had power over, his anger grew, broke in all its awesome fury and faded away just as quickly as it had been roused. And like water falling on sand, he forgot about it just as quickly and completely.

"Yes, Fuchsia's Daughters," Zeus repeated, fighting to recall what that had been all about. Fuchsia sounded like it should be one of the numerous vegetation gods but somehow, Zeus didn't think that was right. Then, as the tractor chugged over a small mountain range, he remembered.

"No, I haven't forgiven you!" Zeus said, a little of yesterday's anger coming back. As if it wasn't bad enough that Apollo had brought a gaggle of mortal women to Olympus, they had seen him naked. And laughed! "You should know better than to bring mortals to Olympus!"

"But Father, they were musicians. Am I not also God of Music?" Apollo asked, drawing himself up to his full height as he sat behind the wheel of the John Deere.

"No mortals on Olympus, Apollo, and that's final. No! No archery champions or painters or anyone else. No mortals!"

167

Apollo skulked as he drove and went through more clouds than strictly necessary while Zeus watched South America slowly disappearing behind them. He must have drifted off because before he knew it, they were over Greece and the huge cleft in the mountains that marked Delphi.

"Here we are Father," Apollo said, putting the tractor into neutral and climbing back to poke Zeus in the shoulder. "Although I don't know what you want with the Muses, since I am head of them."

"Can't a father visit his daughters?" Zeus asked as he climbed stiffly from the flatbed.

"It isn't my fault you knocked up so many virgins that you are practically everybody's father!" Apollo exclaimed, exasperated.

"Impertinent lout," Zeus muttered. "I should have left Leto well enough alone and that's the last time I'm changing into a swan." He rubbed the back of his neck where it was sore from sleeping hunched against the low rails of the flatbed. "I ought to take some of his duties away from him. NO teenager should get to be in charge of the sun, the Muses, music, archery and all the rest." Zeus was still muttering about the evils of teenagers as he drew close to Delphi, the home of his nine daughters, the Muses. At one time, the Muses had lived by the Castalia River in Delphi, but with the encroachment of mortal tourists, they had moved within the rock cleft, making their home from the living rock itself. Zeus squared his shoulders as he strode, invisible among the morals, and knocked politely on the cave wall for entrance.

"My Lord Zeus," one of his daughters murmured as she opened the door. Zeus met her gracious bow with his own. For the life of him, Zeus couldn't tell the nine Muses apart; for all that they were his daughters. He followed her through the winding hallways, noting the fine statues and paintings that filled the halls. She paused at the door to a great library, stepping aside for Zeus to enter first. The room, the size of one of the smaller banquet halls in Olympus Palace, was filled with volumes of all sizes, neatly placed on the shelves that lined the walls from floor to ceiling and also on lower bookcases that made a maze of the interior of the room. As Zeus watched, a team of Hephaestus' androids silently moved among the rows of books; some dusting and arranging the shelves, others putting new tomes away and still others carried sheaves of paper and seemed to be doing an inventory of the library of the Muses.

"If you will wait here, my lord, I will return with my sisters. I am sure that they are anxious to hear the counsel of the Lord of Olympus." Zeus nodded and waved a hand at her, trying for what he hoped was the offhand manner of those used to command. He sank gratefully into a plush armchair and stared at the wealth lining the shelves around him. Even from his chair, he could see that some of the volumes were much newer than others, bound with colorful glossy paper, while others were bound in cloth or leather or wood.

After a moment, the Muse returned, joined by her sisters. A troop of androids followed, bringing trays of ambrosia and silver pitchers of nectar, the sides beaded with condensation. Before Zeus could even rise from his chair, the androids had set up small tables and more chairs for the Muses. *How many of those things did Hephaestus create?* he wondered. The androids working in the library kept to their tasks and here were more that served the Muses. Not to mention those in the Palace and the androids that most certainly worked in the private palaces and sanctuaries of those gods who chose not to live at Olympus.

The Muses sat all at the same time, as if they shared one mind spread throughout their nine bodies. It unnerved Zeus to have them all looking at him with their large brown eyes, upturned noses and sharp chins. Each appeared identical to him yet he knew that each Muse was in charge of a different aspect of creativity, no matter that almost everyone thought of them as a single creativity inspiring entity.

"Daughters," Zeus began, taking a silver cup of nectar from an android. "I have come with a petition of great importance." He set the cup on the small table at his elbow and then rose so he could pace among the chairs and tables.

"It is time that we, the Olympian Gods, reclaimed our position from the One God and his bearded son. It is time—" but he was interrupted by one of the Muses' silver voices.

"Father, we are not Olympian Gods. We are the Muses and not

169

gods at all." She punctuated her words by taking a bite from her cake. Zeus saw her small white teeth bite cleanly through the cake's jellied center.

"In addition," another of them said. Zeus' head swung from the one eating a cake to another daughter, stroking the head of a white cat sitting on her lap. "We are the bearers of human creativity. Without us, the mortals would be lost." The cat raised his head to fix Zeus with a piercing feline gaze.

"Plus," a third Muse began. Zeus didn't hear what her reason was as he strode to the table and took a long drink of nectar.

"Enough!" he shouted as a fourth and fifth voice joined the argument against reclaiming their places as the main gods. "This is not a debate! It is what we are doing. You," he jabbed a finger at the woman with the cat, "are exactly right. Humans will be lost without your guidance. We as gods," his glare dared any of his daughters to argue that they, technically, weren't gods, "continue to serve the mortals, but they do not give us the homage we deserve. I am ordering you to neglect your duties and allow the mortals to try and suffer through on their own." Zeus tried to take another swallow of the nectar, only to find that he had crushed the sliver cup in his massive hands and that the godly liquid was running down his arm and dripping from his elbow.

The Muses exchanged a knowing glance; he hated it when women did that. After a long moment, they rose and bowed their heads to Zeus.

"As you wish it, Father," they said at the same time. Then, they all turned and glided out of the room in a line of swaying hips. Zeus was suddenly struck by the image of a cat abruptly displaced from a lap and how it would stalk off with its tail in the air. He slumped back into the chair and allowed one of the ever-present androids to mop his wet arm with a soft cloth and to replace the smashed cup with a fresh one. Sipping the nectar and scrubbing a hand across his eyebrows, Zeus realized that not all of the Muses had been wearing the white flowing robes he'd expected. In fact, some had even been wearing pants! Then, the impact hit him that they had been nibbling small cakes. Cakes! He grimly stared at the remains of the picnic. He

170

would bet his favorite thunderbolt that their cups and goblets hadn't held nectar but some other mortal drink that they had adopted.

"What are we coming to?" he muttered as he left Delphi. Rather than take another ride in the John Deere tractor with his annoying son, Zeus walked back to Olympus, thinking all the while what god he would next approach with his great plan.

~~~~~

"Athena," Zeus greeted the goddess who entered his chambers the next morning. "Athena, my favorite grey-eyed goddess—why are your eyes purple?" He demanded, suddenly angry at seeing that Athena's eyes were not their expected shade.

"They're colored contacts, Father. Aren't they wonderful?" She ducked her head to admire her new eye color in the mirror that Hera had left hanging on the bedpost the night before.

"No," Zeus said flatly. "Take them out." Athena glanced sideways at her father before sliding her finger into her eye and fishing out the thin plastic. Zeus shuddered while he watched her do the other eye. He pointedly ignored her stonewashed blue jeans and the green halter-top. The post through her navel made him almost as sick to his stomach as watching her poke around in her eyes.

"So," Athena said, settling into a chair and slinging one long leg over the back. She swept her brown hair over her shoulder to examine the ends. "What's up?"

Remembering the debate with the Muses from the day before, Zeus outlined his plan to her all in a rush, before she could interrupt to argue.

"Actually, Father," she said as Zeus paused to gain a breath, "that sounds like a wonderful idea. I've been getting tired of giving wisdom to all those pesky world leaders. They all do the opposite of what I tell them anyway. Except that Nelson Mandela character," she added, stroking her hair over her palm. "Would you like me to approach Apollo and Ares for you?"

"That would be wonderful." Zeus tried to hide a sigh of relief. "Tell Apollo to neglect everything except pulling the sun around the sky. I want the mortals to look to us for answers, not panic when their orbital science suddenly goes awry. Humph!" he snorted

"Using science to explain Apollo's duties. What will they come up with next?"

Athena said nothing, but her grey-eyed stare was suddenly flat, Zeus noticed.

"And what do I tell Ares?" She asked in a too-calm voice.

"Nothing." Zeus pretended not to see Athena's anger. Inside, he cursed for saying that bit about the science; of course the goddess of wisdom would claim the scientific world as her own. "If anything, I want Ares to kick it into high gear. War is good in a time of religious chaos." Athena nodded and sprung up from the chair.

"As the lord Zeus commands," she said, bowing.

~~~~~

From there, it went easily, as one by one the Olympian gods came on board, as well as many of the lesser gods and deities. Zeus' brothers Hades and Poseidon were in full support of taking their place back as the main worshiped gods, even if Hades, being god of the underworld, had nothing he could directly do to help.

"I'll have Demeter come and visit Persephone," he offered. "Having the harvests out of order should help spread the chaos in the mortal's life."

Poseidon agreed saying, "Won't it really mess up their faith if all of the currents in the sea were to suddenly change. Plus, I am the god of earthquakes too. I'll throw a couple of those their way." He banged his trident against the floor of the Palace, causing it to shudder. Three androids fell over from the impact. Zeus nodded and sent them on their way.

"Brothers," he muttered. "On the whole I prefer Hades to Poseidon. Hades at least doesn't go out of his way to damage my palace." Zeus watched as the three androids righted themselves and then carried off the shattered remains of a marble statue of Hera.

He ran through a mental list of the Olympian Gods: Poseidon, changing ocean currents and causing earthquakes; Demeter, visiting her daughter and neglecting her harvest duties; Apollo, sulking, good enough; Athena, on vacation in Greenland; Hermes, taking messages everywhere and coordinating efforts; Ares, causing wars; Aphrodite, called off St. Valentines day, threw the diamond market into upheaval; Dionysus, causing as many bar fights as he could; Artemis, getting all animals to behave badly. Plus, there were the Muses not being creative and Hephaestus causing all types of problems as all mechanical devices from computers to toasters malfunctioned. Any moment now, he expected a great cry from the morals below, beseeching Zeus and the Olympians for aid. Zeus strolled the halls of Olympus whistling and waiting while the mortal world fell to pieces below his feet.

He turned a corner and ran headlong into Hera, her face dark with anger. Recalling their numerous fights and quarrels, he braced himself for the worse, watching her from squinted eyes. She faced him squarely, arms crossed firmly beneath her breasts. Zeus stared into the deep fold between them and at the tops as they gently swelled as she breathed. He sighed, it might be a very long time before he got anywhere near those breasts.

"Hera, my beautiful one," he began, hoping to make his argument before she drowned him out. She raised one hand in his face. He stopped talking, mouth still open, and waited. In their arguments, Hera always dictated what happened and the only way for Zeus to win involved lightning bolts and torrential monsoons.

"Why haven't you cut your hair yet?" She demanded. Zeus took a step back.

"What?" he spluttered, looking to a cleaning android for help.

"If you are going to be the new religious power on the block then you need to look the part. You hair and beard is so very Bronze Age. And don't even get me started on your eyebrows!"

"I'm not trying to be the 'new religious power on the block.' I am the oldest religious power!" He felt like thundering.

"Technically, that would be Hermes. Never mind," she said, waving a hand to dismiss her words. Zeus' jaw snapped shut with a click and he ground his teeth to keep from yelling.

"Now, as I was saying, you really must update your style. We shall have to see about getting you some tailored suits. Armani in pinstripe, I think." Her voice trailed off as she paced a circle around him, one hand trailing suggestively along his waist. Zeus wasn't sure if he should draw away from her hand or lean into it. Hera herself decided, stepping back and changing the subject saying, "You do realize that you shouldn't go out and impregnate any more virgins."

Great, that same old fight, he thought.

"Hera, I am supposed to impregnate virgins. It's part of my duty as King of the Gods." He tried not to sound whiny or plaintive, but he could hear it in his voice.

"Well, it's got to go. First off, rape has been made seriously illegal, and don't tell me that they submit just because you look like a bull or a shower of rain." She held up a hand to forestall his argument. "That's been done and it just won't hold up in a court of law. Besides, virgins don't exist anymore.

"Yes, Armani it is. I shall send someone by to take your measurements. At least you are still in good shape." She patted Zeus' flat stomach and ran a hand across his biceps. He felt another muscle father south flex under the attention. "I'll also send an android by to wax your eyebrows."

"Now," suddenly the shrewish side of his wife appeared. "Why wasn't I invited to take part in this scheme?" Her eyes glittered. Zeus took a step away from her, thought better of it and forced himself to take a step closer. Then another. He inched closer until he towered over her, and she had to arch her back to look up at him.

"You." He made each word a sentence. "Weren't. Invited. Because. Your. Job. Is. Too. Important." There, he'd said it. He resisted the urge to step away from her and run his hands over his body to make sure he still had all his parts attached.

"Too important?" Hera screeched. She jabbed a finger hard into his chest. "What will the world think when they see that I've not supported you in your political endeavor? This will seriously affect our ratings in the polls."

"Nonsense Hera, this is not a political issue."

"It is. Everything is political." She punctuated each word with a sharp jab in the chest.

"Man has worked too hard to lower infant mortality rates for me to allow my war against the One God and his nasty Bearded Son to undermine that." He wrapped her finger in his fist gently but held on

174

securely, unsure of her reaction. To his surprise, she smiled.

"That's kind of you dear." She rose on tiptoe and kissed the point of his nose. He released her hand and drew back. She took a step nearer to him and purred, "I can help in other ways, you know." Her hand was more than suggestive in its actions at his waist. "You may have to forswear virgins, but my marital bed is still warm. Shall we?"

~~~~~

Three weeks after the Olympians began purposefully neglecting their duties, there came a great cry from the mortals that God had forsaken them. All of the religious sects were in upheaval as they tried to justify why the world had suddenly fallen apart.

"It's punishment for eating red meat on Fridays!"

"It's because bacon cheeseburgers aren't kosher!"

"The Flood is coming!"

"It's a delayed Y2K computer virus!"

"An act of terrorism!"

"Women never should have been allowed to vote!"

"It's the fault of the white people!"

"It's because of Capitalism!"

"No, because of democracy! or Marxism! or Communism!"

The only thing the religious leaders could agree on was that they needed the intervention of a higher power since there was no way, scientific or other, to explain the strange occurrences that had been happening. Zeus spent most of his time on the observation balcony of Olympus, staring through the smog with Hephaestus' telescope, chuckling.

"It's going perfect!" he crowed to Hephaestus one afternoon when the religious debate had been especially heated. He had been watching a rally bringing the pacifist religious leaders together in San Francisco that had erupted into a fistfight when Ares had swooped through.

"Perhaps it is time for your intervention, Lord Zeus. If we delay too much longer, there may not be any mortals left to worship us."

"I want the mortals to come crawling back to me." Zeus rubbed his bare chin; he still couldn't believe he'd allowed Hera to shave it. "Still," he paused to listen to a particularly heated argument between a lawyer and a soapbox preacher proclaiming the fall of civilized government. "Still, it wouldn't do for the One God or his Bearded Son to decide to take a hand in matters. I shall make myself known to the people."

"Excellent, Lord Zeus. I'll have Hermes call a press conference."

~~~~~

The mortals must have worked fast, Zeus thought as he strode through the thick crowd of journalists and up to the podium. In the three weeks it took for the world to implode, he'd been taking a crash course in the history of the mortals since the beginning of the Middle Ages and the fall of the Olympian Gods. He knew from the taped press conferences that Hera had provided that this spot was where the king of the United States usually gave his addresses. *The president*, he amended to himself. He was satisfied to see that the political insignias had been removed, but he could tell that they still didn't know what to make of his coming; the wall behind the podium was bare although it looked like a fresh coat of blue paint had been put over the outline of fluted columns.

"Mortals!" he cried when he was in position behind the podium and all eyes, living or electronic had been turned toward him. He had expected to be able to give a little speech about who he was, the King of the Gods, and why he was there, to take back the throne the One God had usurped from him. No such luck.

"Are you really Zeus?"

"Where are your thunderbolts?"

"You look like Sean Connery, not Zeus!"

"The Olympians are just myth!"

"Where's your beard?"

"Since when do gods wear Armani?" Zeus shuddered at that one; he knew he never should have let Hera be in charge of his wardrobe.

"Silence!" he yelled, bringing both arms above his head. His hands felt the familiar weight of lightning bolts. He hurled them without hesitation over the heads of the press and into the back

176

of the room. When the smoke and noise had subsided, the twelve Olympian Gods were in the room, in position along the walls. They looked regal and ancient and very, very powerful. For this occasion, Zeus had insisted that they wore their traditional dress, to impress upon the mortals they sought to convert that they were ancient powers.

"I am Zeus Thunderbearer, King of the Gods!" His voice boomed into the small space, filling it and resounding like thunder. "I come before you angry. You have forsaken the Olympians in favor of the One God and his Bearded Son. Where is your One God now?

"I am here to take back what is mine! You may appease my anger by once again holding to the old ways of worship and sacrifice. If you choose not to, beware the wrath of Olympus!" Power currents shifted in the air as each of the gods tapped into the energies at their command. They did nothing, waiting for a signal from the mortals or from Zeus.

A tall cameraman with hair in a ponytail to his waist was the first to move. He let the camera fall from his shoulder as he folded into himself and sank to the floor. A tiny voice rose from the prone man, calling "Praise Zeus Thunderbearer! Long live the King of the Gods!" When his words seemed to please the scowling Zeus behind the podium, the rest of the room slowly sank to it knees and repeated the words.

"I am satisfied," Zeus said in a more normal tone of voice. The assembled mortals cowered. "Go and tell your people that the King of the Gods has returned."

"Lord!" a small voice called from the back of the room. A tiny lady in a red suit struggled to her feet. "How do we worship you?"

Zeus threw back his head and laughed. The throng pressed their faces into the carpet.

"Seek out your scholars who study the old ways." He paused for dramatic effect. "Although I recommend that no one ever address me so informally and without an honorific again." While the press crowd tried to digest that, each Olympian turned sharply on their left heel and disappeared.

~~~~~

177

At six thirty the following morning, Zeus was roused from slumber by an insistent poking in his left arm. He opened one bleary eye, already thinking of asking Hecate to curse whomever it was who was so rudely poking him awake.

"By thunder!" Zeus roared, coming fully awake when he realized that the poker was a mortal. "Who are you and how dare you wake me!" He flipped the cover off his legs and sprang to his feet. The man glanced down at Zeus' exposed godhead and coughed politely. "You will wake the King of the Gods from slumber by poking him but you cough politely at his nakedness?" Zeus asked the mortal incredulously. When Zeus showed no signs of moving to dress himself, the man half turned away from him, stared out a window and began droning.

"I am Mr. Sylvan. I am the assistant secretary to the President of the United States of America. At this moment, Mr. President is awaiting your presence in the grand banquet hall." Mr. Sylvan coughed again, pulled a handkerchief from his breast pocket and handed it to Zeus.

"By thunder!" Zeus swore again, spitting at the handkerchief. It burst instantly into flames. Mr. Sylvan dropped it and glared at Zeus while he rubbed his scorched hand. "Well?" Zeus asked finally. "What are you waiting for? Go!"

As soon as the man left, Zeus called for the androids. In fifteen minutes Zeus was washed, combed and dressed, the bed had been made and the burnt remnants of the handkerchief had been swept from the polished marble floor. Zeus strode down the hallways of Olympus sending androids and gods alike scurrying out of his way. He slammed the doors to the banquet hall open with a crash.

"Why are you here?" He demanded of the man he recognized as the President. The man calmly set a bone china teacup on a low table and rose from his chair. He adjusted the lapels of his suit before answering.

"I thought we could discuss the State of the Union."

"What?"

"Well, since the Olympian Gods went on strike, the affairs of the world has been, shall we say, somewhat disrupted. I am here to discuss what you are going to do about it."

"Do? The mighty Zeus doesn't do anything." That sounded wrong to Zeus' ears, too much like the position the One God took regarding mortals. "I do what I have always done: throw lightning bolts, impregnate virgins, intimidate puffing mortals like you." Zeus drew himself to his full height, preparing to be intimidating but the President merely waved his hand.

"Bah. That may have been fine two thousand years ago but now people expect their world leaders to be more active. To fight alongside the common man in the trenches, as it were."

"There are no trenches in Olympus," Zeus said icily. He got the feeling that he was missing the little man's point.

"Still—"

"Enough! How did you get here?"

"I flew in my private helicopter."

"Well you'd better fly on home before I throw you from Olympus. Just ask Hephaestus about what happens when I do that!"

The President spluttered something about Zeus having to appear before Congress and that he should apply for a position among the Joint Chiefs before Zeus seized him by the back of the suit and frog marched him from the hall. The President broke from his grasp and ran down the hall to his waiting helicopter.

"Don't come back!" Zeus roared after him. Zeus turned and found himself confronted with half a dozen religious leaders bobbing and scraping. In a rush, they all asked him what he was planning to do to normalize conditions on Earth. It took Zeus five hours just to get rid of them all and they refused to go until he had blessed them each, tasted their national and favorite foods, promised them a tour of Olympus on their next visit and said that he was rooting for Miami in the next Superbowl.

The next day Zeus was poked from sleep by none other than Mr. Sylvan, the assistant secretary to the President of the United States.

"What do you want now?" Zeus demanded, too tired to even push the covers off his body. "Didn't I tell you not to come back?"

"The President has some issues he wishes to discuss with you."

"Fine. Lead on." Zeus rolled from bed and nearly laughed

when Mr. Sylvan blushed. He needn't have because Zeus was fully dressed, having fallen asleep in his suit the night before. A burst of power smoothed the wrinkles from the linen as he followed Mr. Sylvan down the hall.

"Well?" Zeus demanded when he saw the President.

"I am here to discuss the appointment of new gods," the man began without preamble.

"New gods?" Zeus sank into the chair the President had just vacated and accepted a goblet of nectar from an android. He enjoyed the sideways glance the President gave the thing and how he backed away nervously. His voice was as assertive as ever, though.

"Yes, new gods. Some of your duties are very antiquated and we feel that the gods as a body could use some updating."

"Who's we?" Zeus asked, sipping nectar.

"The Senate and the House. And me," he added as an afterthought, looking pleased with himself. "We were thinking that we need a god of Internet. And one of junk mail. And of, course, a god of asphalt."

"No."

"But—"

"No." Zeus reiterated his refusal as he marched the President down the hall, again as he stuffed him in the helicopter and just to be certain the man got it, again when Zeus nicked the rotor blade of the helicopter with a lightning bolt. It would give the man an interesting ride back to the Earth, but wouldn't hurt him. *More's the pity*, Zeus thought as he turned to muddle through the three other political meetings he had that morning, not to mention Hebrew lessons that afternoon, tennis with the President of Brazil and a meeting with the leader of Greece to discuss what to do with the ancient religious sites of Athens, Delphi and Crete.

~~~~~

For the third morning in a row, Zeus woke up to a finger being repeatedly jabbed into his arm.

"The President would see you sir," Mr. Sylvan said to Zeus when he groaned that, yes, he was awake and please stop poking now.

"What?" Zeus asked the President, standing with fists on his hips. Zeus was going for powerful and awesome; the President didn't seem impressed.

"It's come to my attention that your policy on heaven and hell is somewhat vague."

"What?" Zeus said again.

"Well, according to this," the President patted a thick book lying on his lap. In gold letters it said *The Idiot's Guide to Greek Mythology*. "This says that for heroes and those distinguished in battle, the Elysian Fields are to be their final resting place. Or, as I understand it, they stay there, having a perpetual drinking binge, waiting for the last great battle where they all come back to life and tear around the countryside burning and looting. Am I right?" When Zeus didn't answer, the President continued. "This also says that for those people who are evil, there is the land of Tartarus where they suffer for their crimes in life. The example given of Sisyphus was especially romantic." Zeus nearly swallowed his tongue when the man winked.

"But, there is, of course, the matter of the rest of us. The voting public will never accept that the vast majority of them simply hang about in Hades, waiting. We really must do something about this or it is sure to show up in the polls. You could risk not being re-elected."

"The polls?" Zeus said, when he was finally able to form more than one word answers. "Risk not being re-elected? I am not elected! I am Zeus King of the Gods! I am—"

"Yes, that's all well and good," the President said, interrupting. "But what are you going to do about this?"

Zeus was saved from answering—it would have been with a lightning bolt to a sensitive part of that man's anatomy—by the entrance of Hermes who declared that Lord Zeus was needed elsewhere. Zeus followed Hermes' floating shape down the hall, trying not to think about the President's words. Re-election?

"Do you wish you could borrow them and fly away?" Hermes asked over his shoulder, giving Zeus a half smile.

"What?"

"The winged sandals? Where would you go? I hear Tulsa is nice this time of year. Good luck, Sir," Hermes said, leaving Zeus in front of a gold-bound door. Squaring his shoulders he opened it.

For the rest of the day, Zeus faced a never-ending series of etiquette lessons for the Earth's major cultures, language classes in Russian, Spanish, and Navajo. Then he was off to dance classes to learn the salsa, the twist, and ballet pirouettes. In the afternoon, he had curling lessons with the Canadian Head Librarian and a tarot card reading from Bruhilda, the leading tarot expert. Dinner was a formal affair where he sat between the most successful chicken farmer in Argentina and the head of the Classics Department at the University of Arizona.

It was long after Orion was high in the sky that Zeus finally was able to seek his bed. The curled shape of Hera took up one side of the bed but Zeus was too tired to wake her up to have some fun.

~~~~~

Zeus grabbed Mr. Sylvan's pointy index finger before he could use it to jab the god from sleep.

"Yes, yes, yes," Zeus said before Mr. Sylvan could say anything. "I'm coming."

"Mr. President," Zeus greeted him, accepting his goblet of nectar from the android. "To what do I owe today's visit?"

"We need to talk about—"

"I am beginning to hate any statement that begins 'we need to.' What it really means is 'Zeus, you need to do such and such.' Oh well. What's today's crisis?" Zeus settled in a chair to drink his nectar, hoping that his exhaustion didn't show on his face.

"Yes, as I was saying. We need to discuss your upcoming tour. Parades, speaking engagements, press conferences, charity events and so on. And, there is also the matter of holidays. Will they be observed worldwide? By each individual country? Do we do away with Christmas and Easter or will they be incorporated? What about the pagan holiday of Halloween? And so on. As you can see, we have much to get accomplished today. Shall we go to your office?" The man stood and held out an elbow as if Zeus were the wife of some foreign dignitary and the President was offering his arm to escort her to dinner.

"Tour?" Zeus echoed weakly. "What do you mean tour?"

"Well, you are the world's first religious and political leader being accepted across every race, creed, and economical station. I think that that deserves a parade or ten. Now, let's talk about holidays. We'll need to know your birthday so we can celebrate that. And if I'm not mistaken, you overthrew your father to be king of the gods so I suppose that should be its own day. And then of course there is the day you assumed power for the second time. We should put that on in July, say the fifth? That way towns can just make one fireworks order: some for Independence Day and some for Zeus' Ascension Day. Sounds good, no?"

"No."

"No? Of course it sounds good. We are making history, you and I, my friend." The bothersome little man was bouncing on his toes, flapping his elbows like wings.

"No. No. NO! I've had it with all of this. *You* first thing every morning is enough to give even the King of the Gods indigestion. Not to mention all the other leaders I have to face all day. To make matters worse, Hera says that I must be civilized and not throw anything. Not even them! No. Get out! This time I *will* throw you back down to Earth! Go!" Zeus ran after the President. That they must appear comic vaguely passed through his mind as he chased the little man through the halls of Olympus, howling "No parades!"

When the President was zooming away in his jet—he'd left the helicopter for the vice president to use—Zeus locked himself in his private chamber. He looked forlornly in his mirror and summoned Mnemosyne, his favorite aunt. She stepped from the silvered glass looking rather frosty herself. She said nothing to Zeus as she strode to a high-backed chair and sat, arranging her skirts around her. She looked like a queen on her throne. An ice queen.

"I'm surprised it's taken you this long to call upon me, Zeus."

Zeus hurried across the room and knelt at her feet, putting his head in her lap as if he were a child.

"How did this happen?" He asked her, feeling the absence of his whiskers as he rubbed his cheek into the silk of her dress. "I thought I had everything so carefully planned."

183

"Did you think it would be the same now as it was two thousand years ago?" Mnemosyne asked, stroking his shorn hair.

"They're just mortals, Auntie."

"With the abandonment of the One God upon the death of his son, they've learned to be remarkably self-sufficient. The enlightened ones know the truth, of course, but they really have no problem worshipping a god who doesn't listen. How could you not have anticipated the chaos of having a god they could talk to? A god they could see, even touch if they dared enough. Mortals have changed, young one. They have explained away the existence of gods. This came as an unwanted reminder that they are small and weak and that there are beings of a higher power. Besides, the old tricks never would have worked. They expect their leaders, even the bad ones, to be accountable and predictable. They don't need to worship you, Zeus, just like you don't need to be worshiped. Do you?"

He pressed his face into her lap, shaking his head 'no' but still not wanting to admit that he'd become worse than redundant. He'd been forgotten. Even now, with the mortal world in disarray, they still didn't need him to be an all-powerful god, they needed him to be an administrative assistant to macro manage the affairs of the world.

"What do I do?" he whispered.

"If you've called on me, then you already know. Don't worry, child. I am not the Goddess of Memory for nothing. I will make them forget." She waved one hand in the direction of the window. The din raising from far below stopped suddenly, allowing Zeus to hear silence and for the first time really notice the background noise that had been getting steadily worse since the gods went on strike.

"Perhaps it's a good thing that Hephaestus made so many of those androids," Mnemosyne muttered. "They will be of great help to get the world back to its pre-revelation state. Don't worry, Zeus. The androids will make the world right again, they are already working on it, and then the mortals will go back to their lives, forgetting about all of this."

"And the gods, Auntie?"

"The gods will do what they have always done: their jobs. Ares

184

will guide the wars, Athena will counsel the leaders, Demeter will govern the harvest, Aphrodite will counter Ares in love, Hephaestus will give them technology and the Muses will give them poetry. We'll all go back to doing our jobs. Hermes will carry messages and bear souls to Hades, who will accept them graciously. Poseidon will guard the seas and the sailors and Hera will keep their wives. And I? I shall keep their history and teach it to them so they may continue to learn from their mistakes."

"And me, Auntie? What shall I do?"

"You Zeus, shall enjoy your retirement. You've earned it."

Guardian Star
by Candice L. Tucker

No words can form the vision of the woman I longed for. The image is magnificent and beautiful. She is beauty itself, as real as an illustrious mare, yet as mystical as a unicorn. Her eyes are pearls the color of the day's sky; her skin milky and soft for only the eyes to feast upon; her hair, laces of gold, smooth down to the waist; her lips create the sun's wealth when she smiles to the dawn; and the sweet aroma of the powdered perfume upon her slender neck could soothingly wake the dead from their soft slumber.

She is the deity I was meant to spend my existence with. Visions of her would provoke a man to kill another. She is what changes a man like myself, who was once a lying thief, into the uttermost noble and loving man you will ever happen upon.

Many men from the towns that I visited for supplies have mocked me because of the search for my treasure. But disregard them. I forgot them as their cross words reached to tingle my ear and despair my heart. However, for the most part, I traveled through the nature that breathes and sustains aside the sprinkled towns.

I searched for the castle of Amelthia by day on horseback. When the night closed the great eye that watches in the sky and the silver eye opened to look upon me, I rested. I would lay upon beds of luscious grass, with lovely leaves as my comforters, and gaze at the myriad of other eyes in front of the black sheet in the sky.

When I was a young boy, my father once told me that they are true guardian angels that watch over kings, knights, and the noble. Hundreds of legends, which were burned into my mind, were derived from these guardians. Stories like Kathious the King who bravely fought and won battles that raged night and day as well as Luscious the night who perished a prolonged, tragic death on the behalf of his father, the king, for refusing to sacrifice secrets to his enemies. Now they are stars, teaching the living the nobility they know best. They would protect me from dangers that crossed my temple as I slept.

I hadn't known my father well, for he died in battle when I was of the callow age of six. But this ounce of knowledge I gathered from him stuck with me always.

When dawn's lazy eye opened, so did mine. Every morning I would look to my left to see the drowned flame of the camp fire and recall the dream that always lingered fresh in my mind, which soddened the lustiness in my soul. Night after night, I experienced the same dream and that phantasm was my hope day after day.

The dream always started with a new look at the princess of Amelthia in her castle. She stood at the crudely decorated stone balcony, looking beyond the clouds at the winking stars of the empty, quiet night. One candle sat in front of her on the edge of the balcony, illuminating every fraction of beauty upon her fine silk dress, bosoms, and countenance. I didn't know what this angel's name was, but I knew that she was no myth. She was every beauty that existed upon this sacred Earth. Only God could have created such a spectacle, for there was and is no other like this one.

But I've trailed away from the dream.

In my existence I knew that I had a mission. It was told to me in this dream over and over. This beautiful creature would be

188

dispatched without warning and without clemency upon her own balcony. This horrible event was to take spite out on her father by a prisoner of their dungeon below the castle, a man convicted of stealing riches from the royal family to feed him and his starving family.

She stared at the stars, which holds a petite portion of the beauty she has, unsuspecting of the fateful sword that would strike her down. When it does, I give a silent scream for her. I am engulfed in a strong and tormenting pain, suffocating me until I can no longer see. It is like a dull dagger sweeping into my heart, retracting all the love and hope pulsating within me. I wanted her to forever live as an immortal woman like the goddess she was born to be, placed far above in the Heavens. But then we both perish, our flames extinguished by the cruel hand of fate.

Then I would wake.

As I rose that day, the thirtieth day of my journey for her delicate beauty, I gathered my belongings. These included the dirty clothes on my back, the smatter of money in my coin bag and the brute strength that I carried with me at all times in case of an unfortunate encounter. The leaves that I slept on and wood for a fire would be found some place else in the dense forestry.

The journey continued on. I could feel my sore muscles tense as I walked along the unpaved woodland, in search of my horse. After treading through the woods for a while, I spotted an old well, blending in with the rest of the green scenery. It's ivy and moss-covered stone didn't hide what it truly was: a wishing well built by the fairies of Ogosta, and long forgotten by the magicians of the Old World. No mind the age, the magic was still as bright as a cloudless day.

I stepped closer to the well, my heart hammering in my chest. Observing the emptiness within, I dug into the worn leather pouch at my waist, feeling for the biggest coin I could find. I picked it out and gazed at it, turning it to reflect the sun's light into my eyes. I clutched it, closed my eyes and wished:

"May my journey end soon and with success. I wish to wish that I may see this Princess of Amelthia and to save her from the danger that awaits."

I then flipped the golden coin into the mossy black hole and waited to hear a splash or a solid echoing hit on the bottom of the well—a test to make sure if it was a true wishing well.

I heard neither a splash nor a hit. This well was bottomless. This well was no lie. My wish had been granted.

~~~~~

After walking through the singing forest for much of the morning, I descried my horse. He was grazing in an open field off to my left. I smiled to myself, admiring his golden-brown hair and lengthy black mane that shone in the daylight, which was growing brighter after a dreary dawn. I walked with caution through the field so as to not penetrate the steed's concentration on the sweet taste of the dewy green blades.

He was a very attractive animal. If it were not for the aged, stolen reins and saddle attached to the horse, I would've mistaken it for a wild stallion.

Once I came close enough, I gently grasped the reins on the snout of the magnificent specimen. Almost three months ago I found him in an abandoned stable, covered in gory, dry wounds. He was beaten by his old master and so was wary of any human beast.

He wasn't stirred by my touch. Not annoyed from being pulled away from his grazing, yet seemingly still not content with being taken in by his new master.

I had no name for this remarkable animal, but simply what he was: Steed.

After mounting him, we trotted away back into the forest, bearing in mind that this time of year was a dangerous season. Dorthins, large rat-like creatures common in forests and woodland, were in their mating season. I'd heard they tend to become aggressive towards anything that wasn't of their own specie. A bite from their powerful jaws meant a week in agony, their venom inducing a hallucination, which engulfed you within Hell's flames.

Or so I was told. It was more typical of them to be about during the day and never during night, so I was safe when I slept.

I hoped we were nearing the castle.

I knew I would find the princess. I was positive I would. I had staked my life on it. She was as real as the warm air that I breathed, or the flora that I treaded through. I needed her like the air. Her image was a drug in my system, and I was addicted.

I had lived years without a woman in my life, because I babbled on like a madman about the dreams of this one. Why I am just now in search of her is a mystery to me. It wasn't procrastination, but more of waiting for the right moment.

In every dream, her beauty became more prominent. For instance, her glowing cheeks, her fluttering eyelashes, her finely framed eyebrows, the twinkle in her eye, her sweet scent, her soft sigh, and then her bloodcurdling scream. How dreadful and such a piercing tone it was. The last gasps of air escaped her lungs as she lay on the floor and bled to death. Her death was different in each dream (prophecy, or perhaps nightmare, if you will). Sometimes she'd say something to the killer as he condemned her to an early grave. Other times she'd scream and groan as the sword's flashing blade ripped into the soft, scented flesh of her lower back.

My smile faded.

I must save her, I had told myself. *I must. I have to. If I live beyond her life, so help me God will I strike myself dead and retreat to Hell.*

~~~~~

Our candlelight in the sky started fading. As soon as I spotted a clearing, I could make camp once again. I wasn't going to tie up Steed and restrain him like many others would. Besides, every night I camp, he only strayed an hour away, if he did stray at all. I don't believe in censoring the free will of any creature, no matter if it were human or beast. However, as far as I was concerned, the man who planned to defeat the innocence of a defenseless woman is an exception. He is lower than any other beast and acts of immoral abuse to freedom and life.

Steed and I had not run across any sort of dangers that day. However, we hadn't been so lucky before. A few days earlier, we had run across a baby dorthin sitting in our pathway. It was smaller than an adult, yet still its venom is mildly potent. As the infant

191

dorthin hissed and approached us threateningly, we jumped over the creature, but not lucky enough to have escaped unharmed. As Steed flew over the wretched animal, it jumped and sank its teeth into the belly of my horse.

With a fierce squeal and buck, Steed threw me from his back and on my side watching helplessly as he trotted away. Although sore from the drop, I scrambled to my feet and prepared myself for attack. The dorthin leapt and I swatted it away with all my arm's strength as I grunted from the force of the impact. Thudding on its back, the large infant rat rolled over and readied itself for another pounce at my throat. Out of seemingly nowhere, two hooves came crashing down upon the dorthin's world, beating it into the ground. I looked up to see my steed, wild and panicked, yet knowing completely what it was doing.

He stopped stomping the animal and backed away with a whinny, blood staining his front hooves. Entranced by this rescue, I slowly neared Steed and patted his neck. I checked his wound and noticed that he wasn't bleeding much from it. After this, he allowed me to mount him again. He didn't seem to be suffering much, if at all.

How was I to thank a horse? It didn't seem to matter, though. I could feel it in my heart that he knew I was grateful.

Steed had been walking all day with only two short stops, both by two different creeks. Being so tired, he was bound to stay and rest with me during the night. For food, Steed ate the leaves of plants and I ate the more nutritious roots. The taste was undesirable, but how can one be picky if they are miles from any human civilization, poor, weaponless, and starving? One simply can't, or else that picky, spoiled person wouldn't have gotten as far as I did without turning back.

I would never withdraw from saving a beautiful princess' life only because I don't like the taste of creek water and washed roots. Simply impossible! Selfish? Me? Not at all! I am the most giving person anyone will ever meet, even if they steal from me. Maybe *that's* why I am so poor: because I'm far too kind. Far kinder than what I had been. I was a wicked thief with a terrible heart, stealing only because I wished to do so. I swept clean the riches of men and kings, swift enough to never be suspected nor caught. How I wish I could forgive and forget those times.

I reviewed the darkening surroundings for a path to a clearing.

There, up ahead and to the right, I told myself.

I increased Steed's slow, steady pace to a hurried trot. I wanted to gather much leaves and firewood for the night before the silver eye opened wider.

This clearing was mended well. It could have been a field where cattle or horses grazed. I felt in my heart that I must have been on the tail of the dragon. But where was the heart?

Anything past the desolate trees was far too drenched in the night's ebony to see through.

So I stepped off my tired horse and began quickly gathering the firewood and piled it all neatly at a corner of the small clearing. I could still continue to see fairly clear as the day's eye became lazy, unable to keep awake.

I collected the luscious green leaves from the branches still connected to the thick trees. I laid them out gently until the bedding was a few feet long and one inch high from the grass.

By the time I was sitting on my bed of leaves and scraping two sticks together, the silver eye had already awakened to watch over the princess and me. A fire ignited on the dry leaves I added to the firewood. The fire grew larger and illuminated Steed, who had been standing, calm and close by, sleeping in peace. I laid my back upon the soft leaves, hands under my head, and stared off at the distant stars.

For the longest time I could not sleep. I grew so excited, knowing how close I was to the beauty that I had to save from the beast.

I daydreamed about myself entering the room just before the princess was attacked and dispatched the killer. A romance then ensued with the beautiful woman. We would wed and raise six children with the help of her loyal maids and servants. They would each grow to be strong leaders, men and women alike.

And I? I would become a valiant knight, whom only the most brave or the most stupid would challenge, only to surrender at the tip of my sword. The surplus of my radiance would be saved for the princess whom I longed to touch, to hold, and to cherish. Only her and those of my blood, my children, could bring about the soft side that I would hide from the world under the steel armor upon my body.

As I felt the dream begin to descend upon me once again, I opened my eyes for a moment to gaze upon the stars. Then something caught the corner of my eye. It was a small, yellowish flickering. Not like a star. More like a lightning bug. However, the firebugs that dwell within forests are cautious and always moving, for many an animal preys upon them. This one was as still as my dozing horse.

No, this flickering wasn't a lightning bug, or a star.

My jaw dropped in recognition of the light. My heart pumped with excitement and glory.

It was the candle I had sought for almost a month. The light was a beacon, reaching miraculously through the trees.

Focusing in that direction, I realized that it was quite a distance from the ground. Beyond only a few trees lay the heart of the dragon, the woman, waiting for me, although she didn't know that she was. Fortunately, one of us did.

My thin, stinking body sat up and my eyes squinted to get a better look at the candlelight. Above it, I faintly saw the lightly flickering shadows and illumination of her visage. The face that I dreamed of day and night for many years, months, weeks, and days before my journey. It was she; everything that I had imagined, everything that I had dreamed and awaited, and everything that I longed for and was mocked for, truly within my reach.

No time to waste, I reminded myself. *She's in danger*.

How I finally found her on the right night of her brutal murder is beyond me. May it have been luck, destiny, or the wish come true from the ancient well, I did not know nor understand. However, what I did know was that she would *not* depart from this world as she might have. Not if I could help it.

I lifted myself up and ran, as blind as my love for her, towards the flaming candle. I decided that if I saved this fair woman, then she would save me. I knew she would, only because seeing her live would allow me to live forever more.

I ceased running when I reached the castle's moat. I recognized the balcony far above me. I couldn't go out front and simply walk past the bridge and into the castle without guards interrogating me, assuming that the bridge was drawn in the first place. They wouldn't understand and would throw me back into the woods if not directly into the dungeon with the common criminals.

The window in front of me was too small to squeeze through. I pondered what I would do to successfully get inside of the castle. I looked down into the water a few feet from the ground where I stood. The water was black and still, undoubtedly deep to drown intruders. I have heard tales about flesh-eating fish in moat waters, but never thought to believe them true.

Then I had an epiphany. I ran along side the moat to nearly the front of the castle and hid behind a bulky tree close by. I cupped my hands around my mouth and took a deep breath.

"Prisoner! A prisoner has escaped! Guards!" I shouted towards the aged castle.

I continued this until I spotted a full-armored guard appear looking below on his tower. I listened to a few shouts and instructions given by a couple guards and watched the drawbridge slowly anchor down over the moat.

Gloating for a moment, I gathered up my speed and courage and darted for the bridge the moment I saw the last guard clank into the forestry. With my feet barely touching the ground, I flew into the castle, aware of any dangerous turns or tricks there may have been. I knew fully well that I had no time to waste.

I didn't require directions to get to where I needed to be. My instincts told me where to turn, when to turn, and how quick I needed to be.

As quietly as I could, I walked on expensive carpets that lay over the stone floor towards a door. I peaked around the corners of the vacant hallways. I sped to the right side of the hall towards the stairs. I somehow knew the exact place where I was headed. I, again, needed nothing but my instinct.

After rushing up the carpeted stone stairs, I reached the second floor, then the third, fourth, fifth, up and up until I knew where to halt. A hallway illuminated by torches on both walls was past the doorway from the stairwell. At the end was a massive room filled with ancient artwork and furniture. I spotted the door, closed, that belonged to the one I had to save. I was there, doing what I had dreamed of and planned for so long. My heart beat rapidly and my lungs retrieved the air I had lost while speeding through and up the castle.

I rushed down the hallway and clutched the golden handle. I breathed in deeply. Everything seemed to move at an extreme slow pace as pictures of what could be beyond the door rattled and tore through my mind.

My heart pounding even harder against my chest was all I could hear. I shook off any fear I possessed, turned the golden knob and pushed the door wide open.

I saw the unsuspecting princess turning around to the abrupt sound of the door opening, a surprised look upon her flushed face. He was standing there, back facing the door. It was probable that he was contemplating whether he should go through with his dastardly plan. Either that or he was preparing himself for the attack.

Enraged by my entrance, the assassin turned with his sword flashing towards my neck. I didn't realize how near he was to me when I first opened the door, but I could tell I was dangerously close. The blade sliced through my unclean skin. One swipe and my wretched body was decapitated.

The princess screamed. I could still hear, but only for a few more seconds. My headless body crumpled to the floor in a heap and my head bounced beside it. All I could feel was a cold, numb pain.

"What do you think you're . . ." the princess gasped, then stuttered. "Guards! A prisoner escaped! Guards! Father! Come quickly!"

There were many clanking, metal-shoed feet climbing up the stone stairs to the gory, bloodstained room.

The coward ran towards the princess as she continued screaming. Her body froze from fear and her arms covered her face in case any more bloodshed was to befall. But he ran past her and dove from the balcony. He landed rough on his side, then stood and continued to run.

And I died.

~~~~~

The news now is that the man, Jonathan Gumfrey, was caught within the night of the murder. He was hanged in front of the all the people of Amelthia the very next day. Of course there was a small arrogant portion that believed that he was a hero of some sort, but these rebels were warned by the king not to act out in any way. If they did, they would be finished off as well and sent to Hell alongside Jonathan, their bodies placed above the town to be dangled and mocked.

The princess of Amelthia, Kasha, is safe and sound, still living and living well. I told her in her dreams that I was there to save her, and not to destroy her like Jonathan was. Having been convinced of this, she told her father who also believed it. She and her men are constructing a new castle, with more securities and guards.

And I? I am well known around the town as the savior of Kasha. I am a great man. However, not the brave knight like Luscious had been and that I'd dreamt about being with continuous and feverish hope. What I've become is much more of a comfort to me and a rest to my spirit.

Fables and legends were told of how I rescued Kasha. They all instilled bravery in my image. A magnificent sword fight. I had wrestled him with my bare hands. I conducted sorcery upon him. Only Kasha knew what was true, yet allowed these rumors to be spread. My presence was enough to keep her alive and she was thankful for that.

The best painter of Amelthia brought me back to life on a large canvas. I was remade through the oil paints and gentle strokes of a brush from the artist's generous hand. He made my appearance to be as though I were a prophet or wingless angel from God. Perhaps I was, or perhaps I was only a poor former thief with a vision and a wish.

My face became famous and the painting was placed in the new castle of Amelthia. Flowers and gifts were placed beneath the painting as a gracious tribute. I was worshipped. My corpse was dressed with costly nobleman attire and buried in the family's graveyard to prove the king's eternal gratitude.

More rumors spread that I was the lost Son of God. Every picture of me was rewarded with a large sun behind my head, signifying that I was the son of the Eternal One. I never understood, nor wanted this position. I am no more than the man that I honestly was.

Steed was found on the grounds and assumed to be mine. He was adopted and renamed by Kasha. He is now treated as only a god's faithful steed would be treated. He, too, was painted several times beside me or with me astride a fantastic saddle upon his back, holding gold-rimmed reigns.

It was all a beautiful sight, a gorgeous feeling, and an overwhelming sense of thankfulness. However, the greatest and most wonderful thing of all wasn't the gifts, or the flowers, or the praise, but the duty of becoming Kasha's guardian angel.

I could never have been befitted with a greater destiny than to join the guardian stars against the black night's sky.

The Last Word
by Laura Kay Eppin

Up, up, higher and higher I climb toward solitude. The gray dirt collects between my toes, a dust cloud follows my footsteps. I peer down over the edge of a barren cliff and kick a pebble over the edge. As it tumbles down, gaining momentum, I remember Artemis; the huntress always favored me. I was her companion in all outdoor sports; we journeyed over mountains, through forests, and across plains. The scenery was so vast and enchanting; we explored open countryside, a sea of variations of the color green that stretched from ocean to ocean, all ruled by Poseidon. Nothing like that surrounds me now.

Oh Artemis, forever with the giant Orion, you were swift and accurate with your silver bow and prudent in all things. Your entourage of graceful stags and strapping bears was magnificent and powerful; I'm glad you cannot see me now, sulking and cowering alone in this wasteland. I would give anything to see you dance across the hillside in your shining gray shoes, protecting animal

201

babes once more.

I can recall one night so vividly it feels like I could jump in and live in the memory. Dusk was just settling upon us, the moon was glistening over the treetops. You were dancing and feasting with the local wildlife, conjuring up music out of thin air. The very earth seemed to dance with you; all I could do was stare dumbly in awe. Birds leapt from the trees and flew about like bats, singing even though it was night. The naiads and dryads carried torches of different colors; earthy green, blue like clouds mixed with heaven, violet purple, cherry pink, blood red, and blinding white. In a circle the forest gathered and sang your praises as loudly and harmoniously as possible. Flowers that normally closed during the night bloomed in full to observe the nocturnal festivities. Brooks babbled, chattered, screamed!

There was no brook that could talk the way I could.

In the old days, you found my love for conversation not the least bit offensive and cherished our talks, which made the other nymphs amusingly jealous. You were right when you joked that I could talk about anything for hours on end, as long as I had final say. I remember the way your eyes would crinkle with laughter as you recognized my desire for the last word.

~~~~~

I approach an empty cave and walk in to explore further. My senses are being devoured by the sight of darkness, the profound silence, the feeling of dampness, the scent of stagnant air, and the taste of ore. I've decided: this is where I will be staying from now on. I feel suffocated by loneliness.

I imagine this cavern looks the way the inside of Hera's heart must; hollow, dim, and menacing. To experience Hera's jealous wrath is as desirable as a nighttime encounter with the Minotaur, Terror of the Labyrinth, half-bull, half-man, and bloodthirsty.

~~~~~

If I had listened more and talked less I may have heard and learned from the tragic story of Io, Zeus's beautiful mistress with creamy milk skin and hair as black as obsidian. Hera was out for blood when she heard of Io, and would not rest until the poor maiden was suffering. Zeus changed Io into a heifer to hide her, but this was not enough to deter his wicked wife. Hera sent a horsefly to torment Io, biting and irritating the poor creature until she fled to Egypt. This is one account that proves that this gorgeous but jealous goddess, once enraged, derives pleasure by inflicting aggravating and unbearable penalties, which in the end are worse than death.

The marriage goddess found no humor in me the day she sought her husband among the nymphs. Zeus has the tendency to stray away from his spouse, and on that particular day his wandering eye fell upon one of my companions.

Hamadria, a nymph of the oak, was amusing him that day. I had no particular tie to Hamadria, no reason to risk my life for her, except that I knew she would do the same for me. It was not out of a loving friendship that I acted, but obedience to an unwritten law binding my kind to protect each other. We knew that we were food for the gods, even the ones with proud wives. It is a strange relationship we nymphs had, but it is one that has kept us alive for centuries.

Hamandria was pretty, I suppose, but not beautiful like Artemis. Artemis stood tall and took pride in her swift intellect and archery abilities, standing tall with a strong build and fearing nothing. Hamandria, on the other hand, was a wiry spindle of a nymph with dark rings around her eyes and a head of platinum blonde hair. She had a fragile body, which she displayed brazenly in a tight toga with a high hemline. She drank much, which became the cause of her constantly red-tinged eyes. Though always laughing, especially in the presence of men, I couldn't help but feel that she was empty inside.

Zeus didn't see the Hamandria I saw and sought her out many times. Hera may have turned a blind eye on this activity once, perhaps even twice, but after a while Zeus's frequent rendezvous with Hamandria turned Hera into a vindictive huntress, searching for a victim to blight.

~~~~~

Unaware of Hera's history of violence toward Zeus's countless mistresses, I made it my job to delay her search, thinking myself comical to supply no straight answer to her interrogations. When she demanded the location of her wayward mate, I simply repeated her demand. My reply was her query; a game the goddess did not enjoy playing.

She also took note of my need to finish any debate, and because I had become the subject of her frustrations, my punishment was grim; my power of speech was removed, except, ironically, for the capacity to have the last word. I was rendered incapable of free speech, cursed to reiterate what had already been said.

This burden made living unbearable, so I have retreated into the empty cliffs and hills. My desolation has made me no longer care if my body turns to rot and my bones fade away.

~~~~~

I take in the oily red clay soil and bland rock formations. This view is so monotonous, the sheer depletion of green life may prove fatal for me. I scan the scenery to occupy my negative thoughts until an onyx beetle catches my eye; its miniscule limbs squirm to give it motion. I follow it with my eyes with the same intensity with which I once observed a young man, a skilled hunter. The thought of him still grips tightly at my heart, and pulls down on it so heavily I'm afraid it might burst.

~~~~~

I would have paid any price to be able to converse with him, to win him with my knowledge of sport, to seduce him with my charming word games. Alas, this was not possible, so I followed him and his hunting party instead. Not only did Artemis show me how to spot prey, but the silent pursuit of quarry as well, so he did not sense my presence until I allowed him to.

I could not help but pine for him, despite his cruelty and arrogance. He was the son of a delicate nymph and Cephisus, the god of rivers. Narcissus was the most beautiful creature my eyes have ever seen. His hair, wisps of curled gold, was never a strand out of place. Eyes the hue of shallow water, as sharp as a jagged icicle, fell upon me with disgust, while his angelic lips parted into a sneer.

I know not what it was about me that repulsed him. I am told I am quite fair, a tree nymph with limbs like branches and hair the color of spring shoots. Whether it was my orchid eyes or crimson blossom of a mouth that turned Narcissus away, it matters little now. Whatever it was, Narcissus spared not my feelings in his rejection.

I approached him with open arms and wide eyes, only to be mercilessly spurned. "Hands off!" he boomed in protest, his voice more ardent than the lyre of Orpheus. At any given moment I would follow Narcissus to the end of the world, just like the trees that uprooted themselves to hear the minstrel bequeathed by Apollo.

The object of my affection was less than flattered by my attentions. His rejection sliced through me like icy daggers and fiery needles, "I should rather die than let *you* have me!" Tears welled up in my eyes as I pleaded, "Have me," but I was not enough for this demigod. Humiliated, forlorn, I ran away with my head between my hands, wishing for instant death. I have not been the same since.

~~~~~

What's this? My new hermitage has a spring. Water slowly trickles into a pool, which I glance into so I might inspect my wilted features. My hair is dull and unkempt, my eyes are vacant and have lost their sparkle. An unhealthy white has encased my once bark-olive skin, that had been a testament to the beautiful effects of the sun.

~~~~~

Though I can no longer gossip, the fate of Narcissus eventually reached my ears and his heartbreaking tale was recounted against my will by my own shocked lips.

There was a forbidden well feared by all, which Narcissus discovered during his travels. The goddess of vengeance placed a curse (aimed specifically at my love) upon it so that when he looked into it he fell in love with himself. His hand would reach out to touch the astounding reflection, but instead of embracing his heart's desire, the ripples created by his flawless fingers destroyed the image. He felt the pain of wanting what is impossible to have, as I did. Woe struck Narcissus, and obsession took hold of him. Never again did he move from the spot where he knelt in front of the well. He wasted away as he admired himself, ignoring his needs for life and abandoning all logic.

Eventually, his feet literally took to root as his masculinely defined calves morphed into a small, thin stem. Muscular arms flattened and finned, changed into leaves as his face transformed into the corona of a flower. Sunbeam hair became daffodil petals. His heart, already hardened with conceit, sank to the bottom of his being and formed a knobby bulb deep in the ground. Narcissus was turned into another object, equally beautiful and unobtainable as his original form. This newly born perfect being still remains undisturbed, renowned for his beauty. Many onlookers wish to pluck the flower and take it home to gawk at, but to sever it would mean an end to its existence. Instead, Narcissus is preserved, feared, and lamented.

~~~~~

I stare up at the cave's ceiling and shudder with fear of the dark. Darkness has never scared me before, but this is because I have always slept outside. Moonbeams, the gentle silver arrows of Artemis, brought sleep and comfort to me as I lay outstretched on moss or grass. But moonbeams console me no longer; they only make me feel far away from friends.

I lie to myself, saying I can see the stars and smell the lilies that only open after sunset. I wonder if the stars can see me through the roof of the cave, Callisto, are you there? I remember you now, Callisto, raped by Zeus and then hunted down by Hera. You bore Zeus a son, and Hera jealously transformed you into a bear. As a bear, you were a friend to Artemis, until Hera instructed Artemis to kill you. We would have been sisters, alike in misfortune and victim of Hera's temper, except that you were spared, Callisto. Zeus made you into a constellation, safe in the sky, detached from the suffering on earth. I am not so lucky.

~~~~~

My eyelids are steadily growing heavier, I feel as though I am sinking deep into the ground. Sliding, sliding, sliding, further down until I cannot feel a thing, I can't feel my arms or legs, and my head has finally stopped pounding.

My body gives an involuntary twitch: Hera looms over me, gazing down with a haughty sneer. Her long, ostentatious robes are sanguine and gold, magically sweeping around her snowy

206

white ankles in the cave's still air. No sandals cover her feet; she does not need them, her feet do not touch the ground. Hera hovers soundly while her close eyes and tight cheekbones remain icy and unchanging.

A light without source falls upon her head, the blonde locks glisten as specks of light trickle down her blood red tunic.

I may be sick with anticipation. Why is the goddess here, and how did she find me? What does she want from me? Is her purpose to remove my curse or to issue another detrimental decree?

I understand now why she wears that sinister grin. Hera has no intention of speaking to me. This is torture for two reasons, and she knows it; the first is my burning curiosity, which will writhe my insides until I understand why she is here. The second aspect of torture in the odd nocturnal visit is the silence. Billions of words are buzzing in my skull, searching in vain for a means of escape. They will have no outlet unless I am given a sound to copy, until then I am in unnerving agony.

Hera will not initiate dialogue—I cannot—what a brilliantly evil limbo.

My posture is stone-like, but pandemonium reigns in my mind. Please, gods, give me voice! Laughter-loving Aphrodite, born of the sea foam, you can beguile Zeus and sway anyone with your beauty, please convince Hera to restore my voice! Father Zeus, you are the god of gods, surely you can counter the spell of your wife! It was to protect you, oh Lord of the Sky and Cloud Gatherer, that I am in this situation in the first place! Ares, you are the god of action and determination, I beg you, bestow on me some ferocity and mobility, and I will honor you and your horses, Flame and Terror! Hades, your name is feared among all mortals, yet I evoke it now; deliver me from this excruciating state for only moments, just long enough to stand up to Hera, and I will commit my soul to your underground kingdom. I'd go to Hades for an instant of liberation— for that matter, make any trade!

I wait in mock patience for supernatural assistance. None comes. I attune my eyes to search for Hermes, messenger god, with winged heels and a herald's staff, but moments later I still stand before Hera alone.

It is time to take matters into my own hands. I try to jump, to grab, try to kick and punch, to claw and spit and scream. I try to move from the place I've been standing for what seems an eternity, but my body won't budge. I am frozen in place, attached to the floor somehow. I have no control over any appendages and cannot even manage facial expression.

The chaos at present is no longer in my head, but all around me. I am causing none of the destruction; I am victim to a mounting number of calamites. A slithering python is slowly coiling itself around my neck, while the Furies, gnarling dog-headed punishment goddesses, are sharply nibbling my toes. Screeching monkey-like cercopses, tiny terrors from the Underworld, go through my pockets and roughly rustle my hair and out of the corner of my eye I see an awful hag approaching with her own gouged eyes resting in the hand that plucked them—her own. It is the demon Lamia, coming nearer by the second. A great noise sounds, almost knocking me to the ground, a sound of rushing winds and thunder. I can smell fire, smoke, and smoldering skin. The immediate back draft has stolen my breath. Cacus, the fire-breathing giant, is here, and through his own respiration is suffocating me. I can't move, breathe, or cry for help; the only thing I can do is listen for the next terror to arrive and watch my predators march in.

My eyes bolt open— was it only a dream?

No trace remains of the parade of terrors that had just a moment ago been assaulting me.

I clutch my chest and pant heavily. I look around the cave, unwilling to believe that I imagined all the terrors that attacked me. Furies, cercopsyes, demons; they're all in here somewhere. I pace around this dark dungeon, expecting to be ambushed at any second. I know I will not sleep again tonight.

~~~~~

The sun must be up outside, dawn surely has passed. I hear faint human voices outside of these walls of stone, I groan as I realize children are approaching.

"Hello!" a small girl cries. "Hello" I cry back in her meek,

208

adolescent voice. "This is it, then" says a boy in transition from childhood to manhood. "Is it, then?" I retort, using his callow voice against him, making sure to copy the crack and squeak he is ashamed of. "Get her!" calls another voice, male, older than the first two. "Get *her*!" I warn, my voice so loud that walls begin to shake, causing the puny girl to scream in fear. The ground is quaking as stalactites collide with the rough, stark surface of the dirt.

As the dust settles, I see that heavy rocks have piled up into an intimidating heap, barricading the cave. The boulders are so massive that I could never hope to move even one, let alone enough to make a hole for my escape. I hear the little ones scampering safely out in the open. Now I am encased in this pit of misery.

This is the work of Pan. I should have known during the first instant that the hybrid god appeared to me that I would feel his wrath someday.

~~~~

It was a clear day when he entered my life. If it had not been for my heartbreaking encounter with Narcissus a few days prior, I would have thanked the gods for a beautiful sunny afternoon; instead I saw a bleak gap hanging above me instead of the sky.

Emerging from a flowering bush with droopy eyes and a drunken swagger came the goat man in a particularly demanding mood. I had never encountered Pan before, but had been warned to stay as far away as possible. Forgetting or disregarding any advice that I had previously received due to my despair, I did not run away. Nor did I initiate conversation with the satyr; I simply stood in place looking unhappy.

His hideously hairy legs wobbled, his goat horns looked crooked on his chubby human head. I could smell the signature scent of Dionysus, strong red wine, and it smothered me. "Why does such a fair nymph grieve when there is merriment to be made?" "Merriment to be made?" I questioned this query, hoping he would think me simple and walk on, but many more questions followed. With each inquiry I failed to adequately answer, Pan's mood worsened.

"Come now, speak to me your own words! Am I not worthy of a free thought? Do you find Pan so repulsive?"

209

"So repulsive," I replied, deepening the inebriated red on his face.

"I am losing my patience, young one! You are a nymph, it is your job to entertain me!" My eyebrows lifted as I cocked my head to the side and pointed my fingers, as he did, and in Pan's degrading voice commanded, "It is your job to entertain me!"

He took a long, deep breath, leaned back, and tried calmly to ask rhetorically, "Is there a brain in your head, or empty space?" "Empty space" said I, with a nonchalant hint of rebellion. Talking back to Pan was the only thing I had to take my mind off Narcissus, and I intended to exploit it further.

"This is your last chance," threatened Pan, "before you make Pan *very angry*!" I scoffed and rolled my eyes "Very angry?" Little did I know, my fleeting good mood was about to end.

The anxious unease that had been creeping up my spine attacked full force. Logic had vanished from my system. I felt like running and screaming and crying hysterically. These fears were so intense that they froze me in place, left me shaking slightly and panting quickly. I panicked.

He swore at me, he cursed my ancestors and my offspring. Hera's curse forced me, though I do not regret it now, to say the same oaths, damning his family to the vulgar fate he'd committed mine. In his fury, his pipe of reeds swung at his waist, knocking up against me and giving him an idea for the means of his revenge on me. He picked up the fragile instrument and blew into it: a long sharp note that was purposely off key. An impish smile spread itself over his face as he laughed and played more bad scales. He giggled and jumped, almost losing balance on those awkward hooves of his.

Pan ran off to find shepherds to torture with his bad music. Flat notes, long notes, sour notes—all came forth from this flute. Oh, he knew his music was anything but fair, and blamed "a vocal mimic of a nymph" for his troubles. This began a hunting party for the Mimic Nymph, and I was now a detestable legend and notorious cause for a tone-deaf god. Daily I was persecuted by disgruntled humans and their children.

The treatment of Pan and the hatred of the shepherds was my

breaking point. I retreated to the winding hills, where I linger now.

~~~~~

I hear the little ones outside, scrambling about, looking for one another, and fueling their childish fears with legends and tall tales the elders in their village had once told them. A boy with sheer panic in his voice recounts, "Grandfather warned me of a cave-dwelling monster that would disguise itself to look like a rock until you got too close—that's when it pounced on you and ate your insides!" The second boy, who initially tried to stay calm, is slowly losing his nerve, and adds, "My mother warned me of that as well! But she said the monster didn't just eat your flesh, the demon steals your spirit!" From what I hear, they seem to think I caused the rockslide with black magic, which means I plan to eat and rob each one of them in the most painful way possible. They talk about running away, but the boys have yet to convince the child younger than they are to come with them. The third human, the little girl. will not flee with them. I hear fast footsteps and know that the two boys have taken off; the girl remains.

Through a gap in the wall I see her move closer and closer, until only the soft, freckled cheek and supple locks of youth are visible. "I'm sorry you're trapped," she whispers to me, baby pink lips sympathetically supplying the words. "Trapped," I reply with a sigh. "Maybe Pan will stop bothering the shepherds when he hears the Mimic Nymph is no more." "The Mimic Nymph is no more," my sad words are her cue to depart, but she leaves a gift. A single fragile flower pokes through a crack: a subtle, white daisy.

~~~~~

Cracks in the newly formed wall allow scattered beams of light to slowly stream across the cave. I glide over to the barrier and stick my hand under a fragment of sun, hoping to illuminate some part of me.

Have my eyes resorted to trickery, or does my pigmentation match exactly to the dirt underneath me? Whatever the case, I cannot see my hand, which is only inches away from my face.

Anxious, I lightly move toward the pool of spring water I found earlier to look at my reflection. I want to feel the cool water caress my fingertips, but when I extend my hand and submerge it, I barely create a ripple.

With a light head I lean over the water's edge—my image does not stare back. I search the pool for any trace of my features, the glimmer of my eye, a strand of hair. Nothing.

Now that I think about it, I do feel more buoyant, less material. In fact, I feel like a vacuum, with a mouth devouring all life and energy, instead of a solid object that has a place in the world. Emptiness. I am emptiness. Absolutely nothing lives inside me, no light, no spirit, no love. I feel nothing, not longing for Narcissus, not contempt for Pan, not even pity for the race of Nymphs.

I now accept that this is the end of my life, the last time words, though they are trapped in my thoughts and unable to be voiced, will be formed of me. I am nothing of myself without a full will or a voice, simply a Mimic Nymph with no word but the last. I am dying, my corpse will fade into obscurity. I am mortal, my demise swiftly drawing nearer. I am broken, my cursed voice is the only strength I still posses. I am . . . *Echo*.

Hera has stolen my will, solitude has claimed my visibility, but perhaps my voice will remain. This is the only hope of a defeated Mimic Nymph: Let Echo always have the last word.

Don't Be a Bobble-Head, and Other Bits of Guidance
by Timons Esaias

I've been critiquing the manuscripts of both published authors and beginning writers for a couple of decades now, and eventually I realized that I was seeing a specific set of problems repeatedly, and that I was writing the same admonishments over and over. New writers, from inexperience, and established writers, from inattention during the first drafts, are prone to fall into various patterns and into a number of traps. There are many books on writing that wisely teach us to avoid adverbs, eschew excessive numbers of diminishing qualifiers and passive constructions, and drive specially-designed oaken stakes through the heart of the speech tags and Tom Swifties that crop up like weeds if not attended to. Those weaknesses are well-known and one simply points them out by name and they are soon gone. But I became aware of a secondary set of problems, less clearly defined, that also need attention. Eventually I wrote these down in one document so I could cut-and-paste them into critiques as needed, and now I intend to share that list with you.

What follows, then, is a collection of canned lecturelets on certain things that both new and used writers often need to scrub out of their prose.

But first, A Helpful Tactic:

A HELPFUL TACTIC

When working on your first couple of novels, I strongly suggest picking a Template Novel to use as a reality check. It is best if the novel chosen fits the following criteria:

1. A writer you wish to emulate
2. In the POV you intend to use
3. In the style you hope to acquire
4. With the same attitude toward the main character as you intend for your novel.

It might be necessary to select two Template Novels in order to cover this whole list, and if so, choose two.

Once you have your template novel(s) in hand you can use it/ them as a reference on how things should be done. Does your first reader complain about your adverbs? Don't go to a how-to book and see what "they" say about adverbs. Instead, open your Template Novel to a random page and see how your author uses them. Does someone insist that your paragraphs are flabby, with not much happening?? Look in your template, and compare what that author gets done in a paragraph to what you're doing. Does your teacher complain endlessly (and rather pettily) that you have a neurotic obsession with doors??? Open your template and see how many doors are mentioned in a similar scene.

You will find looking at the "real thing" far more useful than looking at how-to books, when it comes to the real nitty-gritty of composition. Read the how-tos for theory, but use templates for practice.

Now back to the traps and snares to avoid:

SOME & ALL ITS EVIL COGNATES

The word *some*, and its cousins *somewhere*, *sometime*, *something*, *someone*, etc., are a threat to vigor and clarity of writing. They are vague. They can distance the reader from the text, because he/she/it doesn't know what to see. I try to make a habit of global searching the string "some" after my first draft of a piece, and try and remove as many instances of it as I can. A perfectly valid, but dangerous word.

PRONOUNS

Many how-to-write texts warn the beginner against larding up the text with unnecessary adverbs, which is sound advice. The pronoun, however, is an equally dangerous snare for the unpracticed, and often for the skilled, so keep your eye on them.

The first problem with pronouns is that we forget to make them agree with the closest previous possible noun or name. This can lead to misinterpretation.

The second problem is using the same pronoun for different things in the same sentence or paragraph. I've seen instances of five characters in one paragraph all being *he*. There are times when the writing can make this perfectly clear, but it [there's a not-very-precise pronoun right there] often destroys readability.

The third problem is just using too many of the damn things close together. Pronouns are already one level of abstraction from the thing being described, and when you fill a sentence with them the readers start losing their grip on the subject. Make sure your poor reader gets a bone from time to time.

DOORS

Many new writers, for reasons that remain a mystery to me, become obsessed with mentioning the opening and closing and passing through of every door in their novel. Doors are often significant, and should be mentioned, but most doors are boring. This is a good thing to check out in your Template Novel, and see how often your ideal writer does it.

TURNING

A favorite verb of beginning writers is *to turn* in all its many forms. The writer is obsessed with letting the reader know which way the character is pointed. This is a form of TV Writing, and almost always requires the reader to pull out to the middle distance, which isn't where you really want them. Turning, alas, is not particularly interesting. It can be dramatic and important in the right circumstances, but generally isn't. Give yourself a Turning Budget for your entire novel, 10 turns, say, or perhaps a dozen. Stick to it.

ANACHRONISMS

This has to do with a technique for period verisimilitude. Basically, if you are writing a story set in the Roman Empire you try not to have objects that wouldn't have existed in that time, but you also try not to use **language** that isn't appropriate. You would not, for instance, use the expression "like a shot off a shovel" because that expression comes from shoveling boiler coal, and they didn't use coal in the Roman Empire. In the case of fantasy or other imagined worlds, it would help keep the reader in your world if they don't come across something that seems jarringly modern, or otherwise inappropriate. A useful tool is the Oxford English Dictionary which gives the first use of words in given meanings in English.

I'll give a particular example that often comes up. Fantasy writers and Historical Romance writers are forever having their soldiers "stand at attention" in worlds ranging from ancient times to the Middle Ages, or their imagined equivalent. But this word, and the concept that goes with it, actually entered the language around 1820. Many readers will find a knight in armor standing at attention to be irritating, so one needs to think about using a different, more appropriate, phrase.

This is not an absolute thing, of course. It's a technique.

POINT OF VIEW

This is a controversial subject. It's up to you if you want to follow my advice completely, because there are writers and editors who just don't care. However, I will strongly argue that the best writers tend not to make this "error." It's the lower tier of writers who do it mostly, and the schlockier publishers.

The essential point is that in first person narrations, and equally in third person personal narrations you should not describe things the POV character could not see. No descriptions of what is around the corner. No descriptions of what's happening behind the wall where the character can't see it. No descriptions of what is happening inside somebody else's mind, unless the POV is engaged in brain surgery. And equally, **no descriptions of what is happening on the POV's face** unless they are: 1. Looking in a mirror, or 2. Deliberately smiling when they would naturally snarl, or some such Highly Self-Conscious Facial Usage.

This kind of thing is one of the elements of what is called Television Writing: namely errors of prose style that come from picturing your story as a television show viewed from the sofa, rather than events viewed through the eyes of the character who is actually seeing the story you are telling in your prose. The thing to remember is that *the camera is behind your POV character's eyes*. If you have them smile, oops, the camera had pulled out for a wide shot. But wide shots are third person omniscient story-telling, and that is not what the reader generally expects.

Having the POV sigh is a similar thing, since sighs are generally unconscious. They are certainly not forefront actions.

I strongly urge you to keep the camera where it belongs. [Note that there are perfectly valid alternate POVs to use, include the in-and-out, and head-hopping techniques, where the changes of camera location (as it were) are clearly signaled. In those POVs, apply the advice above to in-head paragraphs only.]

POSITION IN A SPACE

Another way that visualizing the story from the middle distance creeps into the prose, unhelpfully, is the compulsion to mention the relative position and initial location of every character in a room or other given area. *Compulsion* is the key word here. It is frequently important to set the stage of a scene, putting the commissar behind the desk, the prisoner in uncomfortable straight-backed steel chair, and two reluctant witnesses on a bench against the far wall. But it isn't required in many scenes, and a surprisingly high number of character movements through a room can be left unmentioned. There is no clearly stated rule to learn here, but this is an instance where referring to your Template Novel is in order. How often does Batya Gur, or Stephen King, or Iain Banks describe the precise location of every character? Check a few scenes, and think about what you find there.

VARIOUS BODY TWITCHES

Another form of Television Writing, (or also just lack of experience with Knowing What To Tell) is the myriads of minor bodily functions and actions that are a notable part of stage and screen acting, but are considerably less wonderful in prose fiction. You will learn over time that Fiction Is Not A Transcription Of A TV Program's Visual Elements Onto Paper.

1. NODS

Many new-writers' characters are, alas, afflicted with bobble-headism. They nod a lot. Less often, but frequently, they shake their heads. This is not good. (It's also one of the most common reflexive things that I catch for my professional colleagues, which is why I have a name for it.)

Nods are a perfectly valid element of body language, but they present a number of problems. They are vague, because it is what the nod means to the viewer that is significant, not the nod itself. Nods do not mean the same thing in other cultures as they do in the United States in our time (they are an affirmative gesture to less than half the peoples of the world - except when they see them in Western films, where they know what they signify). That makes them far less universal than many American writers assume. Nods get repetitive, and it doesn't take many to clog all the reader's nod receptors, after which they cease to have meaning and become an irritant. Nods are dull, and become a bad habit in little time. Nods are generally not story-telling.

[Just a momentary aside: Nods are part of the general Body

220

Language Problem. One tends to think that describing a character's body language is showing, as opposed to telling, and a good thing. But actually the reader will begin to feel that the character is suffering an obsessive-compulsive disorder, because they have experienced writing that doesn't dwell on each little pose, twitch, nod, glance, clench, grimace, sigh, eye widening, eye narrowing, blink, flutter, flex, etc., etc., etc.. If you are describing what is important about what is happening, the reader will probably already know what the twitches will be, and being told is both dull and redundant. You need to only mention the Very Significant instances of body language, or the Very Surprising ones. One of the ways the reader has of knowing they are Very Significant or Very Surprising is that you bother to mention it. If you mention them all, well, then the reader has no basis for comparison, and the signal-to-noise ratio goes decidedly south.]

Now in your world you may want to have some sort of formal gesture, that indicates relationship. The equivalent of bowing in Japan and China, or in old Europe, say. That, unlike commonplace nodding, can be very useful for conveying both information and the alienness of the setting. (In *Shogun*, for instance, formal gesture becomes almost an independent character.) If you want to create some specific, named, formal social gestures, that could be wonderful.

Nods, however, should be rare, unless they are the personal tic of a special character. Five or six to a book. No more.

2. GLANCES
These, too, are Television Writing, and vague and compulsive. They often become inaccurate, as well: one mentions that the character merely *glanced* over yon, and then one spends two paragraphs describing far too much for the glance to have taken in.

3. POINTING THE EYES OF THE CHARACTERS
A very common beginner's trait. Again, often a form of Television Writing. Also Not Knowing What To Tell. The basic thing is that readers will know where the character is looking

because of what the character sees. They generally don't need to be told. Rarely, also, is it necessary to mention where the other characters are looking, unless it's an important plot point or terribly interesting. If something important is happening (and it should be, elsewise why are you writing about it?), then the characters will be looking at it. The reader will know this.

So, the rule is: Avoid Compulsively Aiming Your Characters' Eyes.

"Glancing", aforementioned, is a version of this.

4. SIGHING

Sighing is rarely very important, and should be used sparingly. It is a known fact that the population with the most numerous sigh receptors became novel-reading spinsters during the Victorian era. They did not reproduce, and the trait has passed out of existence.

5. SALIVATION

Watering mouths, even in prisoners, are not the stuff of high drama. They remind many readers of Pavlov's dogs (a picture of which I happen to have on the hall wall), and this is not the kind of association you want for your protagonist. Except, of course, for those rare novelists who are using one of Pavlov's dogs as a protagonist.

6. EYEBROWS, EYE-NARROWING, AND THE EVER-POPULAR WIDE EYES

Over-emphasis on these minor changes about the eyes is common, and gives the reader the impression of Twitchy Characters. Yes, body language is significant, but no, describing all these instances of it is not a good idea. You do not want to have *Kirkus Reviews* describe your opus as "a Suspense Thriller about changes of expression in the characters' eyes and peri-ocular musculature."

Also, descriptions of these minor movements suggest that your POV character is staring only at the eyes of the character having the eye movement. In the real world we often are most especially NOT looking at the eyes of the people around us. Only in the soap opera universe is eye-contact maintained with the fierceness that many novelists would require to account for all the eye-business they try to employ.

And finally, with the little eye movements as in all body language, avoid the embarrassing mistake of describing them when the scene (and therefore your characters) are In The Dark!!!! Or in fog, or when mentioning that your POV character's eyes are closed.

7. GRIMACE

I am fighting a personal war against this word, and am in the process of writing "Esaias's First Oration against Grimace" and "Esaias's Second Oration against Grimace." This is a really lazy word that has little precise meaning. *X grimaced*, is the equivalent of writing *The character had a facial expression*, and not much more, though there is a suggestion that it expresses a negative emotion or experience. It also tends to come up in a POV violation. I generally find that it gets used because the writer couldn't think of a way to be precise.

I strongly suggest that you just never, ever use this word, except when describing gargoyles.

If you need a clinching argument as to why, well, I think I need say no more than this: it is French.

8. OTHER CLICHÉD FACIAL EXPRESSIONS, & INTESTINAL DISCOMFORTS

Does your character clench his jaws and teeth in a world with primitive dentistry? Are his or her lips all a-quiver? Are you writing a smile-a-minute novel?? Then you, my friend, have become a victim of the General Body Language Problem, centered on the face.

This is an easy problem to develop for two reasons. First, body language is important in our lives, and it does much to reveal context. Second, it is one of the major methods actors use in television and movies to reveal what is happening. They do this, because they are NOT in a novel where other methods work better. [Again this brings up the mantra that, even though you may be writing the novel from a movie you are watching in your head, A Novel Is NOT A Movie

Transcribed To The Page. *Prose is not film.*]

Don't fall into the trap of reducing the rich powers of prose to the limited palette of TV. That's one thing. The other is that while facial expressions are the very life of TV, they are danged repetitive on the page, especially when they are used over and over and over and over. Significant facial expressions only, please.

You may also be clenching the stomachs and tightening the guts of all concerned, or otherwise trying to wring drama from intestine fluctuations. Please. Remember that bowel movements are an obsession of the very young and the very old, neither of which groups are going to be major elements of your readership.

A BASIC TEST

Here's a field test of the stuff I'm complaining about above: Ask yourself this question: "If I sat all day in a coffee shop and listened to people tell stories to each other, how often do I really think they would mention nods (especially their own), or narrowed eyes, or widened eyes, or raised eyebrows, or leaning back and forth, or glances or sighs or opening and closing doors??" The answer will be Not Very Many, If Any. The reason is because People Don't Find Them Important Enough To Tell In A Story. And there's a lesson in that.

AND FINALLY, A WORD ON FIGHT SCENES

Basic rule: try it at home. Carefully, of course.

The most common mistake in writing a fight scene is inattention to the limitations of reality. No, your character will not see the laser beam coming and dodge it, because when she sees it, by definition, it's already there. No, your bad guy, lying flat on his back, will not kick your character in the chin, unless he has amazingly long legs or your character has stopped to inspect his boots. No your hero's switchblade will not effectively parry the sweeping battle-ax of the time-traveling Viking berserker; it just ain't gonna happen. Block out the motions, invite your friends for pizza and re-enactment, and see if the events are physically possible. You don't want to be laughed at if something amazingly silly gets into print.

CONCLUSION

And that's it. My list of Stuff To Watch Out For. Use liberally, but with discretion. Ignore as needed. Enter 12-step program if necessary.

Then go knock 'em dead.

How to Win Fantasy Fiction Contests
by W. H. Horner

Well, the title above is a bit misleading. I'm not going to show you how to tailor your story to win contests—not even mine—but I am going to talk a little bit about some of my likes and dislikes as an editor of fantastical fiction. If you read this and take it to heart, you may have better luck getting your work published, but I'm not promising anything, and I'm not offering you your money back.

First off, use proper manuscript format (*Double-spaced*; 1-inch margins all around; single-sided; non-proportional font (best is Courier 12pt); paragraphs indented; left-justified, ragged right; plain white paper; author's name, address, phone and email in the upper left corner of the first page (single-spaced); approximate word count (rounded to hundreds) in upper right corner of first page; author's last name, story title, and page number in heading of all interior pages; widows-and-orphans controls turned off (if your word processor does that); and the title centered vertically and horizontally on the first page, with the first paragraph beginning three lines later (this all sounds more confusing than it really is). Section breaks within the manuscript should be marked by one or more hashes (#) centered. Italics indicated by underlining. Send *unfolded* in a 9"x12" envelope. Paperclip, if you like, but *never staple*. **Always include a self-addressed, stamped envelope for reply**.). Why? Because it makes life a whole lot easier on editors who have to do a lot of reading—and we get grumpy when things are hard to read. Whew. (Thanks for the description of proper format, Timons.)

Second—and this one goes hand-in-hand with number one—follow the contest (or publication submission) guidelines to the letter. Read all of the rules. Then follow them. This will help greatly in your quest for publication.

Third, have someone proofread your story. Too many manuscripts arrive on the desks of editors full of common and easy to spot mistakes that irritate and annoy us, and make the author look like a buffoon (even when they are really geniuses—I know that my proofreading buddies have spotted some real hum-dingers in my manuscripts!). Another writer or an editor is probably best, and it's often a good idea to pick someone that you are not highly emotionally invested in, because that dynamic may affect their ability to critique your work (not to mention your ability to accept their critique fairly).

Fourth, be original. We received too many stories that opened with birthing scenes in 2002 (not that none of those stories were good—some were really great—it just gets tiring to read the same thing). We also received a large amount of high fantasy or sword and sorcery type stuff (I blame it on the sudden surge of *Lord of the Rings* to the forefront of popular entertainment). Don't get me wrong. Those things have always been my favorites and I often write in those genres myself, but I'd like to have a little bit of variety in my anthologies, and I know that other publishers want variety too. So, listen up: if you have a story that is different—that takes me someplace unexpected, someplace that surprises me (like, say, Hoboken)—then you are more than likely to get your story included. I'm not saying to stop writing stories about elves and big guys with swords, and demons and dwarves, I'm just saying you'll have to do it really well to beat out a story that is about something "new."

And most importantly, tell a good story. Powerful human emotions are the heart of good stories, but don't force it—it's obvious when you're trying too hard. Pay attention to how the great stories of our world are structured. Notice how every bit of the tale must serve a purpose and keep you invested in it. Pay attention to pacing and emotional timing and how characters and events tug at your heart and soul. Now figure out how to place that on paper and you're golden.

So, what do we have here . . . use proper format, follow the rules, clear your manuscript of as many mistakes as you can, be original, and tell a good story. Each part is important. Don't assume that your beautiful prose will win enough points to outweigh bright pink paper (and especially a bad story), or that a good story will shine through poor writing (it might, but the editor may not have enough time to work with you on polishing your craft and so be forced to allow the story to go on by).

I hope this helps or inspires in some way. If not, at least I could get up on a couple of my soapboxes (Be kind to editors' eyes!!) and preach for a little bit. Best of luck with your writing, and I hope to get the chance to see some of your *Fantastical Visions* in the near future!

Rules for the current *FV Contest* have not been included in this book, due to the fact that by the time it is in print, the submission period will be nearly over. For current rules or news about the contest, please visit our website at www.fantasistent.com.

About the Contributors

Authors

Lisa Swanstrom {First Place Winner} earned her master's degree from the Professional Writing Program at the University of Southern California, where she was the recipient of the Associated Writing Program's Intro. Journals Award for creative nonfiction. Her work has appeared in the *Mid-American Review*, the *Northwest Florida Review*, and *Moxie Magazine*, among others.

Currently, she is a doctoral student at the University of California, Santa Barbara, where she studies science fiction, 20th century Latin American fiction, and the literature of the fantastic. Some of her favorite authors of fantasy and science fiction include Julio Cortázar, Adolfo Bioy Casares, Jorge Luis Borges, Gene Wolfe, Michael

Swanwick, Joan D. Vinge, Octavia Butler, Neal Stephenson, and William Gibson.

Among other things, Lisa enjoys hiking in the Santa Monica mountains and watching Hammer Horror films late at night with her husband Scott and their two cats, Jimmy and The Count. You can find out more about Lisa at www.lisaswanstrom.net.

Angeline Hawkes-Craig received her B.A. in Composite English Language Arts from East Texas State University in 1991. She is a member of the Horror Writer's Association and The Writer's League of Texas. Angeline's fantasy novel, *The Swan Road*, published by Scars Publications, was released in 2002. In December 2002, she was awarded the Editor's Choice award for her alternate history story, "Henry's Daughters", published in Scars Publications anthology, *The Elements*. Her story, "Long Live the Queen", will appear in Double Dragon Publishing's anthology, *Femmes de La Brume: A Collection of Speculative Fiction*, to be released in e-book in April 2003 and paperback in August 2003. Angeline is currently at work on two novels and is in negotiations for a collection of short fiction to possibly be released at the end of 2003. Visit her website at http://home.earthlink.net/~robertccraig/AngieHomePage/ and at www.authorsden.com.

Pamela Hearon Hodges, a Kentucky native, resides in southern Illinois with her husband Dick and two cats. She has three grown children. A twenty-year veteran of teaching, she holds a Master's Degree in Education from Murray State University. She currently teaches 8th grade language arts, and has taught high school English and psychology, and has worked as a guidance counselor and college admissions director.

Since childhood, Pamela's passions have included amateur astronomy and Arthurian legend. Writing science fiction and fantasy gives her an outlet for both. "The Starred Sapphire" is her first published work. A member of The Heartland Writers Guild, she has recently completed her first novel, *The Timestone Key*, an Arthurian fantasy.

More earthly pursuits include avid interests in gardening and travel. She is an admitted Francophile whose favorite vacations include wandering the lavender fields and vineyards of Provence.

Bryan R. Durkin grew up in Portland, Oregon, where he lived for the first twelve years of his life. He began writing at the age of ten, but did not actively pursue a writing career until five years later. When he was twelve, he and his family moved to South America, where they lived for nearly four years. The experiences he obtained there only fueled his passion for writing, and he began to give breath to a dream that he has dedicated his life and most of his energy to. Inspired by such greats as J. R. R. Tolkien and C. S. Lewis, Bryan found his niche in the medieval fantasy genre, and hopes to one day become a successful novelist in this area of fiction. He spends much of his free time in front of his computer, shaping and sculpting words and fragments of sentences into what he hoped will become a world that readers around the globe will be able to enjoy. When he's not writing, Bryan attends college classes and spends a great deal of time reading books by his favorite authors. He also enjoys a variety of real-time strategy games. He now makes his home in Lakeview, Oregon.

Michael Penncavage currently lives in New Jersey with his wife and crazy cat. He is an Associate Editor for *Space and Time Magazine* as well as the editor for the upcoming anthology *Tales From a Darker State*. Fiction of his can be found in approximately 40 magazines and anthologies from 3 different countries such as *Alfred Hitchcock Mystery Magazine* in the US, *Here and Now* in England, and *Crime Factory* in Australia. He is the Treasurer of The Garden State Horror Writers as well as a member of The Horror Writers of America.

Michail Velichansky: he loves a girl named Rachel; he hadn't met her when he first wrote this story. He reads Neil Gaiman, Harlan

Ellison, Terry Pratchett, and many others. His story was probably inspired by Michael Swanwick. Don't you think the variants of the name 'Mike' are far too common? If all were like god, it'd be a classic pantheon; it's probably for the best they aren't.

He thinks that you should not be concerned with who he is, for he is silly, bumbling, and often nervous. He loves to tell bad jokes. He loves to laugh. His writing does not reflect this, and he finds that odd.

He loves to write, and needs to write (except when he hates it, and then only the need remains). He is rather lazy and writes a lot and writes obsessively; his writing is the exception to much of who he is. So it's rather funny, really, in a quiet sort of way.

To a great friend who liked this story when Michail felt broken and alone; to Nancy Jane Moore; to the wondrous-lovely people he's met since the story was written; to friends and somewhat-friends who've made it quietly clear they don't think he will make it, and might be wrong; and again to Rachel—dedication.

Michail Velichansky: he has a long name.

Christine E. Ricketts currently resides in Buffalo, NY and is working on a full-length novel set in the world of "Let Sleeping Dragons Lies," involving her character Jathen Longblade. This is Christine's second publication, and a second glimpse into a gradually expanding world. Read *Fantastical Visions: Short Fantasy Fiction*, for her story, "Jathen Longblade."

Kimberly Eldredge {Second Place Winner} is an Arizona native who loves writing, the color yellow, and hates dust. When not writing, she drinks Earl Grey tea with cream and sugar and watches the neighborhood roadrunner chase the cat. She enjoys traveling to exotic places (St. Petersburg, Russia), speaking Spanish (she's an interpreter in a tax office), and collecting dragons.

Candice L. Tucker was born in Honolulu, Hawaii, and began her passion for writing when she was in second grade. Since then, in Heidelberg, Germany, where she was raised, this young American's passion became on uncontrollable hobby which won her acceptance in the Young Author's Conference for three years.

Determined to make her world hear in any way, Candice depends upon short stories, music lyrics, poems, and the occasional attempt at books to thrust her mind into society's field of vision. A desire for recognition and a strong will to make a difference doing what she loves best is what pushes her to endeavor for success. Inspirations came and went, from R. L. Stine when she was younger, to Stephen King, Marilyn Manson, and Ann Rice.

Now, in her senior year of dreaded high school and still practicing a tasteful use of the English language, Candice lives in a world of her own. In this world, she is heard and known through multiple art forms, under an umbrella of prosperity, and dwelling in the highest tower of contentment. No matter who she must fight with, for, or against, or how hard she must work for it, she will be there one day.

Laura Kay Eppin {Third Place Winner} is 17 years old and a senior in Cardinal McCarrick High School in South Amboy, NJ. She lives in South River, NJ with her inspirational mother, Monica, brutally honest father, Raymond, younger brothers George, who is musically gifted, and Andrew, known for being all-around brilliant, as well as her beautiful little sister Rachel.

Laura plans to be a journalist when she grows up, but hopes to forever be able to write short stories. She also hoped to one day develop a fantastical vision as bright and original as that of her good friend, Garrett Vitanza. She has never won a contest before, and previously considered herself unlucky.

Some of Laura's other aspirations include a high school diploma, a college degree, and to overcome her own tendency to have the last word—Echo isn't the only one that gets in trouble for it, that's for sure.

Illustrators

Lee Seed {First Place Winner} has become one of those illustrators who is brave enough to step out of the box, leaving traditionalism behind, and proving that you can give a new look to fantasy art, and better yet, introduce it into the mainstream.

Lee has been doing art seriously since she was 10 years old, a passion which has led to an amazing career. Her work has appeared inside as well as graced the covers of a large array of fantasy, horror, and science fiction magazines, books, game products, and CD-ROMS.

In 1997, Lee founded the charity organization Art Against Aids. With this organization, she has helped raise money for pediatric aids hospices throughout the United States. From there, Lee went on to compete in and win the L. Ron Hubbard Illustrators of the Future contest in 1998 and has been honored with several other awards along the way.

Last, but certainly not least, for Lee, art is about stepping away from the normality of today's art world and charting a new course. And because of this, Lee Seed is a fantasy artist in every sense of the word!

Fernando Molinari was born in Argentina on November 19, 1963. His entire life has been dedicated to illustration. Painting has become a way of exploring and expressing himself in several ways. He is Self taught; currently works for several publishing houses and advertising agencies in his country and abroad. He acts as an instructor of illustration, graphic specialties, and plastic art.

236

He has illustrated several books—Anne Rice's *Lasher*—art magazines, CD covers, comics, e-comics, etc. He is recognized for his Magic Beans and Fantasy-Art illustrated books.

His artwork has been on exhibition in various art galleries and museums, including The Museum of Modern Art, Buenos Aires, as well as selected galleries and cultural spaces in the United States. He was awarded as best in show 2002 on Leprecon 28, a Sci- Fi and Fantasy Art convention in Phoenix, Arizona. He is also a member of the Henderson Art Association in Nevada.

He has appeared on various television programs, including Much Music in 1999, to present and discuss his artwork as well as demonstrate several techniques.

You can visit the Fernando's artworks at: www.fernandomolinari.com.ar.

Chris Chua is a 24 year-old artist whose goal is to create art that gets a reaction/makes you think. He graduated from the Joe Kubert school of Cartoon & graphic art in 2001. He is extremely dedicated, punctual,hard-working, respectful and cooperative. He enjoys studying all types and styles of artwork. Chris continually strives to learn and improve his artistic abilities. Some of his influences include: Tim Sale, Bill Sienkiewicz, Simon Bisley, Danny Miki, Al Hirschfeld, Sebastian Kruger, David Cowles, graphic art, Asian brush work, cartoons such as Samurai Jack, Disney, and anime.

Upcoming works include: a short story he illustrated in *McCandless & Co: Crime Scenes* to be published by Crusade comics and, along with writer, Kurt Christenson, their creator-owned comic book called *Legend of Liquid Fury*. It is a sci-fi/fantasy martial arts epic. Aspects of this comic include: action, fantasy, science fiction, romance, humor, philosophy, and the heroic ideal. They aim for a fun unpredictable comic with plenty of over-the-top, never-before-seen action drawn in a unique style, pushing the limits of preconceived notions of comic art and storytelling. Their comic should be available by the end of 2003/early 2004.

Stephanie Pui-Mun Law is a freelance artist, whose work consists of fantasy, the otherworld, and the surreal. She has been illustrating since 1996. Stephanie graduated from the University of California at Berkeley in 1998 with a double BA degree in Fine Arts and Computer Science, and her list of clients includes Wizards of the Coast, HarperCollins, and Harlequin Enterprises. Much of her inspiration comes from mythlogy, legend, and folklore, and her art seeks to find a whimsical kernel to reality. As far as technique goes, her usual media include pencil, pen & ink, intaglio printing, watercolor, acrylic, and digital (Photoshop). Her preferred medium at this time is watercolor. In addition to painting into the twilight hours, Stephanie dances Flamenco at any spare moment, plays piano, and burrows through her books like a true bookworm. Influences from her music and dance are also scattered through her art, for she finds inspiration for art and images in everything around her. Her official website is: http://www.shadowscapes.com.

Juan Navarro was born, has lived, and probably will die in Hialeah, Florida, where he handles a myriad of businesses to stay afloat, all the while pumping in as much artwork as he can. He lives in his studio with a fat pug named Chato. (Don't get him and his dog confused).

You can see his art at: www.navarroart.tripod.com and www.hammersmashface.deviantart.com.

Max Bertolini {Second Place Winner} was born on June 6, 1967, in Milan, the city in which he still resides and works. He did not attend art school, so can be considered (in his words) "a true natural talent." His images, where you can often find a concern for the beauty of the naked human form, cover all ranges of imagination, from fantasy to sci-fi, passing through horror/thriller. Max enjoys depicting distant alien landscapes together with his fascinating and graceful warrior women, all of them represented with a deep consideration for contrast and chiaroscuro.

Max has been drawing for the comic book *Nathan Never*, by Sergio Bonelli Editore since 1993, which is a best-selling sci-fi series in Italy. He also does cover art for major publishing houses including Eura Editoale (which include the weekly publications: *Lanciostory* and *Skorpio*) and Mondadori (publications: *I Gialli*, *Sergretissimo*, and *Fantasy*). Max also worked on the Mediaset logos, on the advertising campaign for the De Agostini multimedia language courses, has designed several CD covers for Lucretia Records, and has created many illustrations for the Asics website. His fantasy and sci-fi cover art has been published in France, Germany, and Russia.

In the evenings, when he finds the time, he teaches Cartoon and Illustration at the Accademia dello Spettacolo in Milan. His current work is gradually shifting towards digital illustration.

Essayists and Editors

Jean Graham is a Southern California writer and volunteer senior caregiver whose short fantasy fiction has appeared in *Would That It Were*, the Daw Books anthology *Time of the Vampires*, and *Fantastical Visions I*.

She has been reading, writing and defending fantasy as literature for most of her life, even "setting straight" several grammar school and junior high teachers who tried to disallow Tolkien's work and other fantasy novels as proper book report material.

Jean makes frequent panel appearances at regional science fiction and fantasy conventions, teaches occasional writers' workshops and piano lessons, and lives in San Diego with her husband Chuck and nine thoroughly spoiled pussy cats.

Timons Esaias is a freelance writer and poet living in Pittsburgh.. His short stories have been translated into twelve languages. He has over four-score poems in print, including Spanish and Chinese translations, in markets ranging from Yawp! to Asimov's Science Fiction. A five-time nominee for the Rhysling Award, he was also a finalist for the British Science Fiction Award (Best Short Fiction, 1998). His satires have convinced thousands of readers that the Vatican is moving to Missouri, and that Pittsburgh puts Prozac in the water.

Tim studied biochemistry at Washington University in St. Louis, before shifting to philosophy at UMSL. He then moved on to the normal writerly employments of renovation contracting and building maintenance. He did carpentry and painting for both Stanley Elkin and William Gass, and can be said to have had at least an environmental influence on their oeuvres. Obviously this experience qualifies him to expound endlessly on modern fiction.

He is a member of The Pittsburgh Poetry Exchange and a Member Demeritus of the Worldwrights.

Tim reads far more than is really healthy, though he is occasionally distracted by chess, baseball, historical war games, aikido, learning Hittite or square-foot gardening. For more about him see www.timonsesaias.com.

Courtenay N. Dudek has been writing for the past four years (mainly memoir and poetry). His dabblings in fantasy fiction have brought him to Fantasist Enterprises as an assistant editor with much thanks to William Horner. He recently graduated from Eastern University with a BA in English. He aspires to encourage those he encounters in the writing world to express and fine-tune their art. His life is open to whatever it has coming. There are no current plans with writing and editing, just hopes.

W. H. Horner finds time between two part-time jobs and running a business to work on earning his Masters in Writing Popular Fiction from Seton Hill University, which requires students to write a marketable novel. His fantasy novel has been growing in scope, even as his writing slowed down during the past few, particularly hectic, months. Now that the editorial work for this anthology is over, he plans to retreat to a tropical island with his laptop computer and work on his novel (well, maybe not a tropical island, but a nice café somewhere near home might do the trick).

William enjoys building relationships with writers and artists, and finds much satisfaction in working with them to create the best works that they can—whether that means deep editing on a story or discussing how best to present a critical scene in an illustration without revealing too much. William feels especially good about his job when "his authors," as he sometimes refers to them, let him know that they've learned something from working with him. He would like them all to know that he has learned something from each of them, and has appreciated their hard work and patience through the months it has taken to polish up this anthology.

William currently lives in Wilmington, Delaware. His infrequently updated website can be found at www.whhorner.com.

In appreciation for your purchase, we would like to offer you the chance to purchase our first volume at a discount.

From the streets of modern-day cities, to medieval villages, to the deck of a flying ship, this book will take you there. Meet zombies, elves, kings, and even ordinary human beings, all wrapped up in magical events.

Plunge in now and be prepared to be swept away.

Retail: $9.99   Format: Trade Paperback, 186pp.
Special Price: $6.50   ISBN: 0-9713608-0-4

To pay with your credit card, go to the following URL and enter the login information, below, which is caps-sensitive:

URL: http://fvdeal.fantasistent.com
Login ID: FVII
Password: Special

To pay with a check or money order, follow the instructions below, fill out the required information, and remit form with payment.

Payable in U.S. funds only. Send checks or money orders payable to Fantasist Enterprises to the address below. No cash or COD accepted. Postage and handling in the U.S.: $2.00 per book. International shipping: $4.00 for the first book, $2.00 per additional book.

Fantasist Enterprises   # of Books Ordered: _____
FV Book Deal
PO Box 9381   Postage Amount: _____
Wilmington, DE 19809

Please allow 4-6 weeks for delivery.   Total Amount Due: _____
International delivery 6-8 weeks.

Ship to:

Name: _____

Address: _____

City: _____ State: _____ Zip: _____

Printed in the United States
1356300004B/58-255